"PHOENIX FORCE AND ABLE TEAM WILL BE TURNED LOOSE IN PERU"

"Their mission," Katz continued, "will be to strike at the so-called coalition and inflict as much damage as possible. Collins will be forced out of hiding, and he will react in ways that we can use to track him down."

"What if tht fials?" Brognola asked.

"We have nothing to fall abck on, and the result will be the same as if we do nothing. Mack Bolan, if he is alive, willdie. At some point, Collins will ahve nofurther use for him, and Mack will be eliminated."

"You've all discussed this?" the big Fed asked as he looked around the table.

"We have," Katz replied, answering for everyone.

"I'll take it to the President and see what he says."

D0829360

Other titles in this series:

DON PENDLETON'S
MACK BOLAN®

STONY MAN®

Conflict Imperative

A GOLD EAGLE BOOK FROM

WORLDWIDE®

TORONTO • NEW YORK • LONDON
AMSTERDAM • PARIS • SYDNEY • HAMBURG
STOCKHOLM • ATHENS • TOKYO • MILAN
MADRID • WARSAW • BUDAPEST • AUCKLAND

If you purchased this book without a cover you should be aware
that this book is stolen property. It was reported as "unsold and
destroyed" to the publisher, and neither the author nor the
publisher has received any payment for this "stripped book."

First edition August 2000

ISBN 0-373-61932-4

Special thanks and acknowledgment to
Michael Kasner for his contribution to this work.

CONFLICT IMPERATIVE

Copyright © 2000 by Worldwide Library.

All rights reserved. Except for use in any review, the
reproduction or utilization of this work in whole or in part
in any form by any electronic, mechanical or other means,
now known or hereafter invented, including xerography,
photocopying and recording, or in any information storage
or retrieval system, is forbidden without the written permission
of the publisher, Worldwide Library, 225 Duncan Mill Road,
Don Mills, Ontario, Canada M3B 3K9.

All characters in this book have no existence outside the
imagination of the author and have no relation whatsoever to
anyone bearing the same name or names. They are not even
distantly inspired by any individual known or unknown to the
author, and all incidents are pure invention.

® and TM are trademarks of Harlequin Enterprises Limited.
Trademarks indicated with ® are registered in the United States
Patent and Trademark Office, the Canadian Trade Marks Office
and in other countries.

Printed in U.S.A.

Conflict Imperative

CHAPTER ONE

Northern Peru

It was May in the tropics, but it was still cold at the eight-thousand-foot level in the northern Peruvian mountains. A solid cloud bank at twelve thousand feet almost shrouded the highest of the peaks that surrounded the clearing in the high jungle. A rudimentary landing pad at one end of the clearing had been used to ferry in several helicopter loads of Peruvian government dignitaries and two American observers for the ceremony that was about to take place.

"This is about the most sorry-assed thing I've ever had to do in my entire life," Dan Denning grumbled to the man standing beside him. "And I swear that I've done a lot of sorry-assed things."

Denning was a stocky man whose worn face showed that he had lived a rigorous life. His once dark brown hair was shot through with gray, but he still had the fit body of a field agent, not a desk jockey. Even though he was the head of the DEA's

Latin American operations, he had steadfastly refused to lock himself away in an office like the faceless bureaucrats who were now in the upper echelon of the federal drug-fighting agency. He was proud that he had come up through the ranks as a field agent, and he still kept his hand in whenever he could. But the days of his kind were almost over.

From Denning's perspective, it seemed more and more that politics was the driving force behind the DEA's agenda. Instead of busting drug lords and intercepting shipments, the agency had become an adjunct of the Red Cross and the State Department. Between civic-action missions to teach coca farmers how to grow coffee beans and brokering cease-fires between the various feuding governments and rebel factions in the region, there was little time left for doing what the agency was supposed to be doing—shutting down drug smuggling.

But of all the dumb-assed things he'd had to do in the name of drug fighting recently, this took first prize.

"If this is what the agency's been reduced to," the DEA man complained, "I'm glad that I'll be able to hang up my badge and retire from this shit before much longer."

The ice blue eyes of the big black-haired man standing beside Denning swept the clearing in the high mountain jungle. Surrounded by jagged peaks, the choppers that had brought them there from the capital city of Lima were the only apparent way to get in and out. If he had wanted to design a trap, this was about as good as it got. Not only was the government delegation greatly outnumbered, but they also had no back door if this didn't go off as planned.

"If it hadn't been for Hal Brognola," Denning continued his monologue, "I'd have told Washington to kiss my rosy red and hung it up when this rat screw was first proposed. I still can't believe that the Peruvians are giving up a quarter of their territory to these scumbags. Damn!"

Mack Bolan, the Executioner, known to Dan Denning as Mike Belasko, smiled to himself. He had heard various versions of this tirade for the past two weeks as the countdown to this Peruvian version of the land-for-peace deal progressed. He had said similar things himself to Hal Brognola back at Stony Man Farm, but the big Fed had had his orders directly from the Man. America's interests lay in ending the thirty-year conflict that had all but destroyed Peru, and if this was what it took, the President was willing to go along with it.

The plan had originally called for Brognola to be the senior United States representative at the ceremony about to take place. But, even though the President was firmly behind the proposal, he hadn't wanted to risk the life of his number-one man in the Sensitive Operations Group. Instead, Denning had been tapped for the duty, and Mack Bolan had volunteered to go along as his security man and Stony Man Farm's eyes.

Bolan didn't view the ceremony that was going to create something known as the coalition territory as being a new beginning for peace. To his mind, it was a surrender pure and simple, and the Executioner wasn't big on surrendering. It had been burned into his brain that surrendering never solved anything. If something was worth fighting for, it was worth fighting for to the death. As had been so well proved in Israel, Bosnia, Ireland and a dozen other places where it had been tried over the past few years, giving in to violence only bred more violence.

The Executioner had spent his life combating terrorists and drug dealers the only effective way he knew—killing them wherever he found them. This time, though, he could only stand by and watch while the Peruvians made their own mistake. Hopefully, it would turn out better than all the other times that this gambit had been played. He wouldn't put any money on it, though.

As the minutes clicked down, the half-dozen Peruvian dignitaries assumed their places. Ramon de Castillio, the popular vice president, was the ranking member of the government delegation. Although the land-for-peace plan had originated with the Peruvian president, he hadn't felt comfortable traveling so far from Lima. In fact, the president rarely left his fortified palace unless he was in his armored Mercedes limo and escorted by a full battalion of paratroopers armed to the teeth.

"Okay," the American-educated Castillio muttered as he glanced at his watch. "Let's get this dog and pony show on the road. It's too damned cold up here."

As if on cue, the commander of the PLFP rebel forces shouted a command in Spanish, and his hundred-plus troops shuffled to a semblance of the position of attention. Being jungle fighters and not regular troops, they could be excused for not having the parade-ground routine down. They were, however, armed to the teeth and looked as if they knew how to use their weapons.

In response, the Peruvian infantry colonel in charge of the small military color guard and VIP security detachment called his men to a rigid position of attention. As the two groups warily faced each other, a stocky red-haired man walked out from behind the rebel lines.

Sean Collins was the man of the hour today. This handover of land in the hope of attaining peace was being brokered by White Shield, an international peace group led by the one-time Irish terrorist. Collins had been instrumental in creating the most recent IRA cease-fire in Northern Ireland and had subsequently been nominated for the Nobel Peace Prize. With that success under his belt, he had approached the Peruvian government with a proposal to end the thirty-year civil war with a coalition of rebel groups led by PLFP—Popular Liberation Front of Peru.

In the glare of Collins's Nobel publicity, his personal guarantee that his radical idea would work was critical in convincing the Peruvian government to sign over a large portion of the country to the rebel coalition. With his newly found international status, Collins's long believed, but never proved, association with the infamous Provisional Wing of the IRA had been conveniently forgotten.

As vice president Castillio signed the first document, Bolan let his eyes drift past the onlookers on the rebel side. He wasn't surprised to recognize a couple of major drug cartel players in the coalition's VIP group. Anyone who thought that the rebels would do anything other than continue to grow coca and process the leaves into cocaine was living in a fantasy world. There was hardly anything else that would grow in this particular part of Peru that had any market value at all.

The signing ceremony took no time at all, and no refreshments were offered when it was over. That would have been stretching everyone's tissue-thin sense of trust. As soon as the documents were signed, the two groups immediately separated again, each holding to its own side of the small clearing. The government and the rebels had been at war far too long for either side to feel comfortable fraternizing with lifelong enemies.

When three olive-drab Russian Mi-8 Hip helicopters bearing the blue-and-white cockades of the Peruvian air force appeared, the government delegation quickly boarded for the three-hour flight back to Lima. By the time the third ship lifted off, Denning and Bolan were left standing by themselves waiting for their ride.

When Sean Collins walked up to them, he looked concerned.

"Gentlemen, it looks as if your helicopter is having some mechanical difficulties," he announced to Denning. "The pilot assures me, however, that it will only be few minutes before it is repaired. Is there anything I can do for you while you wait?"

Denning grunted a negative reply. Out of this entire debacle, he resented the presence of Collins most of all. In the IRA's glory days, if a reign of indiscriminate murder could be called that, the terrorists had gotten into the drug-smuggling business as an easy way to finance their operations. Though it hadn't been proved, Denning was convinced that Collins had been in charge of that side of the IRA's operations. The fact that Collins had been granted amnesty for half a dozen car bombings didn't figure as greatly in Denning's mind as did the drug smuggling.

Bolan briefly locked eyes with the Irishman. For a long time, Collins had been on his personal kill-on-sight list. He had been taken off only when the IRA terrorist had publicly hung up his guns and started working to bring about the Irish cease-fire.

From that success he had created White Shield, which was supposedly devoted to ending other conflicts in the world.

While that was a worthwhile goal, it didn't mean that Bolan trusted the man as far as he could spit. He knew full well that murderers like Collins rarely changed their habits. But he had to play the hand he had been dealt this time. That didn't mean that he wouldn't target Collins at some later date if the circumstances warranted it.

Collins caught the look and smiled thinly. He didn't know exactly who this hard-eyed Yankee was, but his time in the IRA had taught him to recognize the type. He was a dangerous man, and he would have to be watched closely. He considered killing him on the spot, but there was the off chance that he might prove to be useful later, so he could live for now.

Walking over to a cluster of rebel troops standing a short distance away, Collins barked a command in rapid-fire Spanish. A dozen of them rushed the two Americans, unslinging their AKs as they came.

"Stand stock-still, gentlemen," Collins warned, "and you will live."

Facing the muzzles of a dozen AK-47s, Bolan and Denning had no choice but to obey. They held their arms out as they were patted down for weapons. Denning was clean. But, in his role as bodyguard, Bolan was packing his Beretta 93-R and two spare magazines in a shoulder rig, as well as a mini-

Glock in a holster in the middle of his back. When Bolan's weapons were removed, the Americans' hands were bound behind their backs.

"What the hell do you think you're—?" Denning was cut off by an AK butt slammed into his belly.

"We'll talk later," Collins said.

As Bolan and Denning watched, the Irishman signaled a rebel who had a radio. A few minutes later, the last helicopter touched down and two guerrillas got into the back. After another signal from Collins, it took off.

The Irishman watched the helicopter as it climbed into the sky over the jagged peaks of the mountains surrounding the clearing. He held out his hand, and one of the rebels put a radio transmitter in it. When the chopper was directly over the highest peak, Collins pressed the transmit button.

A fireball blossomed in the sky where the chopper had been. Burning fuel and chunks of the airframe rained on the jagged rocks a thousand feet below. The sound of the explosion echoed, but hardly anyone bothered to look over at it. It wasn't unexpected.

Turning his back on the burning wreckage, Collins shouted orders in Spanish. About half of the rebel troops broke ranks and headed for the collection of miscellaneous vehicles that had been parked in the wood line. The other half of the troops formed up and started to move into the trees at the edge of the clearing. While the small vehicle convoy drove away to the north, the column of rebels on foot headed south.

Collins wasn't unaware that he was almost certainly being watched by American deep-space satellites. That was why he had specifically chosen to hold the ceremony at that time of year. The mountains were shrouded in clouds nine and a half days out of ten in this season. With the cloud cover blocking visual images, the only thing that the satellites would be able to pick up would be the vehicles, and following them would be fruitless.

"Let's go," Collins said in English.

"Where are we going?" Denning asked.

Collins automatically started to go into a cover story, but stopped himself and laughed.

"What's funny?" Denning snapped.

"I was about to tell you a lie, Mr. Denning. But it makes no difference if you know the truth because you're never going to leave here. I'm taking you to a jungle camp a hundred miles from here for interrogation. When I'm done with you, you'll both be shot."

"You'll never get away with this," Denning said automatically.

Collins smiled. "You sound like a character in one of your Hollywood movies. Of course I will get away with 'this,' as you put it. You forget who I am. A month from now, I will be in Oslo receiving the Nobel Peace Prize for my work to end regional conflicts and you—" he paused "—you might even still be alive. But, of course, that will depend entirely upon you. This will be only as tough on you as you want to make it. Make sure that you remember that."

"You bastard," Denning snarled.

Collins smiled and slipped into an Irish brogue. "As a matter of fact, I'm a proper bastard, as we Irish say. But me poor mum was a bit of a loose-legged bitch, so it wasn't really her fault. She also had an eye for the lads in uniform but, unfortunately in my case, me da was wearing the wrong one. I did track the man down later and introduced myself, but me mum went a bit batty when I brought her both of his ears. She was never quite the same after that, poor girl."

"Jesus," Denning said.

Collins didn't change expression. "I'd do him, too, if I had the chance. He's a bloody bastard, as well."

Bolan kept silent during this exchange. This wasn't the time nor the place for him to say or do anything. For this incident to have a satisfactory conclusion, he would have to play it carefully, very carefully. As far as Collins knew, he was just a hired gun named Mike Belasko, and he would do everything in his power to keep the terrorist thinking that.

"Now," Collins said, "if you're finished insulting me, we have to be going now. You can either walk on your own feet or my men will hang you on a long stick and carry you like a gutted pig.''

"We'll walk," Denning spit out.

Collins looked almost disappointed.

"And as to your original question as to where we're going, we're going down the mountain to a warmer altitude. I'm sure you'll appreciate that."

Since Bolan still hadn't said anything, Collins now turned to him. "Don't you have any smart mouthed questions, mister?

"No," the Irishman answered his own question. "I didn't think so. You're more of the strong silent type, aren't you? But hear me well, boyo—" Collins took half a step closer to Bolan "—I don't really need you, so I would advise you not to do anything that might make me think that you're a liability."

"I understand." Bolan nodded.

Collins locked eyes with him. "I thought you might, SAS man."

Bolan had never been officially associated with the British Special Air Service, Britain's special forces. But he knew that to the IRA, all security men were "SAS men," and to be identified with that name told him what he could expect from this "peace activist."

CHAPTER TWO

Stony Man Farm, Virginia

Aaron Kurtzman arched his back and flexed his muscular arms over his head to ease the tension in his shoulders. He was built like a blacksmith and had earned his nickname of "the Bear" as much for his bulk as for his manner. Having his legs shot out from under him in a firefight had done nothing to mellow him out or lessen his upper-body strength.

When his vertebrae cracked like rifle fire, he wheeled his chair back in front of his keyboard. He was long overdue for the regimen of upper-body exercises that kept him from knotting up with fatigue. Maybe he would find the time to get to it this evening. Maybe pigs would fly, too.

Until this Peruvian thing was wrapped up and put to bed, he would be stuck at his workstation. "What's the cloud-cover situation?" he called over to Huntington Wethers.

"It's still holding zero-zero at twelve thousand

feet," Wethers called back. "So we're not getting anything but IR and radar. No visual contact at all."

The distinguished-looking black computer expert was overseeing the NRO deep-space recon satellite that was keeping watch on the remote clearing high in the Peruvian mountains. And, for once, he was doing it completely aboveboard. Usually, the deeply covert nature of Stony Man operations required that the Computer Room crew "borrow" one of the top secret National Reconnaissance Office's spy birds without bothering to tell them that they were doing so. This time, though, the President had arranged for Stony Man to use whatever was needed to keep an eye on the ceremony.

But the persistent cloud cover in the Andes was getting in the way of their doing that. And not having visual contact with the ground meant that the six-inch resolution cameras in the satellite weren't able to provide them with real-time video of the meeting. The only historical record of the event would be the tape from the single TV journalist the rebels had allowed in to tape the proceedings.

Even with the bad weather, Stony Man Farm's leader, Justice Department official Hal Brognola, wasn't concerned enough about the ceremony to even be at the Farm that day. In his role as the special adviser to the President, he was closeted with the Man and the National Security Council going over the changes to U.S. foreign policy that would result from the Peruvian government's action. No one had any idea what the fallout from this coalition treaty was going to be, so they were kicking around possible contingency plans. They had to have something on hand to fall back on in case the situation down there turned sour.

And Brognola was convinced that it would.

No one could possibly believe that the PLFP would be content with running only a quarter of Peru. Hitler hadn't been content with getting back the Sudan or adding Austria to his empire, either. The rebels were on a winning streak, and as soon as they consolidated their control over their new holdings, they would go after the other three-quarters of the country. But in the halls of government, boundless optimism always reigned supreme. No one ever wanted to look at the cold, hard facts when some half-assed scheme was hatched. Once more the Disneyland syndrome was in full play inside the Beltway.

Fantasy was fine: everyone needed dreams. But when governments got into the fantasy business and those fantasies got out of control, people bled.

"I just got a midair explosion at eleven thousand feet," Wethers almost shouted across the small room.

"Send it over," Kurtzman said curtly.

Kurtzman's screen flashed and changed in an instant to a replay of the IR sensor take from the Keyhole satellite. The brief clip showed a heat source suddenly appearing in the sky directly over the mountains surrounding the meeting place. According to the digital thermal readout at the bottom of the screen, the temperature of the heat source was eighteen hundred degrees.

JP-4 jet fuel burned at that temperature.

"Ah, shit," Kurtzman muttered.

"The radar returns indicate that the explosion was an aircraft," reported Akira Tokaido, who was assisting Wethers with the deep-space surveillance. "From the total mass of debris involved, I'd say that it was probably a chopper."

Kurtzman was well aware that Dan Denning and Bolan had been flown from Lima to the meeting site by a Peruvian army helicopter. He also knew without knowing that the explosion had occurred on their ship. Considering that the rebel coalition had just been given everything it had asked for on a silver plate, nothing else made any sense. The rebels wouldn't be killing the representatives of the Peruvian government, not yet at least. That wouldn't start up again for at least another six months to a year.

Kurtzman's hand shot out to trip the intercom button.

"Price," a woman's low voice answered.

"Barbara," he said, "you need to come down here. We just had a midair explosion in Peru."

"On the way."

Barbara Price came through the door of the Computer Room ninety seconds later. She was a tall, long-haired blonde who looked as if she had stepped out of the pages of a fashion magazine. The faded jeans, men's work shirt and scuffed cowboy boots she wore took nothing away from her beauty and poise. Her attire did, however, give a hint of the fact that she was a no-nonsense type. To be the mission controller for the Farm, she had to be and never more than right now.

"What's our fastest contact with Peru?"

"Through the military."

"Get a status report."

As usual, Wethers was one step ahead of her. "Our Peruvian army contact is reporting that they lost contact with one of the choppers ferrying the peace delegation members back to Lima from the meeting."

"Do they know who was on it?" Price asked.

"They don't have that information yet."

"Do you think it was our people?" she asked Kurtzman.

"I think it's highly likely," he replied reluctantly.

Reaching out for the red phone, Price punched in one of the preset numbers.

"Price here," she said. "I need to speak to Hal Brognola...I don't care if he's in a meeting with God," she snapped. "Get him on the damned phone right now! I have a Golden Haze situation. That's right, Golden Haze, mister. Now move it."

"Idiots," she muttered.

"Hal," she said a moment later. "It looks like Mack and Denning's chopper blew up and went down over the mountains. We picked it up with Keyhole.

"No," she said, shaking her head. "Hunt is working on the confirmation from the Peruvian military right now...We'll be waiting."

A flash of pain crossed her eyes as she put the red handset back on the cradle. Mack Bolan was an important man in her life, more important than she liked to admit. She had always known that he wasn't going to die in bed, but she still wasn't prepared for this.

"He's leaving immediately," she told Kurtzman. "Have you called Katz yet?"

"I got his beeper and left a message."

"When he calls back," she said, "tell him that we need him here ASAP."

Yakov Katzenelenbogen was the most experienced man on the Stony Man team. After leading Phoenix Force for years, he was now the Farm's in-house tactical operations officer, the man behind the plan. As the mission controller, Price had overall command and control authority for SOG operations, but having Katz at her side made her work a great deal easier. There was little that slipped past the old warrior, and he had more tricks than a stacked deck.

"Do you want me to call McCarter and Lyons, too?" Kurtzman asked. If this turned out to be what they all feared, David McCarter's Phoenix Force and Carl Lyons's Able Team would be going into action.

Stony Man Farm was the nation's premier covert-operations unit and operated directly under the President's personal control. The Farm was given the real dirty jobs, both large and small, that could never be allowed to see the light of day.

Because of the level of secrecy that surrounded Stony Man's activities, the men who provided the Farm's muscle were few in number but not in skills. David McCarter led Phoenix Force, probably the world's most dangerous commando group, which specialized in solving the overseas problems. Carl Lyons and his equally skilled Able Team usually worked inside the United States, but occasionally they worked with their Phoenix Force comrades when the situation was too complicated for the other team to handle alone.

Mack Bolan wasn't a member of either of these teams. He usually worked through the Farm, but always retained his freedom of action. Nonetheless, he often joined the SOG missions.

"Give them a warning order," she replied. "As soon as we find out more about what happened, we'll fill them in."

When Wethers turned back, his face was ashen. "The Peruvian army has announced that the chopper involved was carrying the American delegation."

A hush fell over the Computer Room. No one wanted to be the first to voice the unthinkable.

"Pass that on to Hal," Price said.

"I just did."

THE FARM'S BLACKSUIT security chief, Buck Greene, was walking the perimeter of the new poplar-tree plantation that was being planted on the forty-acre plot of land on the east boundary of the Farm. In almost the exact center of the acreage stood a flat-topped concrete building. With the land bare as it was now, it was easy for anyone to see the structure for what it was supposed to be, a mill to make wood chips for pulp mills.

With the phenomenal growth rate of the new strains of poplar trees, cultivating them for wood pulp was a good business to get into. The Farm would do well enough from this venture, but the bottom line wasn't what had prompted it. While fully functional, the chipping mill was really an elaborate camouflage designed to conceal what had been built beneath it.

The development of the new underground facilities—the Annex, as it was being called—was coming along nicely. It wouldn't be long before much of the Stony Man operations would be moving into their new digs. And it wasn't coming a moment too soon to suit Greene. He'd had his plate more than full trying to handle the extra security the initial construction phase of the job had required. But that phase of the work was over, and the last few things left to be done before the Annex was fully operational were being handled by work crews from his own blacksuit security force.

For being professional hardmen, the blacksuits were handy with a variety of tools and construction skills. Since Stony Man Farm was a real farm, they had to be. Their main day job was to keep the farm operating to maintain their cover as an agricultural operation.

Some of the security guards were trying their hand at playing tree farmers. A tractor-mounted drill was boring deep holes in the ground every twelve feet to receive a poplar tree. The outer three rows of trees that were being put into the ground were large trees almost twelve feet tall. It was difficult transporting trees that large and getting them in the ground without damaging them, but Greene had insisted that they have some kind of immediate cover and concealment while the final work was being done in the middle of the forty-eight-acre plot. The trees would also provide a good place to conceal sensors and surveillance equipment as part of a security update.

Greene was watching the last half-dozen trees go into the ground when his com link beeped. "Buck," he heard Price's voice say in his earphone, "you'd better get back here."

"What's the problem?"

"It's external to us here," she said. "I'll brief you when you get here."

"On the way."

Double-timing back to where he had parked his Jeep, Greene slid behind the wheel, fired up the engine and raced back to the farmhouse. As he drove, he keyed his com link and issued an increase in the security status. He had no idea what was going on, but he wasn't a man to take chances.

Peru

THE REBEL FORCE KEPT a fast pace as it headed down the mountain from the meeting site. Bolan and Denning had a personal escort of a dozen guerrillas to make sure that they didn't get any ideas about making a break for it. Since they were in their own territory, the jungle fighters kept up a steady chatter to pass the time.

Bolan knew rudimentary Spanish, but the bits of conversation he overheard were in a language he didn't understand. More than likely, it was Quechua, the language of the ancient Inca people. Their descendants were the majority population in Peru, so that wasn't surprising. It also wasn't surprising to find the rebels carrying AK-47s. Life was hard for the Indian people of Latin America, so they had little to lose by trying to better themselves any way they could.

For many Indian men, that meant signing on with

a drug lord's army or joining a leftist guerrilla group. It was a hard life, but life was already hard for them. Until dramatic changes were made in Latin American society, the life of the Indian people would continue to drive them to guns and drugs.

By the second hour on the trail, the air was considerably warmer than it had been in the mountains, but that only made the going even more difficult. Denning was starting to show the strain of the fast pace. He was fit for his age, but he wasn't fit enough that the forced march wasn't affecting him. He was sweating heavily, and with his hands tied behind his back, it ran into his eyes, stinging them. When Bolan saw his condition, he told one of their guards in Spanish that they needed to take a break.

When the guerrilla came back with Sean Collins, Bolan told him, "If you want us to keep up with you, we're going to need to take a break every hour or so."

Collins stared Bolan down for a long moment. "You get fifteen minutes," he said, "and then we move out again."

"We could also use some water," Bolan said. "Dehydration isn't going to help us keep up with your men."

While Collins would have rather told them to drink their own piss, he knew that the big Yankee was right. They weren't safe until they reached the camp, and keeping the two Americans on their feet was to his advantage.

"Agua," he said to one of the guerrillas, and signaled another one to untie the captives' hands.

The man took a battered canteen from his belt and handed it over.

Collins gave it to Bolan first and watched as he took a short drink, swished it around his mouth and swallowed. When Bolan handed the canteen to Denning, the DEA man drank deeply.

The Irishman laughed and turned away.

"Thanks for getting the water," Denning said as soon as Collins walked off.

"No big deal," Bolan replied. "Collins is a bastard, but he knows that he has to give us water. We're no good to him dead."

"Do you think they'll slow down now that we're a couple of hours away from the meeting site?"

"I doubt it. He's in a hurry to get us under cover somewhere, so he's going to push us as hard as he can."

"Damn," the DEA man said, wiping his face on his sleeve. "I used to think I was in pretty good shape until I got into this shit. This is killing me."

"These jungles'll do that to you." Bolan looked around the unbroken green surrounding them. "You have to be born here not to have them affect you."

"You seem to be taking this pretty much in stride," Denning commanded.

All he really knew about his security man was that he had come highly recommended from the upper levels of the Justice Department. In the week they had been in Lima prior to the ceremony, Belasko had shown himself to be very well-informed, but he hadn't divulged much about his background.

Bolan cracked a brief smile. "Let's just say that I've been in places like this a couple of times before."

"It shows."

"Let's hope that it doesn't show too much," Bolan said. "I don't want Collins focusing on me too much."

Denning didn't quite know what to make of that remark, but he understood it. If Belasko was a seasoned jungle fighter, he might be able to find a way to free them. If Collins noticed it, the Irishman might decide that he didn't need two captives.

CHAPTER THREE

Stony Man Farm, Virginia

Since Bolan's Peruvian mission hadn't been expected to be anything more than a routine diplomatic junket, there was no Stony Man mission alert to cover it in case something went wrong. No one was standing by. With everyone stood down, it would take several hours to assemble the teams at the Farm and bring them up to mission speed.

Hal Brognola was the first to arrive, Washington being only a short helicopter flight away. Barbara Price met him as he stepped off the chopper at the landing pad. His face was set, and he looked as if he had lost his best friend, which in reality he had. He and Mack Bolan went all the way back to the days of the Mafia Wars when they had been on opposite sides of the struggle for America's soul. The friendship had only come later, but it was now the most important one the big Fed had.

"Anything new?" he asked curtly.

"Nothing yet," Price replied, shaking her head.

Brognola placed his hand on her shoulder. "Are you okay?"

"No," she said honestly, "but we have work to do."

As soon as Brognola was clear of the spinning rotor blades, Jack Grimaldi, Stony Man's ace pilot, pulled pitch and lifted off for the Richmond airport to meet David McCarter's flight from Miami. After ferrying the Phoenix Force leader to the Farm, he would head back to Washington's National Airport to pick up Carl Lyons and Yakov Katzenelenbogen. The rest of the Stony Man commandos would be coming in on their own.

While Grimaldi was running the Farm's aerial taxi service, Brognola went to the Computer Room and got to work. The first thing he did was put on his Justice Department persona and get on the phone to the DEA in the Peruvian capital. Ralph Gordon, the senior agent in the Lima office, briefed him on what little was known about the chopper accident.

"All we have at this time," Gordon reported, "is that the chopper that carried them there had some kind of mechanical malfunction at the site. After it was repaired on-site, Denning and Belasko reportedly boarded and took off. They were climbing for altitude to clear the mountains when the chopper exploded in midair and went down."

"What's your take on it?" Brognola asked. "Do you think it's legit?"

"I'll be damned if I know, sir," Gordon replied. "The pilots were Peruvian army, but that doesn't really mean anything. I've got good contacts in their armed forces, but at this point, they don't know any more than what I just told you. The problem is that the chopper was left behind when the others took off, so we don't have any eyewitnesses except for the rebels. What little we do have on the crash is coming from them."

"When do you think they're going to be able to get a rescue team into the crash site?"

"My understanding is that's being discussed with the coalition right now," Gordon said. "The problem is that the rebels are balking about letting the Peruvian military into their new territory even for a humanitarian mission."

"Stay on top of it and give me a call the minute you hear anything, anything at all."

"Will do, Mr. Brognola."

There would, of course, be problems even on something as simple as trying to find the bodies. It was his experience that when something turned to shit, the whole world responded by doing the same.

Peru

WHEN THE REBELS MOVED OUT again after the rest halt, Denning seemed to be better for the water and the rest no matter how brief it had been. Bolan would keep a close eye on him until they reached wherever they were being taken.

As they marched, Bolan surveyed his captors without being obvious about what he was doing. Most of them weren't togged in any kind of uniform, and some of the fighters didn't even have boots. Their web gear and personal equipment was also spotty, and well-worn when they had any at all. As ragtag as they appeared, however, they were all well armed. The men who weren't carrying serviceable AK-47s or U.S. M-16s were packing what looked to be Russian AK assault rifles, the ubiquitous weapon of Third World guerrilla forces. Several rebels also had the equally ubiquitous RPG-7 rocket launchers, and a few even had U.S. M-79 grenade launchers, which was also expected.

The only thing that marked this rebel group as being any different than any of the other South American guerrilla units he had seen was that these men were being led by a European and he wasn't even a Marxist. Bolan hadn't yet figured out what game Sean Collins was playing, but he knew it wouldn't be long before he found out.

THE FARTHER DOWN the mountain they went, the thicker the jungle became and the hotter the air. The overhead cover soon completely blocked out the sun, but the temperature rose to the point that it was almost like being in a sauna. Collins called a rest break every hour or so and made sure his charges got a long drink. Each time, Bolan made sure that Denning got the lion's share of the water because he didn't want to have to carry him if he collapsed.

They had been under the triple canopy for several hours when Bolan spotted signs that they were approaching a camp of some kind. Knowing what to look for, he saw where the brush had been thinned to provide interlocking fields of fire. Fifty yards farther on, he spotted the outer ring of fighting positions all but invisible from the avenues of approach. These well-concealed perimeter positions were backed up by automatic-weapons bunkers connected by communications trenches. Even inside the perimeter, the ground hadn't been clear-cut, but only thinned. In the center of the camp were several buildings of typical jungle construction, wood and bamboo with thatched roofs, and they blended in well with the vegetation.

The layout of the fighting camp reminded Bolan of the better North Vietnamese army camps he had seen in Cambodia and told him that whoever had set this up obviously had extensive jungle-warfare experience. It would take a serious effort to find the place, much less attack it successfully, and that concerned him.

As soon as Stony Man realized that he and Denning hadn't died in the chopper crash, Aaron Kurtzman would start looking for them. And he would start with a satellite recon survey of the area. Normally that would yield fairly quick results, but the density of the vegetation here was going to make the camp very difficult for the NRO satellites to find. Even the radar mapping wasn't going to be able to pick up much through the triple canopy. With the scattered buildings being made of native materials, they also wouldn't show up well on a scan. Their only hope was that there were enough weapons to give strong returns.

As Bolan had told Denning, he had been in jungles before. Usually, though, he had been on his own and under more favorable conditions than he was now. With the DEA man along this time, getting out wasn't going to be easy. In fact, it was going to be damned difficult.

WHEN THE COLUMN PASSED through the perimeter, Bolan and Denning were led away to a sturdy bamboo bar cage in the center of the cleared area. Their hands were untied, and they were locked inside. A few minutes later, an Indian woman carrying two wooden bowls of beans, a leaf stacked high with corn tortillas and two canteens of water walked up and placed the food on the ground next to the bamboo bars.

After the exertion of the trek, the two men lost no time digging into the hot food. When they were finished, the guard motioned for them to put the empty bowls back outside the bars.

"I wonder where in the hell we are," Denning said as he looked around at the shadows. Though they couldn't see the sun directly through the canopy, they knew that dusk was falling.

"From the sun's position during the first part of the march," Bolan replied, "we were moving northeast. I'd say that we're maybe a day's march or so from the Colombian border."

"I don't like the sound of that," the DEA man said.

"I don't like any of this," Bolan replied. "But we'd better get as much sleep as we can. Collins might plan to move us again in the morning."

"I hope not," Denning groaned. "It's going to take me a couple of days to recover as it is."

"Just get all the rest you can."

Stony Man Farm, Virginia

AS SOON AS Jack Grimaldi's chopper delivered Carl Lyons and Yakov Katzenelenbogen to the Farm, the Israeli tactical officer and the Able Team leader joined McCarter and the cyberteam in the War Room.

With a nod to Price and Kurtzman, Katz got right to the point. "How soon will it be before we can get in there and get the bodies out?" he asked Hal Brognola.

"That's still up in the air," the big Fed replied. "The PLFP is balking about letting the Peruvian military into its new territory. They're concerned—"

"What about us going in to get them?" McCarter broke in. "We're not Peruvians."

"That's an even bigger problem," Brognola admitted. "The PLFP—"

"Why don't you call them what they really are," McCarter snapped. "They're bloody terrorists. Nothing that IRA bastard Sean Collins is involved with can be legit. I don't see how in the hell the President could have possibly been stupid enough to get sucked in by that—"

"David," Price said, cutting off his tirade, "let the man finish."

With emotions running as high as they were, Brognola hadn't expected this to be easy. He mourned Bolan, too, but someone had to try to keep things on an even keel until they had enough information to act on.

"Anyway," he continued as if nothing had been said, "the White Shield organization says they're concerned about unsanctioned U.S. incursions, as they put it, into the coalition territory. They say, however, that they are coordinating a joint rescue and recovery operation with the Peruvian military at this time. But the crash site is said to be almost inaccessible, even for experienced mountaineers, so they'll have to use choppers."

"Can my lads make a HALO drop onto the mountain?" McCarter suggested. "If we can get to him, we can snatch him out with a Sky Hook."

"I'm afraid that would be seen as an unauthorized U.S. incursion," Brognola said, "and I'm not sure that the President would sign—"

"We're getting him back," McCarter stated flatly. "And, as T.J. likes to say, I don't give a fat rat's ass if I have to fight my way down from the Panama Canal to do it. You can tell the President that we're going down there to get him, and he'd better reconcile himself to that.

"And—" he locked eyes with Brognola "—if that bloody IRA bastard Collins gets in my gun sights, he dies. I don't have to see it carved in stone to know that he has his bloody hands in this somehow."

"We'll get him back," Price stated flatly, "one way or the other, and Hal isn't saying that we won't. This time, though, with all the international publicity, the ball isn't in our court and we have to step carefully. If we act on our own now, we might cause more harm than good. Like it or not, this time we just have to wait."

"And," Brognola added, turning to Kurtzman and Wethers, "while we're waiting for the situation to clear up, I want you to start blanketing that whole country for communications intel. If the rebels had something to do with this, they'll be burning up the phone lines and I want to know about it. Even if this turns out to be a real accident, I still want to know what the hell's going on down there."

He faced McCarter. "In particular, I want to

know what Mr. Sean Collins is doing. I don't like him any more than David does."

"Will we have NRO cooperation on this one again?" Wethers asked.

"You will," Brognola vowed. "And I'll see that you get access to both the NSA and CIA satellites for the communications intercepts."

When the meeting broke up, Katzenelenbogen went to the Computer Room to read himself into the situation. Over the years, he had lost too many comrades in arms to ever want to sit down and try to count them. At times, though, the faces of dead friends came to his mind and he always smiled as he remembered the good times.

He and Mack Bolan hadn't been together all that many years, but the intensity of their friendship made up for what it lacked in longevity. If—and it was a big "if"—Bolan was dead and his death turned out to be a result of the uncaring face of fate, Katz could live with it. It wouldn't be a loss he'd be able to just put away as he had so many of the others, but he would live with it.

Machines did fall out of the sky, and more than one good man had died because a fifty-cent part had failed at the wrong moment. While it was always a shock when the technology or engineering failed, it would continue to be a fact of life as long as men needed machines to fly.

If that was the case with Bolan, he would mourn, but he would understand.

If, however, the hand of man had been involved in any way, his grief would have a focus, and from that focus would come action, swift and certain. Not even the deaths of a thousand men would compensate him for the loss, but he would extract his vengeance. It would give him something useful to do while he was grieving.

Katz was one of the world's best practitioners of the philosophy of "don't get mad, get even." He also knew that vengeance, as the Spanish so aptly put it, was a dish best eaten cold. So, before he started sharpening his sword of vengeance, he had to see the body. After that, he would determine for himself why his friend had died.

Then, and only then, would he make a decision to act or not. And if he did decide to take action, nothing on Earth would stop him from taking vengeance.

Peru

AFTER ORDERING his captives to be taken away, Sean Collins went directly to the sizable bamboo building that served as his jungle headquarters. Now that the first part of his operation had been successful, it was time to implement the rest of it.

Being the senior American DEA agent for Latin American operations, Dan Denning was an invaluable asset. It was unfortunate that he'd had to sacrifice two of his old IRA comrades to pull off this coup, but it had been a necessary price to pay. The chopper had had almost a full load of JP-4 fuel on board when the thermite grenades went off in the tanks, so there would be little left to be identified when the wreckage was investigated. But what remains that would be recovered from the crash site had to be from Europeans, not Latins, for the deception to work.

With the American drug authorities believing that Denning had died in the crash, there would be no reason for them to change their way of doing business. They believed that their antidrug programs were gaining ground, so they wouldn't disrupt them. It was true that whoever the Yankees sent to replace Denning would have his own way of doing things, but any changes he made to their procedures would be gradual. And by that time, Collins would have some of his people on the inside, so it wouldn't matter.

Collins considered letting his American guests have a good night's rest before he started asking questions. That tactic was designed to drive home the fact that they were helpless and would lower their resistance to interrogation. Normally he would go along with that procedure, but this time there was another factor he had to take into consideration. The cartel representative was due to arrive in the morning, and he would want to know what Collins had discovered about upcoming DEA operations.

Collins wasted no time regretting the fact that

he'd been forced to make an alliance with the cartels to secure the financing he needed to get his Peruvian project off the ground. He had long ago learned that the end always justified the means. Capturing Denning had been worth five million of the cartel's dollars. The information he intended to get from the man was worth another five.

He knew that ten million was merely pocket change to the drug lords, but to a man who knew how to get the most out of a pound, it would go a long ways to getting his operation up and running. But to get the money, he had to deliver the information, and there was no time like the present to start that process.

He called to the rebel guard on duty outside his door. "Bring the old one here," he said in Spanish.

"Sí, patrón."

CHAPTER FOUR

Stony Man Farm, Virginia

With everyone settled in at the Farm, Jack Grimaldi was completely at loose ends for the moment, so he decided to drift over to Cowboy Kissinger's armory to hang out and burn time. The thing about being the Farm's resident pilot was that when there were no planes to fly or maintain, there wasn't a hell of a lot for him to do. When, and if, a mission was mounted, he'd have his hands full again. At the moment, though, he wasn't even needed for consultation.

In the armory, John "Cowboy" Kissinger was going through the motions of keeping busy by re-cleaning already immaculate racks of small arms. He stayed on top of the Farm's weaponry and perimeter defense systems, and unless a mission was in the making, there usually wasn't all that much for him to do beyond the routine—particularly anything that would take his mind off the circumstances at hand. Mindless fieldstripping and cleaning weapons did, though, give his hands something to do.

He hadn't worked in the field with Mack Bolan on a regular basis like Phoenix Force and Able Team, so he couldn't say that he knew Bolan as well as they did. He had, however, come to know the man from working on his personal weapons and brainstorming with him when they were developing mission-specific items. He had also spent enough downtime with Bolan to have a feeling what the man was like off the job. He liked him and had the greatest respect for him.

Kissinger was very much aware that if, and he still thought of it as a big "if," Bolan actually had been killed, life at Stony Man Farm would never be the same, could never be. The President would still order McCarter's and Lyons's teams to go in harm's way to do America's dirty work, but an indefinable element that had characterized their operations so far would be lost forever.

Bolan was more than just another gun around this Farm.

"You got your coffeepot up and running, Cowboy?" Grimaldi asked as he walked in. "I can't take any more of the Bear's Computer Room crap."

Kissinger enjoyed the first smile that had crossed his face since the news from Peru had come in. "What's the matter, Jack, you getting old on us?"

Grimaldi shook his head. "I've been too old for that shit ever since the first day I had a cup. I don't see how those guys over there can stand it. It's no wonder Brognola practically mainlines Maalox."

Kissinger held his smile a moment longer. Kurtzman's disreputable coffeepot and the bitter, acidic product it dispensed were infamous. Not even the worst Army mess hall coffee could invoke the grimaces that the mere mention of the Computer Room brew could.

"There's a good reason that I go out of my way to procure my own coffee fixings over here." The pilot went straight to the armory pot, grabbed a clean cup and poured.

"Do they have confirmation on Striker yet?" Kissinger asked the only question that really mattered.

Grimaldi shook his head. "Not yet."

"Do you think it's true?"

"No way. I'm going to have to see the body for myself before I buy into that crap."

Kissinger wanted to climb on board the pilot's optimistic bandwagon. He wanted to believe so much to make himself feel better, but he just couldn't allow himself to do it. He was afraid that if he got his hopes up too high, and they turned out to be for naught, the fall would hurt even more. Every man had to die sometime, and not even Bolan could escape that.

He wouldn't, however, put his attitude on the pilot. If Grimaldi could find comfort in his hope, he wouldn't rain on his parade.

"It's going to be a long wait, isn't it?"

Grimaldi nodded over his steaming cup. "Sure as hell is."

"Well, you're welcome to hide out here."

Peru

DENNING WAS EXHAUSTED and had gone to sleep immediately after eating dinner, but Bolan stayed awake to observe the camp at night. The time-proved rule of thumb for prisoners was that they should try to make their escape as soon as they could create an opportunity. Usually a person would never be in better physical and mental condition than he or she was right after being captured.

Had he been alone, that's exactly what Bolan would have done. The bamboo cage they had been put in wasn't his idea of a serious containment area, but he'd signed on as Denning's bodyguard and his code wouldn't allow him to leave the man behind.

From what he had seen of Collins's forces so far, they were the usual guerrilla troops he was accustomed to seeing in Latin America. They were hard men, most of them Indians, with nothing to lose but their lives by taking up arms. They looked to be experienced and, for such a ragtag group, were very well equipped. Along with the M-16s and the ex–Soviet Bloc AKs and RPGs he had seen on the march, he had spotted more modern weapons, including U.S. M-60 machine guns and 81 mm mortars in the camp. On top of that, every guerrilla he had seen on duty had been carrying hand grenades.

Even though their clothing was no kind of uniform and there was a decided lack of personal equipment, someone had been pouring money into outfitting these men with the only part of a military force that really mattered—firepower.

Since he had recognized several cartel players in the PLFP party at the ceremony, it was obvious that most of Collins's financing had come from the drug lords. The cartels had been buying protection from the local insurgent forces for some time. It was cheaper than fielding their own forces to protect their operations. Usually the rebels of both the right and the left of the political arena didn't care where their money came from just as long as it came. And if there was one thing that the drug lords had more than plenty of, it was hard cash.

With cartel involvement, there was always a chance that a survivor of one of his many cartel hits would recognize him. His best chance of survival was to get away from wherever he was as quickly as he could. If he escaped on his own, he knew that he stood a good chance at freedom. The opposition was good, but he had spent much of his life in the jungles of the world, as well, and was confident that he keep ahead of them. But if Denning was also to survive, the DEA man had to go with him and that was the sticking point.

The march into the camp had shown that Denning

wasn't up for the jungle, and trying to take the agent with him would doom them both before the first day was out. So, for now, Bolan would stay put, but it was always good for a prisoner to have escape on his mind. It kept him from giving in to the situation. This time, though, he wasn't sure how it was going to play out.

BOLAN HEARD THE GUARDS approaching their cage before he could see them. The rebels were keeping good discipline in the camp, and they were used to moving in the dark.

"Dan," Bolan said, shaking the older man's shoulder, "wake up. We have company."

Denning woke and forced himself to sit up. "Ah, shit. What now?"

"Collins probably wants to talk to us. That's the way these things usually go."

"What time is it?"

Since their watches had been taken, Bolan could only guess. "You've been asleep about an hour and a half."

"Better than nothing."

There were four guards, and two of them stayed outside the cage with their AKs leveled while the other two unlocked the cage and dragged Denning out.

BOLAN WAS STILL AWAKE when the guards carried Denning back to their cage. The DEA man had been thoroughly beaten and was unconscious. The soldier quickly checked him over and, except for his nose, didn't find any broken bones or serious injuries. It looked, though, as if his hands had been stomped on. So, while Denning was still out of it, Bolan pulled two of the man's fingers back into joint.

After making him as comfortable as he could, Bolan wetted the tail of his shirt with water from one of their canteens and tried to clean the blood from his face. The man awoke in the middle of these ministrations and jerked his head away.

"Easy," Bolan said. "You're okay now."

"The hell I am." Denning spit blood and saliva. "I feel like I got hit by a fucking truck. But I didn't give them a damned thing."

"What did he ask you?"

"Nothing, actually." Denning coughed and clutched his side. "In fact, he wasn't even there. I think the bastard had his goons beat me up just for the hell of it."

Bolan seriously doubted that. Inflicting pain, but not asking any questions in the process was an old interrogation technique. The DEA man had been silently beaten to fix in his mind the fear of future torture. Every man had a breaking point, and fear helped to quickly reach it. No matter how tough anyone thought he was, there was always some point beyond which he simply couldn't take any more.

It was also true that too much pain left some men

psychotic to the point that anything they finally did say was useless. That was why it was so much faster, as well as easier, to obtain useful information by using chemical interrogation. But Collins didn't seem to want to do things the easy way, and the question was, why?

Bolan didn't read Collins as a sadist. So far he hadn't shown any of the signs of that particular twist of mind. The soldier saw him as too cold and calculating to get off on another person's pain, and this beating proved that assessment. He hadn't even been there to watch Denning being hurt. The beating had been ordered specifically as part of an interrogation process. The questions would come later.

That was also why Bolan hadn't been given the treatment tonight, as well. It was devastating for the beaten man to see his comrade whole and in one piece. He would know that he, too, could be safe and out of pain if he would only answer his questioners. It was a crude technique, but Bolan knew that it was often effective.

Since he hadn't worked with Denning before, he had no idea how much the man could take. But the way this was going, he didn't think that he would survive too much of Collins's interrogation methods. It was apparent that the agent was a stubborn man, maybe too stubborn for his own good, and he wasn't likely to talk. Collins didn't look to be willing to grasp that fact, which would only result in

Denning being beaten to death. And once the agent was dead, Collins wouldn't have any reason to keep Bolan alive.

Right now, he was serving both as Denning's nurse and as a vivid reminder that the DEA man didn't need to suffer as he was doing. It wasn't a job that was going to last very long.

"Wash your mouth out," Bolan said. "And then try to get to sleep again. I'll keep an eye out."

"The bastards," Denning mumbled.

Stony Man Farm, Virginia

"HAL," BARBARA PRICE said over the intercom.

Brognola could hear a tremble in her voice. Knowing her as he did, he knew what was coming next. "What is it?"

He heard her take a deep breath. "We just got a report from the Peruvian army. One of their mountain-rescue teams reached the crash site, and there are no survivors. The bodies—what was left of them—were described as having been almost completely incinerated. They're being taken out now by helicopter."

"I'll be right down."

Brognola sat for a long moment, his eyes unfocused. He'd had a very different relationship with Mack Bolan than had the commandos of the Stony Man action teams. He had known the Executioner from the earliest days of the Mafia Wars, first as a

Fed on his tail, then later as an ally in his fight against the crime lords. He had also been the one who had brought him into Stony Man Farm when the President had asked him to create the SOG.

He had always known that this day would come sooner or later. Mack Bolan was never going to die in a comfortable bed with his boots off and maybe with a loving woman or a faithful old dog by his side. No matter how many times he had earned it, men like him never died that way.

He was grateful, though, to whatever powers there were that Bolan had died in an air crash and not from coming out second best in a firefight. Even though the chopper crash had more than likely been caused by enemy action, it had been through no fault of Bolan's. He hadn't faltered in any way, nor had he been anything other than on top of his game when it happened, and that was good.

As he got to his feet, Brognola felt old. Now that Striker was gone, he was finally going to have to take a hard look inside himself to see if he wanted to continue as the director of Stony Man Farm. It had been a good run and he had enjoyed it. But much of the pleasure had been because he had been working with Bolan.

Now, though, he had to go downstairs and do what he could for the people Bolan had left behind. He would have preferred to shoot himself rather than have to face them and tell them the news, but he was still their leader and burying the dead was one of the things that went with the job title.

THE WORD FROM PERU had flashed through the Farm like a lightning strike. Everyone from the cooks to the blacksuits on patrol knew that the big black-haired man with the ice blue eyes but calm, friendly manner was gone. Some of them knew who he was in detail, and some of them only knew one or the other of his cover stories. They all knew, though, that he was at the heart of everything they did.

When Brognola reached the War Room, he found it packed to the walls with people who normally weren't allowed into the Stony Man briefings. Apparently, Price had let them in because no one wanted to be the last one to hear the fate of Mack Bolan. For this once, he let her decision stand.

The room was starkly quiet when he walked in and took his place at the head of the table. He paused for a moment to steel himself so he could speak clearly. The time for emotion would come later.

"There are no words I can say that will make this any easier," he said. "According to our best information at this time, Striker died in the crash of that chopper."

A collective groan came from the room, a deep sound of pain, but still no one spoke.

"His remains," Brognola continued, "along with

those of the DEA official he was accompanying and the two crewmen, are being taken to Lima for forensic examination. A report on those findings will be issued in due time, and as soon as I have that report, I will pass it on to you."

"As to what effect this will have on our operations here, I can't say at this time. Stony Man still has a mission, and that won't change at any time in the near future. We have lost one of our own, but we are at war and men die in war."

"Do you have anything on what brought down his chopper?" McCarter asked. "Was it enemy action?"

Everyone wanted to know that answer. If it was enemy action, they would have a focus for their anger.

"I don't have anything on that at this time," Brognola said, "and I don't want to speculate. My information is that the Peruvians weren't able to bring out any of the wreckage for examination. They had limited resources and were more concerned about recovering the bodies. They said that as soon as the weather clears, they'll make another attempt to recover the wreckage. As soon as that is accomplished, we'll examine it and determine what caused the aircraft to go down. Until then, we just have to wait."

No one wanted to hear those words, but they all knew that Brognola spoke the truth.

CHAPTER FIVE

Stony Man Farm, Virginia

Aaron Kurtzman wasn't a man who was comfortable waiting around for information—not as long as he could reach out and find his keyboard. Latin America in general, and Peru in particular, wasn't located at an on-ramp to what was being called the Information Superhighway. For them, it was more like being a wide spot along a badly rutted dirt road. Nonetheless, even the most remote corners of cyberspace were as close to him as the ends of his fingers.

It took a while, but Kurtzman was able to find an Internet link to the hospital in Lima that the bodies from the crash site had been taken for examination. After he logged on, he didn't encounter any local security systems, so it was child's play for him to make his way to the computer in the morgue where the forensic examination was being conducted.

Because two of the bodies were thought to be those of high-ranking U.S. representatives, the Peruvian pathologist conducting the examination was being careful to do a thorough job of it. He was dictating his findings to an assistant who was entering the information into a computer so they would have a record of the proceedings.

Kurtzman read along as the data was slowly entered. A Spanish-English cybertranslation program designed for the CDC was spitting it out for him in something he could read. When the pathologist started in on the osteologic section of the exam, Kurtzman almost came out of his chair.

PRICE LOOKED UP from her desk when she saw Kurtzman at her door. "What do you have, Aaron?"

Kurtzman looked grim as he wheeled his chair into the room and locked it in place by the side of her desk.

"It isn't him," he stated flatly.

"What do you mean?" she asked. "Do we have the DNA testing back yet?"

"No," he answered, "and we don't need to wait for it. The two bodies that the Peruvians identified as being Striker and Denning were European Caucasians, all right. But I just got their femur measurements, and neither one of them are him. The bones spec out as belonging to individuals who were well under six feet tall."

Price slumped in her chair. She knew that the length of the human femur bore a direct relation to the height of the individual. Bolan was over six feet tall.

"How about Denning?" she asked.

"He was over six feet, too."

"What do we do now?" She felt weak as the relief flooded through her, but she still had to stay on top of this development.

Although Kurtzman's arena was his cyberempire, Price knew that he had a devious, steel-trap mind, and she had learned to value his assessments in situations like this. His idiosyncratic mind-set could see around corners when no one else could even see the building.

"The first thing I think we need to do is let everyone know that he's still alive."

"Including the President?" she asked. Since this was another politically inspired debacle, she was reluctant to compound the screwup by putting it back in the hands of the politicians.

"Even him." Kurtzman nodded. "We're going to have to go proactive real hard, real fast, and it'll be a lot easier if we don't have to bump heads with him or try to do it under the table. He'll grease the skids if he knows.

"But," he cautioned, "beyond telling him and only him, we have to keep this tightly to ourselves. Since we don't know what happened down there, we can't trust anyone else in Washington and run the risk of tipping off the opposition that we're onto them. I recommend that we go ahead with the public brouhaha about the loss of two such valued public servants in a tragic accident, *yada, yada, yada*. The whole political dog and pony show, including a fancy funeral for Denning in Arlington, would be just fine.''

"Have you told Katz and Hal about this yet?''

"No.'' Kurtzman's eyes softened. "I thought you might like a chance to absorb this alone before the whole crowd gets involved.''

Kurtzman pretended not to notice the tears of relief welling in her eyes. "I think we can afford to give you fifteen minutes to yourself.''

"Thank you, Aaron.''

EXACTLY FIFTEEN MINUTES LATER, the War Room was ready when Barbara Price walked in and took her seat at the conference table. She could tell by the faces that Kurtzman had told them of his findings and, while they were relieved, they were out for blood.

As the tactical adviser, Katzenelenbogen had already worked up a contingency plan and was ready to present it. "The mission is to get Striker and Denning back ASAP,'' he said. "That much is straightforward.''

There were growls of assent from almost everyone on that point.

"The problem we're facing,'' he went on to explain, "is similar to what the U.S. Army faced in Vietnam in the late sixties and early seventies. They were looking for COSVN, the Central Office South Vietnam, the headquarters for all the Communist forces fighting in the region. They knew the general area it was in, but in spite of the best efforts of the world's best ground-recon teams, aerial recon, EINT and communications intercept, and the sixty-thousand-man Cambodian invasion of 1970, they never did find it.''

He looked up from his notes. "In our case, we know that Collins's coalition has a camp somewhere in northern Peru. And, for a number of reasons, mostly political, we cannot call upon the U.S. Army to help us find him. We have eight field operatives and a handful of support people we can call upon. It is true, though, that we have technology that would have been unimaginable during the Vietnam era to help us. Because of that, our only chance of finding him in time is to create panic in the opposition so they will help lead us to him.''

He locked eyes with Brognola. "I propose turning Phoenix Force and Able Team loose in Peru to go on a rampage. Their mission will be to strike at the so-called coalition everywhere and anywhere they can find them and to inflict as much damage to them as possible. The expected result will be to bring Collins out of hiding or to make him react in ways that we can use to track him down.''

"What if this fails?" Brognola asked.

"Should this fail, we have nothing to fall back on and the result will be the same as if we do nothing. Mack Bolan, if he is still alive, will die. At some point in time, Collins will have no further use for him. And even if he doesn't find out who he is, he's too dangerous to be left alive, so Collins will have no choice but to eliminate him just to be on the safe side.''

Everyone in the room knew these facts and had run them through their minds more than once. Hearing them spoken so matter-of-factly, though, was a shock. Leave it to Katz to put everything on the table, warts and all.

"You have all discussed this?" Brognola asked as he looked around the table.

"We have," Katz answered for everyone.

"I'll take it to the President and see what he says."

"As long as you're going to be asking," Katz said, "tell him that we really need 'get-out-of-jail-free' cards this time and the complete cooperation of all of the U.S. agencies in Peru."

Brognola nodded. The infamous "get-out-of-jail-free" cards were a remnant of the covert cold war. They weren't so much a card as they were a letter of instruction telling every American federal employee from the lowest janitors to the ambassadors to instantly obey any order of the bearer. They were signed by the President and the heads of all of the Armed Forces and federal intelligence and police agencies. They were rarely issued nowadays, but when they were, they were taken very seriously.

"I want to launch Able Team on this as soon as possible," Katz continued, hitting the next item on his list. "And it would be nice if we could borrow a State Department VIP transport for a quick trip down to Lima. It would add a certain caveat, as well as being a quick way to get their mission equipment down there without having to be too obvious."

"That shouldn't be a problem."

"And lastly," Katz added, "tell the Man that I strongly advise against bringing the Peruvians in on this at this time. Their president can't be trusted to take out the trash, much less keep something like this to himself. He'll sell it to the coalition in a heartbeat. He's trying to ride to glory on Collins's Nobel Prize coattails."

"What about the VP?"

"We can tell him what went down after it's all over because I have a feeling that the prez is going to end up on the wrong side of this thing, and Castillio will be taking over before too long."

"Anything else?"

Katz shook his head. "That should do it for now."

"Anyone else?" Brognola looked around the table.

"The chopper's waiting," Price said when she saw that he had no takers. Katz had spoken for everyone in the room this time.

"I'm going." He shut his briefcase and headed for the door.

"Do you think the Man will sign off on it?" Barbara asked as Brognola disappeared down the hallway.

"It doesn't really make any difference one way or the other," Katz stated, smiling grimly, "because we're going in no matter what he says. It will be a lot easier for us to pull off, though, if he agrees to it, so I hope Hal's on his best form this time."

"I think he'll be convincing."

BROGNOLA RETURNED to the Farm in record time. He wasn't smiling when he stepped off the chopper, but he wasn't frowning, either.

"It's on," he told Katzenelenbogen and Price. "The Man gave us everything I asked for, and then some."

"About damned time," Katz said.

"Have Carl and David meet us in the War Room."

In the War Room, Brognola turned to the Able Team leader. "Carl, get with Kissinger and prep for at least a two-week operation in Peru. I want you there tomorrow afternoon. And I got your get-out-of-jail-free cards, so you shouldn't have any trouble with any of our people down there. The embassy and all federal agency offices are being told to provide every assistance."

"That'll be a nice change." Lyons smiled. "I get

tired of having to fight our own people all the time, as well as the bad guys.''

''When does Phoenix launch?'' McCarter asked. It made good sense to send Lyons down first to pave the way, but he didn't want to be left too far behind.

''You need to be ready to move out tomorrow, and you'll be staging out of Panama City. Jack will fly you down there to pick up your mission equipment and your ride to Peru.''

''We're ready now.''

''In the meantime,'' Brognola said, ''I have a funeral to attend tomorrow. Dan Denning of the DEA is to be laid to rest in Arlington National Cemetery as befits a fallen national hero. The remains of the other man are being cremated and will be laid to rest in a private ceremony at an undisclosed location. As far as official Washington goes, that will close the incident and Collins won't have to worry that we're onto him.''

''I'm onto him,'' McCarter vowed.

IT WAS A WARM spring day at Arlington National Cemetery, America's final resting place for its most honored heroes. It had rained the night before, and the air was clear enough to see the Capitol dome in the distance across the Potomac. The Robert E. Lee house, surrounded by the white stone markers of thousands of Civil War dead, gleamed in the sun.

Hal Brognola stood at the open grave site next to Robert Wilton, the head of the DEA, as the horse-drawn caisson bearing the flag-draped casket slowly approached following the Army honor guard. Dan Denning had both served in the Army and had died in his country's service, so he was getting the full treatment.

"It's a damned shame," Wilton said for the third time in the past half hour. "Dan only had a year and a half left to go before retirement."

"It is a shame," Brognola agreed yet again.

"Is there going to be a service for the other man, his bodyguard?"

Brognola shook his head as he fielded the question. "His family requested a private cremation. They didn't want any official presence, and we honored their request."

"He should be here, too." Wilton shook his head. "He earned the right. It's a damned shame."

Brognola agreed that Mack Bolan well deserved to rest in Arlington if any American did. But he also knew that it would never happen. When Striker finally did die, he'd be laid to rest as anonymously as he had lived most of his life. No matter how much he deserved it, there would be no national mourning for him. That was just how it would be.

For a man with no immediate family, Denning's funeral was well-attended. Like many federal cops, he was divorced, but he had made many friends during his years of federal service, and they all came to say goodbye to a comrade.

"Who's the State Department type?" Wilton

asked, looking across the open grave to a late-thirtyish man in a charcoal gray suit and a lightweight London Fog raincoat who was standing back out of the way

Brognola looked, but didn't recognize the man. "He sure looks like one of the Foggy Bottom Georgetown whiz kids to me," he said. "But I don't think I've ever seen him before. Maybe he was one of the geniuses who promoted that Peruvian-coalition treaty and is here to do penance."

"I didn't like that damned thing from the first," Wilton growled. "It's a hell of a thing for Dan to get killed over something as stupid as that. We should be out there busting those bastards' chops, not rewarding them by giving them legitimacy."

"I couldn't agree more," Brognola said thoughtfully. "And do me a favor, will you?"

"Sure."

"Find out who that guy is and get back to me immediately."

Wilton knew better than to ask why Brognola wanted that information. He knew, though, that it would be put to good use whatever it was.

"Can do."

THE SERVICE WAS the military's standard version given by one of the old guard's chaplains. As soon as he closed his Bible, the seven-man honor guard brought their rifles to their shoulders on command and fired the three volleys of the final twenty-one-gun salute. As the last crash of the rifles echoed away, the lone trumpeter on the knoll brought his instrument to his lips and the clarion notes of "Taps" sounded as they had so many times before over this hallowed ground.

When the last golden note faded, Brognola turned to go. This was the only time he had ever walked away from an Arlington grave site feeling good. It was true that this still might become Dan Denning's grave, but for now it was empty. And he would move heaven and earth to keep it that way.

He only knew Denning by reputation, but he'd do his best to rescue him along with Striker.

TRENT CARLSWORTH KEPT his face as solemn as the occasion warranted as he walked back to his car. Working at the State Department gave a man valuable experience in hiding his true feelings about almost everything. Denning's funeral would make it on CNN tonight, so the coalition headquarters in Lima would pick it up and pass the information on to Collins. And with this out of the way, the Irishman wouldn't have to worry, which meant that he wouldn't have to, either. When Collins worried, he had a way of passing it on.

As Carlsworth walked to his car, he didn't notice that Robert Wilton had him in the viewfinder of a 35 mm camera with a zoom lens.

Brognola had asked Wilton to find out who he was, and the camera was DEA standard issue for taking field-surveillance mug shots. As the agency's director, he didn't spend much time in the field anymore, but he still carried his camera in the glove box of his company car.

After taking five shots to insure that he had what he needed, Wilton drove away. The photos would be developed as soon as he got back to his office, and IDed for Brognola.

CHAPTER SIX

Lima, Peru

The U.S. State Department VC-20H Gulfstream IV jet taxied to the part of the Lima International airfield reserved for diplomatic flights. Before the pilot even locked his brakes and chopped his throttles, a black Mercedes limo with tinted windows escorted by two 30 mm autocannon-packing armored cars and two trucks full of heavily armed Peruvian paratroopers drove out to meet it.

"That's quite a reception party," Herman "Gadgets" Schwarz said as he looked out the plane's window at the paratroopers piling out of the trucks and taking up positions surrounding the plane. "Someone down here must really like us."

Carl Lyons snorted. "Someone down here has been told that if anything happens to us on the way to the embassy, the shit is going to hit the fan, big time," he stated accurately. "I'm surprised that they have only one company of troops and two pieces of armor here."

The President of the United States took a very dim view of being made a fool of. And until it was discovered exactly what in the hell was going on in Peru, he was taking no chances. The U.S. ambassador in Lima, as well as the Peruvian ambassador in Washington, had been told in no uncertain terms exactly what was expected of them until this matter was cleared up. And part of what they were to do was to insure the absolute safety of the personal representatives the President had sent down to conduct an investigation for him.

"If you look out to the fence," Rosario Blancanales said, "you'll see the rest of the welcome."

Another dozen armored vehicles, including several French-made AMX-30 main battle tanks and what looked like at least a battalion of camouflage-uniformed infantry, could be seen. Overhead, a pair of AH-1 Cobra gunships cruised by, barely clearing the telephone poles.

"The only thing missing is the marching band," Schwarz said.

When the troops had formed their cordon around the plane, the Mercedes drove right up to the jet's door. A man in a tropical suit and sunglasses stepped out, took off his sunglasses and held up his ID card so the pilot could see it from the cockpit window. When the pilot was satisfied with his identity, he had the in-flight attendant open the door and lower the steps.

"I'm Rich Baylor, State Department," the man

said when he entered the cabin. "Your car is waiting, gentlemen."

"What about our luggage?" Blancanales asked. The baggage in question mainly consisted of items that usually didn't make it past foreign customs police. "We don't want the Peruvians going through it."

Baylor was on top of that sensitive issue. "It's been declared diplomatic pouch and is being transferred to the car right now."

"Let's go, then," Lyons said.

The sun was baking the tarmac as Able Team walked the few steps to the air-conditioned car.

"I don't see any Twinkies," Schwarz said, looking around the spacious interior of the limo. "I specifically said that I wanted fresh Twinkies on the ride to the embassy."

When the State Department man blanched, Blancanales smiled and shook his head. "Don't pay any attention to him, Mr. Baylor. He's always wanted to be a rock star, and he read somewhere that Culture Club always had Twinkies waiting for them in their limos."

"It wasn't Culture Club, man. It was—"

"Dammit, Gadgets!" Lyons snapped. "Knock it off and leave the man alone."

Baylor looked about as confused as a career foreign service officer could be. He had drawn the short straw to pick these people up from the airport, and he had no more idea than the ambassador did about what was going on. All he knew was that he had been told to treat these men as personal representatives of the President and to follow their orders as if they had come directly from the Oval Office. But if these three were working for the President, Washington was in worse shape than he thought.

THE TWO PERUVIAN army Cobra gunships shadowed the convoy as it sped through the streets of Lima. All of the highway intersections along the route were blocked by armed motorcycle police to give them free passage through the city.

The American Embassy was on a tree-lined boulevard and it looked to have been recently fortified. The sandbag positions on each side of the main gate looked brand-new. The two AMX-30 tanks flanking them weren't new, but their 90 mm main guns looked serviceable and the commanders in their hatches were scanning the surrounding rooftops with binoculars, looking for targets.

Inside the embassy gates, the Marines of the guard detail were in their full battle dress and armed. Whatever instructions the President had given the ambassador were being taken seriously.

"If you'll follow me, gentlemen," Baylor said as he opened the door of the limo and quickly led them up the steps into the building.

The conference room Baylor took them to was set up with a massive silver coffee service and a generous cold-cut and fresh-fruit platter. "Make yourselves comfortable, gentlemen," the aide said. "The ambassador and the station chief will be with you immediately."

Since they had eaten well on the flight down, the Able Team commandos passed on the cold cuts and contented themselves with coffee, which was excellent. It was hard to beat mountain-grown beans.

According to the briefing Brognola had given them at Stony Man, the ambassador was a middle-aged woman, the widow of a prominent senator. The favors that had been owed to her deceased husband at the time of his death had been paid off by giving her the ambassadorship. She wasn't a bad woman, simply unversed in international affairs.

"Gentlemen," she gushed officiously as she swept into the conference room, "I'm so glad to welcome you to Peru. The President asked me to give you the 'run of the house,' as they say, so anything you need, just ask."

"Thank you, ma'am." Lyons extended his hand. "We're glad to be here. I'm John Weiss."

"Samantha Biggins," she replied.

"Joe Verde," Blancanales introduced himself.

"Jim Braun," Schwarz said.

The man standing behind the ambassador stepped forward and introduced himself. "Cary Rockhill, station chief."

Though Rockhill was known to the outside world as the embassy's "cultural attaché," he was the

CIA station chief, and he was not paid to gush. "If I can see your credentials, gentlemen?"

"Oh, I don't think that will be necessary, Cary," the ambassador said. "The President said—"

"Actually, ma'am," Lyons said, interrupting her as he popped open his briefcase, "I prefer that he does check them. That way there won't be any awkward questions later."

One glance at the get-out-of-jail-free document bearing the President's signature was all Rockhill needed to see. "Will you be calling upon my office for assistance?" was all he asked. He didn't want to know their mission.

"Only for background intelligence at this point," Blancanales said. "And perhaps for certain items of equipment later. We came prepared for our primary mission."

Rockhill kept from grinning. He knew a wetwork team when he saw one. Whoever these three guys really were, because they sure as hell weren't Justice Department flunkies, someone was going to feel the sharp end of the stick before this was over. And as far as he and his staff were concerned, it couldn't come too soon.

"You've been cleared for an in-depth backgrounding," the CIA man said cautiously, "but I'll have to okay any extensive equipment requests."

"We expect that," Blancanales said smoothly. "The acting director has been briefed, and he'll support any requests we might have."

Rockhill raised an eyebrow. If Langley was in on this gig, he'd be sure to play any kind of ball these guys wanted to play. His tour of duty in Lima would be over in a few months, and he had aspirations to advance to a comfortable office in Building Number One. Maybe if he handled this well enough, he would get an office with an outside view.

The ambassador was looking a little confused at this exchange. She still hadn't completely come to terms with the fact that her cultural attaché answered to the director of the CIA rather than to the State Department. Not understanding what the spy agency had to do with cultural affairs, she found it all a bit silly.

"I guess I should leave you with Cary, then," she said lamely.

"Thank you for the welcome, Madam Ambassador," Blancanales replied. "You've been most gracious."

"You're welcome," she replied.

"If you're ready, gentlemen," the station chief said, "we can retire to my briefing room."

"Let's do it," Lyons said.

The station chief led Able Team past the ambassador, down the hall and into his secure room. "Now we can talk," he said as he closed the steel door behind them.

"She doesn't have a clue about what's going on, does she?" Blancanales hooked a thumb back in the general direction of the ambassador they had left behind.

"I'm afraid you're right." Rockhill shook his head. "But at least she keeps the hell out of my way most of the time. All she knows about you people is that the President told her to bend over backward and drop her knickers if you so much as even hinted."

Lyons couldn't keep the grin off of his face. "I think we'll pass."

Rockhill smiled back. "I rather thought you might."

"By the way," Lyons warned him, "we're only an advance team. There may be others joining us later."

"The more the merrier," Rockhill said. "But can you give me enough of a heads-up so I can tell my people what to keep their eyes out for?"

"You know those two DEA reps who went down on that chopper at the coalition treaty signing?"

"Dan Denning and his security man?"

Lyons nodded.

"That was a goddamned shame. I knew Dan pretty well, and I caught his funeral on CNN. It was a nice send-off for one hell of a good drug cop."

"They aren't dead," Lyons told him. "They were taken prisoner, and the Man wants them back."

"I'll be a son of a dirty bitch," Rockhill said softly. "I told Dan to watch his ass up there."

"We think it was a setup from the get-go, and they didn't have a chance."

Rockhill's jaw was clenched. "I knew there was something wrong with that arrangement. From the very start of the negotiations, the PLFP insisted on having a senior U.S. representative present at the treaty signing. We just figured that they wanted to rub our faces in their shit. We had no idea that they were planning to pull something like that."

"Obviously no one did," Lyons said, "or the President wouldn't have thrown his support behind it."

"My initial report to Langley about the proposal was as negative as I could make it," he said. "But I understand that someone in the State Department sanitized it before it went forward."

"Do you know who?"

"No," Rockhill said, "but I sure as hell intend to find out. Like I said, Dan Denning is a friend."

"His bodyguard is a friend of ours," Lyons admitted, "and we intend to find them both."

"Anything we can do to help, we will," Rockhill vowed. "On or off the record."

"First off," Lyons said, "we need a safehouse in town here, then we need a target list of all the PLFP facilities in Lima and vicinity."

Rockhill didn't blink at the words "target list," but it confirmed his first assessment of this trio. They were someone's clandestine muscle, and they had come to Peru to take vengeance. There had been a day when the CIA had taken care of chores like that. Since political considerations kept the Company on a very short leash nowadays, he didn't mind them operating on his turf at all. In fact, he envied them.

"You mean coalition facilities, don't you?"

Lyons's eyes turned icy. "I mean the assholes who are behind this, whatever they call themselves."

Rockhill smiled. "Got you covered."

THE CIA's LIMA SAFEHOUSE was a small walled villa on a side street a few blocks away from the embassy. Its cover was that of a summer house for a Mexican businessman who had extensive holdings in Peru. That explained why the security men who watched over it while the owner was away all spoke Mexican Spanish.

Rockhill not only put the villa and its security men at Able Team's disposal, he also provided a Chevy Blazer four-wheel-drive and a Buick sedan for their transportation needs. The larder was fully stocked, as was the bar, so Able Team quickly settled in.

They had barely carried their luggage inside when Rockhill himself showed up with a briefcase handcuffed to his wrist. "This should get you started," he said. "But if it's not enough, call me anytime day or night."

As soon as the station chief left, the trio started in on the background material.

Lyons soon found that the PLFP had a liaison office in the suburbs of Peru's capital city and figured that would be as good a place as any to start cracking heads. They would start off small and quickly work up to the bigger jobs. The recently sanitized PLFP rebels who manned the office might well have the information he was after. But even if they didn't, hammering them would be a good-warm-up exercise for the main act.

THE NEXT MORNING Able Team took the Buick out to make a recon of their first target. The coalition office turned out to be in a newly built Peruvian-style strip mall, a long block of two-story cinder-block buildings.

While Lyons and Schwarz cruised the neighborhood to familiarize themselves with the street access, Blancanales did the face-to-face canvass. Dressed in local clothing, he was able to keep from attracting too much attention as he reconned both the front and the back of the office and talked to the shopkeepers in the mall.

An hour later, they regrouped and headed back to the safehouse.

As they drove, Blancanales made his report. "It's going to be difficult to hit them during the day without creating a lot of collateral damage. And at night, there's not much worth going after in there except for the two night guards and maybe the files.

"But," he added, smiling, "according to the locals, the PLFP honcho who runs the office leaves every evening to go visit his girlfriend. He always takes the same route down a narrow side street, and they say you can set your watch by him. They say he's *mucho hombre* with the women."

"It sounds like he wants his girlfriend to know when to have dinner warmed up and waiting for him." Schwarz grinned. "I like a man who keeps to a time schedule. It makes our work so much easier."

"We'll take him down tomorrow night," Lyons said.

BACK AT THE SAFEHOUSE, the trio completed their map recon and picked out the ambush site.

"What do you want to do for an encore?" Blancanales asked. "Once we kick this thing off, we're going to need to keep hitting them before they can recover."

Lyons shuffled through the thick file Rockhill had provided them. "Let's pull this job off first, and then we'll take a look around and see what's worth blowing up."

"How about leveling everything the rebels have going here?" Schwarz suggested.

"Hal might consider that a bit excessive," Blancanales replied. "We're just supposed to make a few waves, not wipe Lima off the map."

"Damn," Schwarz replied. "A guy can't even have any fun with him around."

CHAPTER SEVEN

In the Jungle

Sean Collins didn't particularly like Sayed Mamal, but in his line of work, he didn't particularly have to like his associates. The thin, hatchet-faced Palestinian had always given him the willies. And considering his background, it took quite a lot to make him uneasy. But like it or not, the Arab was his partner now and had to be briefed on his progress.

Mamal was the first of the representatives from several organizations who were due to arrive at the jungle camp over the next several days for a conference on the future of the new coalition territory. Since Collins's fledgling empire would be fueled by a percentage of the drug lords' future profits, it was critical that he learn about the DEA's current drug-interdiction plans as soon as possible so he could brief his new partners. Denning, however, was being a great deal more stubborn than Collins had anticipated.

"I can make the infidel talk." The Islamic Brotherhood official laid his hand on the hilt of the curved dagger in his belt. "They are always weak to the sight of their own blood."

"I do not doubt your expertise," the former IRA terrorist said carefully, avoiding the fact that he, too, was an infidel and had seen his own blood on more than one occasion without it making him weak. "But I can get Denning to talk my own way. I need to have him intact for what we have planned to work properly."

The Palestinian didn't let his disdain for what he saw as infidel squeamishness show on his face, but Collins knew the man well enough to know that it was on his mind. The infamous Islamic Brotherhood always sang the same song when it came to shedding blood. The more blood they spilled, the happier they were and they didn't particularly care whose blood it was.

The Irish Republican Army, particularly the Provisional Wing Collins had been an operative for, was no stranger to shedding blood. The difference was that the Provos made sure that every drop they spilled, friendly or enemy, served a specific purpose even if that purpose was simply to spread terror. Collins had no qualms about killing. He had killed by his own hand many times, and he would continue to do so whenever it suited him. He would kill anyone who interfered with his plan.

He wouldn't, however, kill in either a drug or religiously induced frenzy. He detested drugs and religion equally. The irony that he had to depend on both drugs and Islamic fanatics to make his plan work wasn't lost on him. But he was a man who concerned himself with the end game, not the route it took him to achieve those ends.

His personal turn-on was power, and he was on the verge of having as much of it as he wanted. In just a little over a month, he would be awarded the Nobel Peace Prize for his work with White Shield in bringing about the cease-fire in Northern Ireland, as well as in Peru. He would become noted in the history books with such modern luminaries as the Reverend Dr. Martin Luther King Jr. and Nelson Mandela.

He always laughed when he thought about the Nobel Peace Prize winners of the past few decades. Most of them were nothing more than terrorists or Communist activists who had learned to play the game. Renouncing his ties to the IRA and forming White Shield had been in the best traditions of the famous Nobel Peace Prize–winning "peacemakers."

The hypocrisy of it all was enough to gag a maggot. But once the prestigious award was in his hand, he would be bulletproof as far as being suspected of any wrongdoing. Nobel gold washed away sins better than the Pope.

Under his guidance, the coalition territory would become a showcase of how a Third World nation could be developed. The fact that its economy would be backed up by drug and terrorist organizations would make no difference. All the world would see was that a war-ravaged, poverty-stricken nation was forging ahead into the twenty-first century. It would make wonderful press copy, and he had learned early on how to warp the media to serve his interests.

From his base in Peru, he would be able to bring other areas under the control of White Shield in the name of peace. Panama might be a good next move, or even Bosnia or Thailand. He had no intention, though, of ever getting involved in Africa. A man had to know his limitations. There was no nation in Africa that was even halfway stable enough for his organization to work. The unremitting savagery of Africa didn't lend itself to brokered peace deals.

"I will have another session with Denning this morning," Collins told his terrorist guest. "And I will supervise it myself. He will talk."

WHEN DENNING WAS BROUGHT back to the cage this time, he was in worse condition than he had been the night before. Again, Bolan tended to him as best as he could with what little he had to work with. He could do little for him, though, beyond cleaning up the blood.

"I don't know how much more of this I can take," Denning gasped through smashed lips. "You're going to have to kill me so I don't talk."

"We'll talk about that later," Bolan said. With

Collins and an Arab watching them from a dozen yards away, this was no time to be overheard.

COLLINS AND MAMAL WATCHED when Denning was taken back to the bamboo cage. "One more session should do it," the Irishman predicted. "He thinks he's tough, and he is. But every man breaks."

Mamal was turning away when he caught a clear view of Bolan tending to the DEA man. He stopped dead in his tracks and thought that he had to be seeing a *djinn,* one of the shape-changing spirits from Arab folk tales. That was the only explanation he could think of when he saw Collins's other prisoner. The Yankee was a dead ringer for the man who was known in the world of the Islamic Brotherhood simply as Al-Askari, "the Soldier."

There were as many stories about this man, and as far as he was concerned, most of them were embellished. If everything that had been said about the man was true, there would be no freedom fighters left alive anywhere in the world, and certainly no Brothers of the Islamic Revolution. That didn't mean, however, that the deeds attributed to the man were completely a figment of overactive imaginations. Mamal himself had been in the hands of a merciful God one night when Al-Askari had come calling.

The Black September cell he had belonged to at that time had been massacred. Almost two dozen fighters had been slaughtered less than half an hour before they were to launch an attack on an Israeli agricultural settlement across the Jordanian border. He had been delivering a last-minute message to their headquarters when Al-Askari struck, and so he had survived. His comrades hadn't been so lucky.

Finding him here was another act of a merciful God, and one that he wouldn't let slip from his hands.

"You know, Sean," Mamal said in his Oxford-accented English, "I would say that you have your hands on a real prize, and I suspect that you don't even know it."

Collins frowned. "You mean the DEA man?"

"No—" the Arab thrust his chin in Bolan's direction to point at him "—his bodyguard."

"What are you talking about?"

"He is a dead ringer for the man known throughout the Arab world as Al-Askari, the Soldier. He has been a premier Yankee assassin for many years."

"Why would the Americans send him here?"

The Arab shrugged.

"Are you sure that he's this Al-Askari?"

"I swear by God."

Collins wasn't much on oaths, but he knew the Islamic Brotherhood took such nonsense seriously.

"Our price for what you want of us is Al-Askari," Mamal said ominously. "My people will give you anything you can possibly want for him.

We owe him much, and it will be a pleasure to have the chance to repay him even a small portion of it.''

"I'm going to investigate him before I decide anything,'' Collins said.

"Don't take too long,'' the Arab warned.

BOLAN SAW the Arab stare at him and saw what he thought was a look of recognition pass over his face. He didn't think that he'd ever seen the man before, but that didn't mean anything. There were many men he had never met who knew of him, and if he'd been made, all bets as to the outcome of this were off. Collins would have to know of him under one of his field names as he had brought the IRA to account for their actions several times. There was nothing he could do but ride this out and see what happened next.

He briefly considered telling Denning who he was, but dismissed it. The DEA man had enough on his plate right now without having to try to hide that information, as well. In fact, the DEA man's only hope of living was to spill his guts.

"How are you doing?'' he asked the agent.

"I'm afraid that I'm gonna live,'' Denning replied, his voice slurred as he tried to talk around busted lips and a swollen jaw. He locked eyes with Bolan before continuing. "And I'm serious about your killing me. I don't think I can take much more of this.''

"Look—'' Bolan sat down beside him "—you

can forget about my killing you, but I really think that you need to change your tactics here. The way this is going, you're not going to last too much longer.

"I've been here before," Bolan said intently. "I know how this system works. You're determined that you're not going to talk, and he's going to beat you to death."

"Are you saying that I should tell that Irish scumbag what he wants to know?"

"It's the only way you're going to stay alive," Bolan said bluntly. "And he's not going to get much use out of anything you tell him anyway."

"What in the hell are you talking about?" Denning asked. "I know more about DEA operations in this theater than even the director does."

"That's true," Bolan said. "But it no longer matters. Every U.S. agent in all of Latin America had been put on alert since we were captured. And we aren't the only ones who know that we are still alive. Whoever they turned over to the embassy as our remains won't go unexamined, and I can assure you that my supposed remains won't match my DNA file."

"Why's your DNA on file?" Denning frowned. Most federal agencies hadn't yet started DNA identification files for their own personnel.

"It's a long story," Bolan said.

SEAN COLLINS MADE a hard decision the way he always made them—instantly. If Belasko was really the mythical warrior Mamal thought he was, he was a far greater prize than the DEA man. In fact, he could be the most valuable man on the planet, and there was no way that Collins was going to turn him over to the Islamic Brotherhood. And that meant that the Arab had to have an accident.

It was fortunate that the situation in Peru was still so unsettled. He knew that he couldn't risk alienating the powerful Islamic Brotherhood, but Mamal's death could be attributed to whichever group hadn't signed on to the cease-fire. Before he did that, though, he needed to check out the Arab's story. And even though he was in a completely uncharted jungle, miles from even the nearest small town, modern technology made that childishly simple.

Taking out a powerful satellite cellular phone, he placed a call to a beeper number. There was a pause as the signal went to the satellite and back down to Earth before the recorded message said. "You have reached 555-0688."

After the beep, Collins simply said, "Wrong number, I wanted 0866," and hung up.

It was less than three minutes before Collins's phone rang. "I had to leave a meeting to take this call," an American-English-accented voice said. "This had better be important,"

"It is, Trent," Collins replied. "I need you to look into someone for me. I have a man here named

Mike Belasko, Denning's security man. I need to know exactly who he is and how he was picked to come down here. This is very important, and I need the information immediately.''

"It may take me a while," Trent Carlsworth of the State Department replied cautiously. "I'm in a conference right now on what is being called the New Look of Peru. Since I was the pointman on the coalition proposal, I have to be there to continue promoting White Shield.''

"You have nothing more important right now than getting that information for me," Collins said in a cutting tone. "Make sure that you don't forget that again. Trina Wilson's father still wants to know how and why his daughter died.''

"You'll get the information," Carlsworth promised.

"Make it soon.''

Washington, D.C.

IN WASHINGTON, State Department employee Trent Carlsworth folded his cellular phone and stared out over the Capitol Mall.

There was no way that he could have known that Trina Wilson had been planted on him. He had been one of the U.S. observers at the final rounds of the IRA–Northern Ireland peace talks when he met her at a cocktail reception. Hell, he hadn't even known that she was British. She'd said that she was a print journalist for an Irish publication, and he wasn't good at recognizing the subtle difference between the educated Irish and the British accents.

He had always prided himself on being a bit of a ladies' man—the family money, the Georgetown connections and a personal trainer made that possible. Therefore, he hadn't been too surprised when she had fallen for his charms at a cocktail party for the media and the negotiation team. She was the one who had suggested that they go back to her place, and he had been more than ready to top off the evening.

The evening that followed wouldn't have been remarkable in any large American metropolis, but Carlsworth hadn't known that Irish women were so interesting.

The next morning, he had awakened to find her in bed next to him stone-cold dead. His eyes immediately went to the coffee table where the remnants of the cocaine she had snorted the previous night dusted the glass-topped coffee table. He hadn't done much more than sample the nose candy she had offered, but she had sucked it up off and on all night to fuel her exertions.

He was still trying to input all of this information when the phone suddenly started to ring the characteristic double ring of British phones. His first thought had been to ignore it, get dressed and get the hell out of wherever he was. Force of habit, though, made him pick it up.

"Hello?"

"Trent Carlsworth?"

"Yes."

"This is Sean Collins." After having sat across the table from the Irish peace activist for several days now, Carlsworth didn't fail to recognize the name. "I would like to speak to Trina, if I may."

On the edge of panic, he'd said the first thing that came to his mind. "Ah, she's in the shower right now. Can I have her return your call?"

Collins laughed. "You're in a serious spot of trouble, aren't you, boyo. She's lying on the bed stone dead, and you don't even know what to do next. You don't know if you should try to slip out and pretend that you were never there, or if you should call the police and throw yourself on their mercy. Let me tell you that doing either one is going to put a rope around your neck."

Collins chuckled. "Hanging's not a pretty way to die. But buck up, boyo, things aren't as bad as they look. I have an easy way out of your dilemma. Just stay there and I'll come to you."

"I'll be here," Carlsworth said, taking the out.

"You had better be," Collins warned.

And the Irishman had been as good as his word. The body had been disposed of, and he had been spirited out of the building without being seen. All it had cost him for this service was his soul. Collins had taken a series of photographs of him, the body and the room as insurance that Carlsworth would stay bought.

Trina had been the only daughter of a prominent British politician, but her death was still officially an unsolved murder. It would remain that way, though, only as long as he did whatever Collins told him to do. Not a minute longer. That meant that for as long as he lived, Trent Carlsworth would be owned by the Irishman.

CHAPTER EIGHT

Lima, Peru

Able Team's takedown of the PLFP official's car went flawlessly. After all, it was one of the standard moves in their world championship playbook. This time, though, they used the Claymore variation to deal with the escort car. In line with Katzenelenbogen's plan to rattle a few cages, Lyons was after the maximum effect, and the Claymore was sure to get someone's attention big time.

While the M-18 Claymore was a decidedly low-tech weapon, Gadgets Schwarz had rigged a high-tech trigger to the powerful directional mine. When the lead car passed the kill zone and broke the laser sighting beam, rather than go off, the detonator would merely note its passing and get ready for the next vehicle that tripped the laser beam. Only then would it send its microsecond electrical charge to a tightly contained, unstable chemical compound.

The men of Able Team had parked the Blazer to give them good observation of the approach to their kill zone, and their targets appeared exactly on time. As Blancanales had been told when he canvassed the PLFP office, the lead car was the black Lexus owned by the rebel honcho. The silver Acura following it belonged to his backup muscle.

With the target confirmed, Schwarz hit the switch to activate the mechanical ambush.

The Lexus tripped the laser beam and passed through unscathed, as was intended. Five seconds later, the second car hit the beam again. Even at forty-five miles per hour, the Acura traveled only three feet before the Claymore detonated.

Since the mine had been affixed to a stucco-over-concrete wall, the mine's normal back blast from the explosion was converted into additional forward force. Propelled by a pound and a half of C-4 plastic explosive, seven hundred .25-caliber steel balls moving at the velocity of a machine-gun bullet hit the escort car like a rainstorm from hell. A 5.56 mm Squad Assault Weapon with a 500-round magazine and the trigger held down couldn't have done a better job.

The silver Acura slammed to a halt as abruptly as if it had rammed a concrete wall.

Nearly every three-inch square of its front and left side had a .25-caliber hole in it where one of the Claymore's deadly steel balls had penetrated. And that included the bodies of the four PLFP bodyguards who were riding inside. The tires on that side of the car were shredded, the lights shot out and steam hissed from a riddled radiator.

Before the three occupants of the lead car could react to the sound of the explosion behind them, Lyons drove the Blazer in front of it, blocking off the narrow street. From the Chevy's passenger seat, Schwarz sent a single burst from his over-and-under M-16 IM-203 combo, taking care of the two men in the front seat of the Lexus, the driver and shotgun rider.

The man in the back seat was still trying to figure out what was going on when the door was ripped open and he was jerked out of the car. A buttstroke to the forehead from an M-16 made him a lot more portable. Lyons grabbed him, slung him over his shoulder and carried him back to the Blazer and tossed him into the back seat.

Leaving the cars and the bodies where they were, Schwarz powered the Blazer away from the scene of the crime. Just as none of the locals in this neighborhood had gotten involved with the takedown, Lyons knew that no one would trouble themselves with the corpses they had left behind until morning. It was only when they impeded the normal use of the street that anyone would even notice them.

As was the case in too much of Latin America, paying too much attention to the inconvenient dead in Lima was a good way to join them.

"IS HE AWAKE?" Carl Lyons asked as soon as the captured rebel was secured to the chair in their safe-house.

"He is now," Schwarz replied as he broke a capsule of ammonia under the prisoner's nose.

Ricardo Pena, one time PLFP fighter and now a front man for the coalition, sputtered and woke to a nightmare. He found himself strapped to a chair with several electronic devices attached to various places on his body. He didn't know enough about such things to know if they were to torture him or to betray him if he told a lie.

Pena was a hard man—only hard men survived the brutal insurgency that had devoured Peru for so many years. He had lost count of the men, women and children he had killed over the years, many of them up close and personal. He had suffered minor wounds himself on several occasions, but not until now had he felt that he was in serious danger of losing his life.

These three Yankees, and they could only be Yankees, weren't the frightened peasants or young draftees of the army he had killed before. He didn't have to be told that these were experienced men; he could see it in their eyes. The blonde with the cold blue eyes was the most frightening.

Blancanales stepped forward to handle the linguistic chores for the interrogation. Spanish was his first language.

"I will need your name," he said, "so I will

know who to notify that you have been taken captive by the Committee to Free Peru.''

''What committee are you talking about?''

Blancanales looked surprised. ''Didn't Mr. Collins tell you? There are some of us who are not happy with what he is doing here.''

''But you are not Peruvian,'' Pena stated, recognizing Blancanales' foreign Spanish accent.

''You do not have to be Peruvian to love justice,'' Blancanales said. ''Freedom is in danger here, and we intend to see that it does not die.''

He leaned over their prisoner. ''We do not, however, care if you die or not, so your fate is completely up to you. My friend—'' he pointed to Lyons, who had his .357 Colt Python in his hand ''—wants to kill you, but he has agreed to let you live as long as you answer our questions.''

Pena looked into Lyons's cold eyes and gulped.

''Now,'' Blancanales went on, pulling back, ''if you want to start earning the right to live, you can begin by telling me your name.''

''My name is Pena, Ricardo Pena.''

PENA HADN'T LIVED as long as he had by being a fool, and he quickly told Blancanales everything he knew about Sean Collins's operation. The problem was that he knew very little. His office was more of a PR stunt for the international media to show the new ''openness'' of the coalition than it was an operational office. It was true that he had once been a midlevel field officer of the PLFP, but he hadn't been given a role in the coalition beyond playing front man for curious locals and the media. And, as such, he wasn't privy to information such as where Collins's base camp was located.

After Blancanales finished questioning him, Schwarz put a blindfold on Pena and the team left the room.

"That was a complete waste of time," Lyons growled. The chance that this gig would break the situation open quickly and get Bolan back had just faded.

"This will still throw a scare into somebody and may make them react in a way we can exploit," Blancanales reminded him. "Remember what Katz said about stirring up the nest to drive the rats out into the open."

"So what do we do with Pena?" Schwarz asked.

There was no question about what they all really wanted to do with him, but this wasn't the time or the place. Plus, he might have some use later.

"Let's find out if the local DEA office has a holding facility," Blancanales suggested.

"No." Lyons shook his head. "They're probably infiltrated with Collins's people through their Peruvian counterparts. I'll call Rockhill and ask him to put this guy on ice for us till this is over."

ROBERTO RICHART PUT down the phone in his office in the White Shield headquarters and leaned back in his leather chair. He had come a long way in a very short time and wasn't about to be panicked by a minor setback like having Pena being snatched off the streets. Pena was a low-level pawn he could afford to lose as long as it was an isolated incident and not a sign of cracks forming in the cease-fire treaty.

Richart had been a law student in Santiago, Chile, when Marxist Chilean President Salvador Allende had been assassinated during a U.S.-backed coup, his government deposed and a military dictatorship put in its place. Richart's family had been Allende supporters and lost everything but their lives in the turmoil. He was shut out of the university because of his socialist parents and had been forced to flee himself. After doing a stint in one of the armed groups opposing the junta, he decided that fighting a guerrilla war was a good way to get killed and left the country.

Making his way to Colombia, he presented a forged law-school degree and signed on with one of the smaller drug cartels to handle their legal problems. The idea that drug lords needed lawyers wasn't that ridiculous. After all, even in the most repressive banana republic, the courts could still be an obstacle to living a life of crime. Unless, of course, the judges were properly taken care of, and that was where he came in. In other words, Richart become a bagman.

He quickly graduated from bagman to front man, the guy who legally bought properties and made investments using the drug lords' laundered funds. He also quickly became comfortably rich the easy way. With the drug lords behind him, he didn't have to skim the cartel's money, which was never a smart move. He merely had to mention their names and things happened for him. It was a perfectly legitimate way for a Latin American lawyer to do business.

In the course of his duties for both the cartel and himself, Richart found himself in the gunrunning business. When the cartels discovered that they could hire local insurgent groups far cheaper than they could recruit and outfit their own security forces, they did. Since the war chests of most rebel groups, both rightist and leftist, were chronically running low, the cartel stepped in to take care of their outfitting. Again, Richart learned the business quickly.

Before long, Richart's arms dealing brought him in contact with the Provisional Wing of the IRA and a terrorist named Sean Collins. It didn't take him long to figure out that Collins wasn't just another crazed Irishman raised on ancient tales of blood and past wrongs and thirsting for vengeance that was always out of reach.

In Collins, he found another man who could see further than the next assassination or car bombing. Because of that, he wasn't surprised when the Irishman left the Provos and became a peace activist. What better cover for money-making operations than a do-gooder peace organization? He was a bit surprised, though, when Collins contacted him after negotiating the IRA cease-fire and briefed him about the venture he was about to embark on in Peru.

After hearing Collins out, Richart had taken the plan back to his cartel bosses. They had liked it enough to sign on immediately and send Richart to Lima to be their representative to White Shield. His public role was to be the coordinator for the various groups who had joined together under the protection of the coalition. He was also currently in negotiation with several other groups, both Latin American and Middle Eastern, who wanted to join in on the spoils.

He wasn't surprised that the apparent capture of Ricardo Pena was causing concern within the ranks of the PLFP. The truce was supposed to have put an end to the factional fighting until a final agreement could be worked out to everyone's satisfaction. All of Peru's major armed factions, both leftist and rightist, had sworn that they would abide by it. The problem was that after such a long period of social unrest, there were more splinter groups than there were major factions, and not all of them had signed on for a cease-fire.

Sean Collins was particularly angry when he was informed. For his plan to work, he had to have peace in Peru for at least six months. It would take that long for him to get in the men and materials he needed to adequately defend his territory and go on to the next stage.

His immediate response had been to order Richart to investigate the incident. If there was a rogue rightist group that wasn't abiding by the agreement, he would have to have them taken out immediately. If it was a leftist group, he would let the PLFP handle them. But, either way, incidents like that couldn't be allowed to continue.

Another thing Richart did was to arrange for the security at the White Shield headquarters to be increased considerably. Collins had originally wanted to try to preserve as much of the traditional non-involvement stance expected of a peace organization as he could and hadn't wanted a visible security force. The public perception of his organization was essential, and he was afraid that having machine-gun bunkers and armed guards out front would spoil their image. But in this instance, Richart had been able to convince him that pragmatism had to prevail.

Getting the Peruvian army to provide that security for them had been a stroke of genius. Now, anyone who attacked them would face the full force of the government, such as it was. The fact that White Shield intended to destroy that very same government was a fine irony.

As a Latin American lawyer, Richart appreciated such ironies.

AS THE PHONE CALLS FLEW back and forth across Peru and Colombia, their electronic echoes shot out into space as did all electronic signals.

Anyone in the galaxy could, if he waited long enough, receive the entirety of humanity's radio and TV broadcasts. All it would take was a wide-band radio/TV receiver and lots of time. Since cellular phones were nothing more than small two-way radios, their calls were also subject to being overheard from outer space.

Since things of interest to the national security of the United States were often discussed over cellular phones and radios, the NSA had developed a series of deep-space electronic spy satellites to listen in on what America's enemies and potential enemies were saying to one another. It was simply a matter of equipping the satellites with wide-band receivers and telling them what frequencies to listen to. Onboard computers made sense of the signals, sorted them out and retransmitted them back to ground stations.

Not content to rest on their transistors, the wizards of space spy technology then went on to develop a way to detect the changes in the electromagnetic field of a telephone wire when it was in use. These magnetic field signals were much fainter than cellular phone transmissions, but EM radiation was EM radiation. All it took was fine tuning to be able to distinguish what emitted from phone lines and what came from, for example, electric shavers.

Once that was done, more NSA satellites were shot into space.

To a certain degree, these intercepts could be foiled by scrambler technology. But good scramblers were expensive and were temperamental to use, so only the most paranoid went to those lengths. After Prince Charles was overheard talking dirty to his girlfriend, everyone learned that cellular phones weren't secure. But people who really should have known better continued to talk openly over land-line phones.

In the cold reaches of space, an NSA Big Ear satellite dutifully intercepted and recorded those calls and stored them until the next time a ground station came over the horizon.

Stony Man Farm, Virginia

AT STONY MAN FARM, Akira Tokaido was intercepting the data flow from the NSA electronic-surveillance programs. They had authority to have the feed legitimately, but it was more fun to keep his hand in by tapping it.

The raw-feed signals were put back into voice communication form, then the audio was run through a translation program. As soon as the printer spit out each intercept in English, Hunt Wethers started to plot their points of origin. The termination point of any one particular transmission was more difficult to plot, but it, too, could be done with a certain amount of accuracy.

Before long, a pattern started to develop. It would take some time before the picture was clear, but it was forming.

CHAPTER NINE

Peru

Mack Bolan waited that night until Dan Denning was sleeping soundly before making his escape. Even though he was certain that the Arab had recognized him, he hadn't wanted to burden Denning with that information. Nor had he told him of his plans tonight. The man was trying to hide enough as it was without adding to the load.

Bolan had tried to explain to the DEA man that his only chance of survival lay with his cooperating fully with Collins, but he knew that Denning would continue to resist. The agent was of the old school where a man didn't give an inch to an enemy, but this was one time when that kind of courage wasn't a virtue. It was only going to get him beaten to death.

Bolan wasn't going to use his escape to go for help. He was confident that Stony Man knew that they had been captured and was already working to locate them. Also, leaving the area would surely doom Denning. The only way he could help keep the DEA man alive was to stay in the area and create so much trouble for Collins that the terrorist would delay questioning the agent and shift his focus to trying to kill the escaped prisoner.

It was a risky tactic, but it was worth trying.

There wasn't much in their cage that would be useful in making his escape to the jungle. He would, though, take one of the canteens so he wouldn't have to stick close to the water sources. He had also managed to retain a battered stainless-steel spoon from one of their meals. It wasn't much of a weapon, but it might have its uses. Anything else he needed, he would try to find on his way out of the camp.

First and foremost on his wish list was a weapon, any kind of weapon, but preferably a firearm. One of the AKs he had seen most of the rebels carrying would do very well. But if he couldn't score an AK, at least he had to find some kind of knife. Of all the tools ever invented, a knife was the most essential, particularly in a jungle.

Since the camp was so dimly lit, his night vision wouldn't be greatly impaired in the first few critical minutes after escaping. Once he was free of the perimeter, it wouldn't be very long before it was a hundred percent again. First, though, he had to get out of the cage and make his way through the camp unseen.

Collins had placed a guard on his prisoners, but

the sentry was standing under a tree twenty yards away. Better yet, he was watching his comrades around the campfires more than he was keeping an eye on the occupants of the bamboo cage. Watching two men sleep wasn't very exciting.

Keeping low, Bolan crawled around to the back side of the cage and quickly brushed aside the layers of dead vegetation that made up the floor. Getting out of the cage wasn't easy, but the stolen spoon helped to break up the layers of soft earth so they could be scooped away.

Since he had to stay on his belly while he dug, it took more than an hour to scoop out enough dirt with the spoon and his bare hands to create a gap under the bottom of the bamboo bars. It was a tight squeeze for a man of his size, but he wriggled through without losing too much of his exposed skin in the process.

Outside the cage, Bolan hugged the ground again and waited to see if he had been heard or seen. When it was obvious that the guard was oblivious to what was going on, he got to his feet and silently moved in on him.

With the guard's back against the tree, Bolan wasn't able to approach from directly behind him. This time, he'd have to come in from the side to make the barehanded kill.

The rebel sensed something at the last moment and turned his head, but it was too late. Bolan's right hand clamped down over his mouth and jaw like a vise and jerked the man's head toward him. At the same time, his clenched left fist struck a powerful blow to the base of the man's neck, right behind, and under, his ear.

The blow dislocated the guard's vertebra at the base of his skull, severing his spinal cord. His feet silently kicked as he died suspended by the Executioner's hands.

Bolan lowered the body to the ground and sat him upright against the base of the tree as if he were asleep. He had noticed that the guard on their cage hadn't been changed the previous night, so the corpse probably wouldn't be discovered until dawn. By that time, he'd be miles away.

Slinging the sentry's AK-47 over his shoulder, Bolan carefully worked his way through the camp, avoiding looking directly into the dim light of the dying fires. He was armed now, but the last thing he wanted was to have to shoot his way out. Slipping from tree to tree and shadow to shadow, he reached the ring of hidden bunkers of the inner perimeter. There might not be many guards on duty inside the camp, but he was certain that the bunkers would be manned.

As he worked his way closer, he smelled burning tobacco from the bunker in front of him and heard low voices. This one was occupied. Moving to the left until he was behind the next bunker in line, he paused again to look, smell and listen carefully.

This time, he could detect no signs that any rebels were in the bunker.

That didn't mean, though, that someone wasn't keeping an eye on this sector of the perimeter. Dropping to the ground, he rested the assault rifle across the tops of his hands for ready access and started to pick his way through the scrub brush. This was the slow way to travel, but he was safe down in the dirt. A hundred yards from the bunker line, he got to his feet and disappeared into the jungle.

The farther he went from the camp, the more he heard the sounds of the jungle night, the nocturnal hunters and their prey. That told him that Collins didn't have patrols out guarding the approaches.

AFTER TWO HOURS, Bolan found a tree and climbed up high to spend the rest of the night. The South American jungle was a good place to hide, but at night it was wise to get out of the way of the predators.

The vegetation also served to block his body heat from anyone looking for him with IR sensors. He hadn't seen any of the rebels carrying anything that high-tech, but he couldn't rule them out. Collins was obviously being financed by the cartels, and good night-vision goggles were available on the open market.

IT WAS THE WOMAN who had been tasked with taking food to the two captives who discovered that one of the Yankees was missing. As she was reporting this, a rebel coming to take over the prisoner guard detail discovered that the man he was supposed to replace was dead.

"I told you that he was trouble," Mamal told Sean Collins. "The stories always say that he moves like a cat in the night. Only the Soldier could have escaped without leaving a trace like that."

"He left a trace," Collins snapped. "He dug his way out of the cage, and the man who was supposed to be watching him was killed."

"But you said there was no blood on the guard," Mamal replied. "Al-Askari kills without shedding blood. There are those who say that he can kill with just a—"

"No matter who he is," Collins said, abruptly cutting him off, "he won't get very far. My men were born in these jungles, and no one can escape from them. They'll track him down before the day's out."

"Bring the old man in anyway," Mamal said. "He will tell us where his comrade has gone."

"Denning isn't going to know a damned thing," Collins pointed out. "If Belasko is who you say he is, he will have known better than to tell the DEA man where he was going, but I will talk to him."

"I'LL TELL YOU as much as I can," Denning told Collins when he was invited to talk, "but he didn't tell me that he was planning to try to escape much less where he was going once he got out.''

''Why are you so willing to talk now?'' the Irishman asked suspiciously.

Denning shrugged. ''I don't want you to beat me to death. It's as simple as that. If you're going to kill me, I'd much rather it would be a bullet to the head. It's quicker.''

''Where did Belasko come from?'' Collins changed topics.

''What do you mean?''

''How was he chosen to accompany you on this mission? Did he have any special qualifications?''

''To be honest,'' Denning said, ''I don't really know. He was assigned from the Justice Department, and I just assumed that he was from some kind of pool of security officers.''

''But why not have someone from your own agency, the DEA, protecting you?''

Denning looked thoughtful. ''You know, I never thought to ask that question. If you'll remember, there was some kind of high-level go-around about who would be the senior U.S. representative at the signing. My understanding is that you wanted the head of the Justice Department to be your witness, but the President nixed that idea and nominated me instead. Belasko had already been tasked with the job originally so, when we switched principals, he stayed on because he had done the preliminary ground work.''

"Did he ever say which specific agency within the Justice Department he worked for?"

"No," Denning answered honestly, "and I didn't think to ask. He had the proper credentials, though."

"You and he were in Lima for about a week before the signing, weren't you?"

"We were."

"What did you two talk about during that time?"

"Mostly about what a stupid idea it was for the Peruvians to sign on to this program of yours. And when we weren't talking about that, we were talking about where we were going to eat that night."

"What did you two talk about after I brought you here?"

Denning looked the IRA man straight in the eye. "Mostly about what a bastard you were and how long it might take for us to be rescued."

"You won't be rescued," Collins said flatly. "Both of you are going to die right here. How hard your death will be depends entirely upon you. As for Belasko, he's going to die real hard unless he's lucky enough to catch a bullet first."

Denning was confident that Belasko wasn't going to prove to be an easy man to kill, but he kept that belief to himself. This game had taken an abrupt turn, and all he could do was ride it out.

"Like I said," Denning said, shrugging, "since you're going to kill me anyway, I want an easy death."

BOLAN HAD AWAKENED before dawn. Though he couldn't see the sky, the changing background sounds of the jungle told him that the sun was on its way overhead again. The denizens of the night were going back to their lairs to give way to the predators of the day shift. But of all the dangers of the jungle, it was the two-legged animals that all the rest feared. And those upright predators who carried cold steel were to be avoided at all costs.

The secret to surviving in the jungle was simply not to try to fight it because it couldn't be conquered by any man. As the overused sixties cliché went, a person just had to go with the flow. For the Indians who made up most of Collins's guerrilla force, this was something they started to learn from the moment they were born. The main difference between them and the animals of the jungle was that they walked on two feet. Beyond that, they were equally at home in it.

This intimacy with an entire ecosystem could be learned by outsiders, as well. It just took a lot longer. It involved creating an entirely new mindset and impressing an entire new set of expectations onto it. To be truly at home in the jungle, a person had to know it to the point that he or she became just another animal in it.

Bolan had learned this art and was comfortable in the jungle. It was true that to the average American, *comfort* wasn't a word that would be used to describe this steaming, green hell full of things that cut, bit and stung. But, like so many other words, comfort was a relative term. If your life depended on it, a person could be very comfortable while a six-inch-long, poisonous centipede crawled across a bare hand.

It was Bolan's comfort level in this environment that made him almost impossible to spot as he lay in wait along a major trail leading away from Collins's camp. He knew that the rebels would expect him to stick to the established paths instead of breaking brush as he tried to escape. They would be following these trails looking for signs of his passage, and this time they wouldn't be disappointed.

He had found a slight rise in the ground that gave him good observation and fields of fire over that trail. Parting the vegetation enough to see clearly, he sighted in his AK-47 and lay down to wait.

Though it had been designed as a select-fire, short-ranged assault rifle, the AK family wasn't that bad at aimed single-shot fire out to four hundred meters. Beyond that distance, though, the 7.62 mm cartridge wasn't very effective. But, since he'd be lucky to get even a hundred-meter shot in jungle this thick, that wasn't going to be a problem. Ammunition, though, was.

A successful jungle ambush usually required a high volume of fire. The guard he had taken the AK from, though, had only had one magazine that contained twenty-eight rounds, so full-auto fire wasn't an option. But being forced to aim carefully before squeezing the trigger would give Bolan a better shot-to-hit ratio. Most automatic fire merely served to keep the enemy's head down and rattle him. There was something about a single-shot kill, though, that was just as psychologically effective if not even more so. With the thick vegetation muffling the report, it was also more difficult to locate a lone gunman firing single shots.

He had learned these jungle-fighting lessons a long time ago. One shot, one kill was still a favorite mantra of his, and those old skills would serve him well in this jungle.

THE GUERRILLA POINTMAN was moving cautiously, but setting a good pace. After all, this was his home turf and he knew what he was looking for. It wasn't misplaced confidence on his part and, had he been up against anyone other than the Executioner, he might have been okay. As it was, Bolan had spotted his movement as far away as he could see through the jungle.

Bolan lay motionless while the rebel continued up the path, waiting until he moved into the initial kill zone.

With the AK's iron sights set at one hundred meters, Bolan took a sight picture on the man's upper torso before aiming a little low to compensate for the shorter range, took up the trigger slack and started to track his target. When the guerrilla paused

to look closer at something along the trail, Bolan
squeezed the trigger.

The 7.62 mm round took the pointman right under the heart. He cried out and went down, coughing
blood. The lung shot might not kill him, but he
wouldn't be doing much more than fighting for air
for some time.

To their credit, the rebels didn't all start firing
blindly into the jungle. They were too accustomed
to setting ambushes themselves to make that mistake. All that would do would be to let Bolan know
where each one of them was located. Now he would
have to find the extent of their formation the hard
way by probing their flanks.

When Bolan caught an obvious glimpse of movement, he knew it was a ruse to draw his return fire,
but he fired anyway, knowing that he was giving
his position away.

Now that they had him spotted, the rebels opened
up with a blaze of gunfire. Most of them fired short
bursts, though, showing experience and fire discipline as they raked the jungle around him.

Bolan was already low to the ground and moving
backward, so the rounds passed harmlessly over his
head.

Once he was clear of their zone of fire, he kept
low and slowly worked his way to the right, looking
for the end of the enemy patrol.

He found the rebel on drag splitting his time between watching their back trail and trying to see

what was going on up ahead of him. He appeared to be much younger than the others, barely a teenager, so he could be excused for his inattention. Because of his age, the soldier gave him a break and went for a wounding shot, not a kill.

It took at least two men out of action when one was wounded. But, to make it work, it had to be a serious wound. Rather than gut shooting the boy, he aimed carefully and put a round through his thigh, taking the leg out from under him. The guerrilla yelped in pain as he went down and started shouting for his comrades to help him.

That was Bolan's signal to fade back into the bush and break contact.

Now that he had established this area as his territory by defending it, it was time for him to move on. Animals were usually trapped because they stayed in their home territory, and Bolan didn't intend to be trapped and killed. Specifically he was going to go back to the main camp. No one, neither Collins nor the rebel commander, would expect him to do that. And with most of the rebels beating the bush looking for him, the camp should be lightly defended.

Bolan followed the track the rebel patrol had taken for several hundred yards before breaking off and heading back the way he had come the night before. Since he had just left a rebel patrol bleeding and broken behind him, he didn't expect to run into trouble. Nonetheless, he'd continue to stay off the main trails.

It would be more difficult that way, but taking the easy route was what had gotten that rebel patrol in trouble.

CHAPTER TEN

Lima, Peru

Able Team's drive-by recon of the White Shield building revealed the difficulties they had signed on for by deciding to make it their next target. Unlike the suburban PLFP office, this was a spacious residential villa surrounded by a colonial-style solid masonry walls topped with broken glass. That all the villas in the neighborhood had such walls told volumes about Lima's recent troubles. A squad of Peruvian soldiers was stringing razor wire on top of the glass to make it even more difficult to get over, and another squad was busy off-loading filled sandbags from an ex–U.S. Army two-and-a-half-ton truck. Yet a third group of troops was stacking the sandbags in bunkers on each side of the main gate.

"Do we really want to mess with this place, Ironman?" Schwarz asked as he slowly drove their Buick sedan past the wrought-iron front gate. "They've kind of got us outnumbered this time."

As if to underscore Schwarz's concerns, another dozen infantrymen marched around the corner. If they joined the villa's guard force, that would bring the numbers up to at least fifty troops.

"How about a stand-off attack?" Blancanales suggested. "Maybe we can borrow an RPG and half a dozen rounds. There should be enough of them around here."

"I'd rather borrow a tank," Lyons muttered.

"Ironman," Schwarz replied, "that's perfect. The Peruvians have those French tanks on damned near every corner around here, and all we have to do is to get Pol to talk them into letting us borrow one."

"Wait a damned minute," Blancanales said, "I don't know if an armored attack is going to fly with Hal. Plus, we're supposed to be on the same side as the Peruvians."

"We're not going to hurt their damned tin can," Schwarz said with a grin. "We're just going to borrow it for a while. When we give it back, we can leave a few bucks in the driver's seat to pay for the ammo and gas we use up."

"And the crew?"

"That's where you come in, Pol. You can figure out a way to talk our way into it without anyone getting hurt."

Blancanales was known as the Politician because he had a way with words and people. When Able

Team needed a front man or a gentle persuader, the job fell to him.

Lyons let a smile cross his face. "You know, Pol, Gadgets has a pretty good idea this time. We don't want to hurt the Peruvian troops guarding that place, and we sure as hell don't want them hurting us. So, if we show up in a tank, we can blast that place to the ground and not have to worry about getting in a firefight with them."

Blancanales hated to admit it, but his teammates had a point. "Ah, shit," he muttered, "here we go again."

"Good boy," Schwarz said as he patted his shoulder.

THE FRENCH AMX-30 equipping the Peruvian army was classified as a light tank, but that was because of its relatively small size and the thickness of its armor. The long-barreled gun sticking out of the small turret was a high-velocity, autoloading 90 mm, and that was a main battle tank gun by anyone's standards.

Hundreds of these versatile vehicles had been sold to Third World nations because they were the biggest bang for the buck available on the international market for armor. With its lightweight chassis, its multifuel engine and the big main gun, it was perfect for regions that had unimproved roads and less than adequate bridges for heavy armor. Several Latin American nations had bailed out of their older, heavier U.S. tanks when the AMX-30 went on the market at an attractive price. Peru was one of those nations that had found it to be the answer to the need for armored, mobile firepower.

One of the key elements of the little tank was the autoloading feature of the main gun. The high-velocity 90 mm round was fed from a magazine similar to that of a chain gun and eliminated the need for a crewman to load each round by hand before it could be fired. It also eliminated the need for that crewman altogether, allowing the turret to be rather small.

They were perfect for the task Able Team had in mind, and finding one to borrow turned out to be easier than they had hoped.

THE PERUVIAN ARMY tank park was located in an industrial suburb north of town. Like any army's tank park, it was a clutter of vehicles with men swarming over them, making repairs and performing routine maintenance. A close look, though, told Able Team that it wasn't going to be easy for them to sneak one out of there.

As they watched, a tank rolled up to the main gate and was waved through. As it rolled past them, the Able Team commandos saw that the two crewmen they could see in the driver and commander's hatches were wearing dirty mechanic's coveralls. They had to be mechanics making a test run rather than the tank's regular combat crew.

"That's the one we want," Schwarz said. Giving the vehicle a hundred-yard lead, he pulled out to follow it.

The tank rumbled down the street a quarter of a mile before turning onto a side street. When Schwarz drove past the turnoff, he spotted the armored vehicle parked in front of what looked like a neighborhood bistro.

"Let's do it," Lyons said.

Parking their car half a block away, the three men got out and walked to the tavern. Schwarz and Lyons waited outside as Blancanales walked into the little bistro. He greeted the mechanics in Spanish and expressed curiosity about the vehicle parked outside. After buying them a beer, they proudly offered to show him "their" tank.

Blancanales hung back when they stepped out into the sunlight to find Lyons and Schwarz pointing guns at them. Being good soldiers, they put their hands up and went back into the bar. In the meantime, Blancanales's weapon had convinced the barkeep to put his hands up, as well.

The captives' hands were quickly secured behind their backs with plastic riot cuffs, and a strip of surgical tape over their mouths insured silence. The Peruvians were taken into the back room and seated comfortably on the floor.

"We'll close your front door," Blancanales told the bartender, "so thieves don't come in. And we'll call the police to free you in an hour."

After locking the door behind them and sliding the key back under, the Able Team commandos got in the armored vehicle and drove away.

IT TOOK SCHWARZ a few blocks before he got the hang of handling the tank's braked differential steering. Fortunately he clipped only a couple of curbstones in the process and managed to miss all of the vehicles parked along their route. By the time they closed in on their target, he had the tank under control well enough to maneuver around an ice-cream vendor's cart without even nicking the crowded bus passing him in the other lane of traffic.

With Schwarz driving and Lyons acting as the gunner, Blancanales was left as the man in the commander's hatch. His job was to be on the lookout for serious threats in the form of other Peruvian tanks or government troops with rocket launchers. For them to pull this off properly, they couldn't afford to get into a firefight with the good guys. If another tank showed up, they would have to turn tail and hope they could get away before they got a 90 mm round up their rear end.

"Okay," Lyons said over the intercom, "it's right around the corner. Time to button up."

Schwarz dropped his driver's seat and closed the hatch over his head. "Ironman," he said as he tried to peer through the vision blocks set at eye level to the front and to both sides of his head, "this ain't exactly the best view in the world from inside here.''

"You aren't going to be able to see anything if one of those guards blows your head off with a machine gun.''

"Got it.''

Lyons had the turret control stick in his right hand. Twisting it from side to side traversed the turret, back and forth raised and lowered the gun tube. The trigger under his index finger fired the 12.7 mm coax heavy machine gun, and the button on top fired the main gun.

The targeting optics were lighted, so he had no trouble seeing the target, but he didn't bother to try to figure out what all the yellow numbers and stadia lines in the gunner's scope meant. Since he intended to fire from less than fifty yards, he didn't think he'd have too much trouble hitting something as large as the villa.

He also hadn't had time to determine the type of ammunition in the gun's ready magazine, but again, it didn't really matter. Both armor piercing or high explosive would punch holes in the masonry walls. He would just start firing and let whatever came out of the cannon's muzzle surprise him.

"Okay, guys,'' Schwarz warned over the intercom as he hauled back on the laterals to lock the tank's treads, "here it is.''

The Peruvian troops had noticed the AMX drive up to the main gate, but they weren't concerned.

Tanks in the streets of Lima weren't uncommon. The whine of the electric-motor-driven turret as Lyons laid the gun on target didn't even cause too many heads to turn.

The sharp whipcrack of the 90 mm gun, though, sent them all scrambling for cover.

The first shot hit the double doors of the ornate entryway, sending masonry, plaster and the thick, polished mahogany doors flying in a cloud of dust and splinters.

Using the turret controls, Lyons slowly traversed the gun from the far left corner of the first story to the right. Every ten feet or so, he paused and triggered the gun again. The magazine was apparently loaded with a mix of ammunition types, because each shot did something different to the building. The AP rounds punched nice round holes in the stucco wall, but the HE rounds blasted wide gaps.

By the second shot, the Peruvian troops had recovered their surprise and opened fire on the tank. The effect inside was like someone dropping a fifty-five-gallon drum of marbles on a tin roof from a great height. Since it was all small-arms fire, though, the effect, though noisy, was just as harmless.

Lyons had finished blasting the first floor to rubble and was starting on the upper levels when Blancanales shouted over the intercom, "Ironman! We've got an RPG team coming up on our right front!"

"Okay, Gadgets," Lyons said as he threateningly swung the main gun to cover the approaching Peruvian troops and watched them scatter, "let's go."

"And we have a tank coming in from our left," Blancanales added.

"Get us out of here, fast!" Lyons ordered.

Schwarz slammed the automatic transmission into reverse and stood on the throttle. The multifuel engine bellowed black smoke as the steel treads sparked against the cobblestones, seeking traction. Halfway through the intersection, Schwarz shifted to first, hauled back on the right lateral control stick and slammed the left one forward.

The little tank whirled like a top as one track spun forward and the other in reverse. As soon as he was aimed in the right direction, he released the laterals, stood on the throttle and the AMX-30 shot forward. By the time it had cleared the block, it was moving at forty-five miles per hour, its top speed.

As Schwarz fled, Lyons traversed the turret to point the 90 mm gun over the rear deck and cover their retreat. He wasn't going to fire on the other tanks, but he wanted them to think that he was. With the turret providing him cover, Schwarz opened his hatch and ran the seat up to the stop so he could see to drive.

The Peruvian tank commander was slow to figure out what was going on. But after the guard troops yelled and pointed at the rapidly retreating vehicle, he figured it out and took up the chase.

Schwarz had a good lead on their pursuer and was making the most of it. The streets were fairly crowded, but the local drivers weren't about to challenge him. No one in his right mind was going to get in the way of a madman driving a speeding tank, even a small one. Having the right of way wasn't worth getting tank tread marks across your hood.

"Hang a sharp right at the next corner," Blancanales called down from the command hatch.

Hauling back on the right-hand lateral control stick and shoving forward on the left, Schwarz spun the AMX on its treads and shot down the side street.

"Take another right!" Blancanales shouted.

Since his teammate had a better view from the top of the turret, Schwarz again followed orders. They had turned into a section of town that looked to be a light industrial area. A number of small factories and repair shops flanked both sides of the street. At this time of day, they had the street to themselves while everyone took a midafternoon siesta.

"Pull in there." Blancanales pointed to an open gate in a sheet-metal fence surrounding what looked like a junkyard. As Schwarz drove in, Blancanales pulled himself out of his hatch, dropped onto the deck plates, then to the ground to close the gate behind them.

"End of the line," Schwarz said as he shut down the multifuel engine and pulled himself out of the turret.

"You know," he said as the trio peered around the edge of the gate to see if the way was clear, "we should think about getting one of those for our own. It might come in handy again."

"YOU GUYS DON'T mess around, do you?" Cary Rockhill said admiringly. The attack on the coalition compound was headline news all over Lima, and the station chief couldn't resist visiting the safehouse to talk to the urban-demolition firm of Weiss, Verde and Braun. "That bit with the stolen tank was great."

"What was the body count on that?" Lyons asked.

"Actually, it wasn't that high," the CIA man stated, sounding regretful. "Only three dead and half a dozen wounded. But the coalition is looking at the real-estate listings right now for new digs. You guys pretty well demolished that place."

"Tanks are good at doing that." Schwarz smiled.

"What's the word on the street about who was behind the attack?" Blancanales asked.

Rockhill grinned broadly. "The word is that it was one of the minor rightist groups that didn't sign on to the so-called cease-fire. The government caving in to the PLFP wasn't a popular move in many circles."

"Good," Lyons stated. "That's what we want them to think. Maybe that will encourage some of the anti-Marxist splinter groups not to give up too soon. From what we read, the coalition treaty had pretty much taken the wind out of their sails.''

''If I might ask, what are you guys planning to do for an encore?''

''For the moment,'' Lyons said, ''we're done here in Lima. What we need next is another safehouse where we can open a second front. Something out in the country between here and the coalition territory. It needs to be isolated enough that we can get a chopper in without everyone in the neighborhood knowing about it.''

''Who's coming to town?''

Lyons locked eyes with him. ''A small group, but no one you want to know about in case you're ever questioned about what's going down here. They're completely off the radar, officially and unofficially, just like we are. So, if you have any questions about it, you'll have to ask Langley.''

''I think I know just the place for you,'' Rockhill said. ''It should accommodate a dozen people and enough gear for anything you might need to do. It's a safehouse we've loaned out to the DEA on occasion, so it has its own generator and is fully security wired.''

''That sounds about right.''

''Damn,'' Rockhill said wistfully. ''I sure as hell wish that I was cleared to get in on whatever you're doing. It's been a long time since I've been able to do anything useful around here.''

Lyons sympathized with the man. Wishful thinking had been the backbone, if one could use that analogy, of U.S. foreign policy in the region for a long time now. And wishful thinking didn't leave much room for doing anything useful about the all-too-apparent problems.

"Believe me, you're doing something useful by supporting our operation. And if we're successful, there won't be any public kudos handed out, but you'll be able to tell that we won this time."

Rockhill grinned. "That's good enough for me. I already have a stack of 'atta boys' in my personnel file."

"I'll see that you get another one signed by the President this time."

"That and a couple of bucks will get me a cup of latte in an airport."

CHAPTER ELEVEN

Stony Man Farm, Virginia

Aaron Kurtzman was tracking the Peruvian reports of Able Team's activities in Lima. So far, the guys had gotten off to a good start. He turned when he saw Hal Brognola approaching his workstation. "What's up?" he asked.

"My Washington office just had an interesting inquiry from the State Department, of all places," Brognola told him.

"What was that?" Kurtzman turned his chair around. Anything connected with the State Department could automatically be considered bad news.

"Well, a Mr. Trent Carlsworth from the Latin American desk called and said he needed some background information on a security officer named Mike Belasko."

"You're kidding me!"

Bolan's Belasko field persona had been carefully worked out so the Executioner would have a cover name he could use that had an existence somewhere on paper. Any inquiries about Mr. Belasko were forwarded directly to Brognola through the Justice Department.

"He said that he needed the information because State is going to award him some kind of medal for getting killed while in service to the department."

"That's got to be the biggest crock of shit I've ever heard from one of those morons," Kurtzman growled, "and that's saying a lot."

"You've got that right," Brognola readily agreed. So much of the trouble Stony Man was called upon to set to rights originated from State Department screwups that it was sometimes difficult not to think of them as the primary enemy of peace and order in the world.

"What's that guy's name again?" Kurtzman asked, his fingers poised over his keyboard.

"Trent Carlsworth from the Latin American desk."

"Let's take a look at who that boy is."

What normally passed as adequate cybersecurity at most government agencies didn't slow Kurtzman for more than a couple of keystrokes. He had all of the major federal security codes loaded into his system, and, of all of them, the State Department's was the weakest. Their classified personnel files opened up as fast as he could hit the keys.

"I've seen that guy before," Brognola said when the file photo of a younger Carlsworth flashed up on the screen. "I spotted him in the crowd at Denning's funeral and I asked Wilton from DEA to find out who he was for me. I've been so busy, though, that I haven't gotten back to him to see what he came up with."

"What in the hell was a State Department rep doing at a funeral?" Kurtzman asked. "Those bastards never honor their screwups. They'll turn their backs on you in a flash once you're down."

"That's what I asked myself at the time," Brognola said. "But I think we have an answer now. We've found a rat in Foggy Bottom."

"Only one?" Kurtzman snorted.

"So far."

"What do you want to do about him?"

"For right now, nothing," Brognola said thoughtfully. "But keep him in the center of your radar so we know where to find him if his name comes up again."

"With pleasure."

Peru

IT WAS TWO HOURS past dark by the time Bolan got back to Collins's jungle camp, and he found the situation to be just about what he had expected. In the low glow of the cooking fires, he saw very few fighters other than the handful who were walking their guard posts. At night as Collins's prisoner, he had seen dozens of the rebels spending their early-evening hours lounging by the fires, drinking, playing cards and flirting with the women. Tonight it was mostly just the women and their children around the fires.

Even so, there were enough men left that he would have to take precautions. Looking into the lights of the camp, even as low as they were, would affect his night vision. And he would have to make sure that he was well concealed because he knew how well even dim light could show a man against the dark.

He pulled back into cover to make what preparations he could before going any closer. Scraping away the decayed vegetation until he reached the red earth of the jungle floor, he poured water from his canteen into it to make mud. After working the mud into a thick paste, he applied it to every inch of his exposed skin and face as field-expedient combat cosmetics. It would dry quickly and flake off, but for an hour or so, it would work well to kill the sheen of his skin so it wouldn't reflect light.

That done, he scouted his sector of the perimeter until he found a depression in the ground at the edge of one of the cleared fire lanes eighty yards from the bunker line. With the low light conditions and the iron sights on his AK, that was as far as he could be from his targets and still expect to hit with every round. Pulling back into the remaining vegetation, he found out a good firing position and waited.

His first target was a lone sentry walking his rounds inside the bunker line. The guerrilla wasn't expecting trouble, and his mind wasn't really on his duties. As often as he peered out into the jungle, he looked back at the women talking around the campfires. With most of the rebels sleeping in the jungle tonight, his chances of scoring a bed partner were way up.

Even had the guard been carefully watching his section of the perimeter, frequently looking back at the fires seriously degraded his night vision. He was about to get a lesson on properly performing night-sentry duty, but it would be the last lesson he would ever get.

With the ammunition situation being what it was, every shot had to count tonight, so Bolan took his time getting a good sight picture. Night firing with nonilluminated iron sights could be tricky.

When the guard paused to light a cigarette, Bolan fired.

The 7.62 mm round took the man high in the left chest for a heart shot, and the guerrilla dropped where he stood.

WHEN DAN DENNING HEARD the shot, he smiled in the dark. Belasko was back. He finally realized why the security man had left and what he was trying to do. He had escaped to cause trouble for Collins so the terrorist wouldn't concentrate on making him talk. Instead of running for safety, the man was risking his life to try to help Denning stay alive.

Denning was as tough as a veteran DEA cop

could be, but for the first time in longer than he could remember, he cried tears of sheer relief. He vowed that if he survived this, he would do everything in his power to insure that Belasko's selfless sacrifice wouldn't be in vain.

THE FIRST SHOT ALSO TOLD Sean Collins that Belasko was back. The coalition territory had been cleared of all opposition groups, and the clanging of the alarm bell told him that it wasn't an accidental discharge from one of his own men. What he couldn't figure out was, why? He couldn't see what the Yankee hoped to gain by attacking the camp by himself. He hadn't taken him to be a madman, but nothing else made any sense.

Killing the kerosene lamp by his desk, he snatched up his AK-47 and rushed out to take command of the camp's defense.

MAMAL WAS RELAXING with one of the Indian women in what Collins laughingly called his guest quarters when the camp went on alert. He didn't have to ask who had fired that first shot—he knew. He was absolutely certain now that the mysterious Yankee calling himself Belasko was, in fact, the feared Al-Askari. No one else would even think of attacking an armed camp completely by himself. He also knew that the Irishman was wasting his time and the lives of his men trying to go after him tonight.

If he were Collins, he would take his operation back to a city where he could be adequately protected. The jungle was home to a man like Al-Askari, and it was foolish to play another man's game when the stakes were life and death.

And since his life was now on the line, as well, he pushed the woman aside and took up his assault rifle. If Al-Askari was after him, he wasn't going to die defenseless.

BOLAN WAS OPERATING in what Pentagon spokesmen always liked to refer to as a target-rich environment. There was no shortage of targets for him now that every gunman left in the camp was responding to the alarm. The problem was that each time he fired, his weapon's orange muzzle-flash gave away his position. The assault rifle didn't have a flash hider on the muzzle, so the flash would also be seen from the side, as well as from the front.

After loosing two more carefully aimed shots, he rolled to the side and started to crawl to the right as return fire started snapping over his head. He crawled some twenty yards before finding another good firing position.

HEARING BELASKO'S carefully spaced single shots, Ramon Sabatas realized that the Yankee was low on ammunition. That lessened the danger considerably and made this more of a nuisance attack than a serious threat.

Calling over one of his more experienced men, he ordered, "Take three of your best men and try to get around behind the Yankee. He is low on ammunition, so try to take him alive if you can. But if you can't, kill him."

"Yes, sir."

Now he would see what this Yankee was made of.

BOLAN WAS ALSO KEENLY AWARE of his dwindling ammunition status. Every round he fired was one he couldn't easily replace. He had allotted himself eight rounds for this attack. He had expended three in the ambush earlier and after firing eight more tonight, he would have only seventeen rounds left to last him an indefinite period of time.

Spotting a stationary muzzle-flash from the base of a tree well inside the perimeter, he aimed an inch above it for a head shot and returned the fire. No more rounds came his way from that position.

With the barrage of fire coming from the camp, Bolan almost didn't hear the four men coming up on his flank. It was only when one of them caught a flash of reflected light that he spotted them.

Rolling onto his back, he triggered the AK-47, and the round took the lead guerrilla in the chest.

Bursts of return fire tore into the jungle floor where he had been lying just seconds before.

Continuing to roll out of the way, Bolan tracked and fired again to take out the second man.

The third attacker lurched backward, trying to catch Bolan in his sights when the Executioner fired a third time.

When the third man went down, the sole remaining rebel fled back into the jungle. Though he didn't have a clear line of fire at him, Bolan sent an insurance shot after him anyway to keep him running.

He had fulfilled his mission tonight—to alarm the camp and cause a few casualties—and it was time for him to move on. But, even though he needed to move on before another hunter-killer team came looking for him, there was something he had to do that was even more important. He hadn't expected the windfall the dead rebels presented.

Only one of the guerrilla bodies was fully dressed. His field belt held a canteen, a magazine pouch and a fighting knife in a hand-sewn leather sheath. It was almost as if Bolan had stumbled into a supply room in the jungle. Stripping the field belt from the corpse, he belted it around his waist before moving on to the next body.

After salvaging the ammunition from the pockets of the other two corpses, Bolan now had eight magazines for his AK-47. Some were only partially full, but he still should have roughly two hundred rounds all told. With the extra canteen and the knife, he was now equipped well enough to conduct a real harassment campaign.

Bolan faded back into the jungle like a cat. He

had accomplished his mission, and it was time to find a tree to sleep in again.

SEAN COLLINS'S JAW was clenched as Ramon Sabatas reported the casualties from the attack. Six men were dead with nothing to show for it at all. The survivor of the team Sabatas had sent out claimed that there had been at least three men out there, but he knew better. One man who was fast enough could easily look like three in the dark.

"Set some listening posts out tonight," he said when Sabatas was finished, "to make sure he doesn't come back. And in the morning, give me a plan about how you are going to find and kill this man. I do not care how you do it, but I want it done. With the people I have coming here, I cannot afford to have him running loose out there shooting the camp up whenever he wants."

"*Sí, patrón,*" Sabatas replied.

THE TWO INDIAN PLFP fighters saw Ramon Sabatas approaching and fell silent. They followed the rebel officer with their dark eyes until he passed out of their view.

That was the second time in the past few minutes that Sabatas had seen that look, and he knew that he had to put a stop to it quickly. He had also overheard some of the Indians saying that the Yankee was some kind of jungle demon.

Most of the time, it was hard enough working

with the Indians without having to put up with their primitive fears. Most of them were nominal Christians, but he knew that only held true as long as they were within half a day's walking distance of a church or a priest. When they were in the jungle, they reverted to being the superstitious savages they had always been. Without a doubt, they were good jungle fighters, but they saw spirits and demons everywhere they looked. A jaguar's cough or a crash of thunder in a clear sky could put them in a state of panic.

If he didn't put a stop to this, he knew they would start vanishing from the camp like a mist. They would play on one another's fears, and the story would build with each retelling. The defections would start with the most fearful man slinking away, and as soon as he was gone, others would soon follow. To keep that from happening, he had to do something about this Yankee and quickly.

Sabatas had much more Spanish blood than he did Indian, but he had been raised on a plantation in Indian country and it was the Indians who had taught him to survive in the jungle. Though he was their protégé, he had the advantage of not being subject to their tribal superstitions. He appreciated the jungle for the truly dangerous place that it was, but he knew that the dangers were all of this world, not of an invisible spirit realm. And this time, the danger was from one very well trained and dangerous Yankee.

Unlike many of his leftist comrades, Sabatas didn't denigrate the Americans. They were, without a doubt, the most powerful people on Earth at this time. It was true that most of them were stupid, greedy and soft beyond any man's understanding, but not all of them. It was true that their government could also be stupid, greedy and soft. But when their government decided to act, it didn't matter that their reasons for doing so would only serve a corrupt few and not the people. Even a stupid, greedy and soft giant was still a giant, and lesser nations needed to take heed.

To deal with this particular Yankee, he needed to bring in some non-Indian fighters. One of the drug lords allied with Collins had an experienced, well-trained private army, most of whom were white mercenaries or Cuban exiles. His main camp was right across the coalition territory's border with Colombia, and he would ask to borrow several jungle tracking teams from him to put an end to this nonsense.

CHAPTER TWELVE

Lima, Peru

U.S. Embassy Station Chief Cary Rockhill was more than a little puzzled when he walked into Ambassador Samantha Biggins's office and saw that she was smiling. The silly old woman didn't make a habit of inviting him into her inner sanctum. Not unless she was going to chew his ass about some trivial piece of something that was usually none of her business. Something strange was going on here.

"You wanted to see me, Mrs. Biggins?"

"Please, Cary," she said pleasantly, "have a seat. Can I get you a cup of coffee?"

"No thanks, ma'am."

The pleasantries over, the ambassador got right to the point. "Do you know where those three men from the Justice Department are staying?"

"Ma'am?" Rockhill frowned.

"Those men who came to see you—what were their names, Weiss, Braun and Verde?"

Leave it to this old social-climbing bitch to remember those rather obvious, throwaway cover names, Rockhill thought. "No, ma'am, I don't," he lied.

"Well," she said, looking disappointed, "if you should happen to see them, would you tell them that I'd like to talk to them, please?"

Rockhill was stunned. What in the hell was going on here? "If you don't mind my asking, ma'am, about what?"

"A man from the Latin America desk of the State Department called me and said he would like to talk to them."

"But I don't understand," Rockhill said carefully. "Those men were from Justice, not State. If this guy wants to know what they're doing, shouldn't he be going through interdepartment channels to talk to their superiors?"

Since the ambassador was in well over her head in her job, she was always big on "doing things the right way," as she put it. That usually meant passing the buck both up and down the ladder at the slightest opportunity. There had to be some very pressing reason for her to be so willing to act on this.

"Well," she said offhandedly, "Trent Carlsworth called me because his father and I are old friends, and he thought that I might be able to help him get in touch with them faster than if he tried to do it through regular channels."

She leaned closer and lowered her voice. "You know how things can get so messed up back in Washington, Cary. It's just terrible."

Rockhill instantly smelled a rat—in fact, a whole damned nest of them. If this State Department flunky had to make a long-distance call halfway around the world to find out something he should be able to get with a local crosstown phone call, something was dead-assed wrong. Plus, what in the hell was he doing checking up on a deep-cover, wet-work job that had to have been cleared at the National Command Level?

"I'll see if I can locate them for you, ma'am," Rockhill said, "but can you tell me the nature of the State Department's questions, so I can let them know what to expect?"

"Oh, that's all right," she said a little too quickly. "Trent specifically asked me to handle this myself. It's politically sensitive, you know."

Damned straight it was, the station chief thought. It had to be some kind of State Department "cover your ass" program, and it had to be tied in with the coalition.

"I understand," he said, and he did.

"I guess I can tell you, though, that he wants to talk to them about that poor Mr. Belasko, the man who was killed in the chopper crash."

Since it was the crash that had brought Weiss, Braun and Verde to Lima, Rockhill realized that this conversation had just become explosively dangerous.

"If I run into them, ma'am," Rockhill said as he stood to go, "I'll tell them to come by and talk to you."

"Thank you, Cary," she said sincerely.

Back in his secure communications room, Rockhill chased out the duty radioman and placed the scrambled call to safehouse.

GADGETS SCHWARZ WAS closest to the scrambled radio in their new safehouse and took the call. "This is Cary Rockhill," the voice said. "Let me talk to Weiss."

"Just a second."

Lyons crossed the room and hit the transmit button. "This is Weiss."

"I thought you'd like to know that you've got someone from the State Department bird-dogging your activities down here," Rockhill said.

"How's that?"

Rockhill quickly recounted his conversation with the ambassador almost word for word and added his thoughts on the strange request.

"You'd better keep that old bitch out of our way," Lyons warned him. "If this goes wrong and she gets in the cross fire, you're going to need a new boss. And if she's doing what I think she's doing, you're going to get a new one anyway, because she's going to be out of here on the next plane north. The State Department has absolutely no part in this operation, either in the planning or in command and control.''

''I didn't think so.''

''Sandbag her,'' Lyons said, ''and let me know if she asks any more questions about us.''

''Will do.''

''Damn,'' Lyons muttered as he reached for the satcom radio mike to talk to the Farm. ''We don't need this shit.''

Stony Man Farm, Virginia

HAL BROGNOLA INSTANTLY SAW what Carlsworth was trying to do and recognized it for the threat it was.

''I'm going after Carlsworth right now,'' he told Barbara Price. ''We've got to get this guy before he takes this any further. He knows too much as it is, and I have to make sure he doesn't get anyone else involved.''

''Are you planning to go after him alone?''

''No. I'd like to have Ironman here to help, but it can't wait that long. This is twice now that his name has come up asking questions about what we have going on down in Peru. I know Striker's rule about that, but I'm not going to wait for the third time to confirm that it's enemy action. I'll take Buck with me, and we'll make the snatch inside the State Department building.''

"Why don't you take Cowboy with you, as well?" she suggested. "He cleans up pretty good and should pass without too much comment in Washington."

"Good idea."

KISSINGER WAS GLAD to be invited to the party. It wasn't often anymore that he got a chance to get his hands dirty.

"What kind of hardware do you want to take?" he asked. His chief concern was first, last and always the weapons.

"I have my old Airweight .38, and you two take what you like. But remember I want this guy alive at all costs. Unless he starts firing, go light on him."

"I always pack my old .45," Buck Greene said, "so I hope he doesn't take a shot at us because I don't miss too often."

BROGNOLA'S COMPANY car, a late-model, full-sized Buick sedan, was in his parking slot at Andrews Air Force Base. The three climbed in and headed for the Capitol and the State Department.

"Remember, guys," Brognola said as he drove, "I need this guy in one piece."

"Can I thump him a little?" Kissinger asked. "If he's involved in Striker's disappearance, he's earned a couple of bruises."

"Only if the situation requires it."

Kissinger smiled. He had rarely seen a takedown that didn't incorporate a bruise or two in the process.

TRENT CARLSWORTH CHECKED his watch and put his phone on call forwarding before he left the office. He was walking down the hallway when he saw three men approaching him. Something about the way they looked at him set off the alarms.

The guy in the middle looked like one of the faceless, cookie-cutter, upper-level, career public servants who kept Washington from drowning in its own incompetence. The guys on either side of him were dressed, more or less, as lower-level government employees, but they didn't have the bland look that came with a midlevel GS rating. They looked more like some kind of federal cop.

Carlsworth stopped when they got closer. "Can I help you gentlemen?"

The older man whipped out his wallet and flipped it open to show a badge. "Are you Trent Carlsworth?" he asked.

"And you are...?"

"Hal Brognola, Justice. You're under arrest for suspicion of violating the National Security Act."

Turning on his heels, Carlsworth raced down the hall for the fire door.

Kissinger and Greene immediately raced after him.

A door opened right in front of Carlsworth, and

a young woman stepped out. Grabbing her arm, he swung her out into the path of his pursuers.

Both Kissinger and Greene tried to avoid a collision with her, but she slipped on the carpet and stumbled into the men, taking both of them to the floor with her.

Carlsworth reached the door and slipped through it. Slamming the door behind him, he activated the electronic antiterrorist lock that had recently been installed to seal off the floors of the building in case of infiltration.

As Greene and Kissinger got untangled from the woman, Brognola held his badge out and the spectators started fading back into their offices. No one wanted a piece of whatever was going down.

"The door's locked!" Greene shouted.

"Blast the lock," Brognola ordered.

"It's a steel door."

"Try it anyway."

Holding the muzzle of his Government Model .45ACP close to the lock to prevent ricochet, Greene fired. The heavy .45 slug drilled into the lock and stopped an inch inside, shattering the mechanism.

When the door continued to resist being opened, one of the onlookers helpfully stepped up. "They put one of those new electronic antiterrorist locks on that door, sir."

"Who has the code?" Brognola snapped.

"Ah, I guess security."

Brognola was reaching for his cellular phone when three armed Capitol police security guards rushed into the hall summoned by an alarm. Brognola held up his badge. "Justice Department," he called out loudly.

"Put the gun away!" the guard with the M-16 said nervously.

Facing the muzzles, Greene slid his .45 back into his shoulder rig and put his hands down at his sides.

TRENT CARLSWORTH HURRIED through the lower level of the State Department building without seeming to do so. Running would only make people take notice of him. But if he looked like just another self-important, midlevel flunky late for a meeting, he would be all but invisible.

Outside, he hurried to the nearest taxi stand and slipped into the back seat of the first cab in line. He couldn't risk going back to his apartment for anything. If they were onto him, they were sure to have someone watching his place. The same went for his car. He gave the driver the address of a bank in Arlington that he knew wouldn't be watched because he didn't have an account there, only a safe-deposit box under one of his cover names.

The safe-deposit box in the bank contained two U.S. passports, both valid and under different names, his financial passbooks to his offshore accounts, ten thousand in cash and identity documents to back up the passports with credit cards to match.

Putting all this in the soft-sided briefcase in the box, he exited and hailed another cab outside the bank, telling the driver to take him to Dulles.

In the airport's ticket lobby, he quickly scanned the international-departure screens. The two best avenues of escape for him were through either Venezuela or Mexico. Trying to fly directly to Peru or Colombia would cause the U.S. authorities to check him over much more carefully. The backup plan was to travel through one of the Caribbean islands.

There was an Air Mexico flight to Mexico City leaving in an hour and a half. That was longer than he wanted to wait, but he decided to take the chance. It would be faster for him to get to Peru through there than from the islands. Plus, if he was somehow tracked down there, it would be easy for him to disappear in the world's largest city.

Producing one of his phony passports, he used an equally phony credit card to pay for a coach ticket. After passing through security, he spent the time before boarding in a sports bar drinking mineral water and watching a soccer game on TV.

"WE REALLY HUMPED the pooch on that one," Buck Greene growled as the Stony Man trio drove back to Andrews Air Force Base. "I must be getting too old for this shit."

"That was my fault," Hal Brognola admitted. "I should have called for more backup and had the Capitol police secure the damned building first."

"But that would have given away the ball game," the blacksuit chief reminded him.

"We've done that anyway," Brognola replied. "Now the whole damned State Department knows that we're after the bastard, and they're asking me why. I'll have to get to the President and ask him to tell them to stay the hell out of it."

"Where do you think he'll go?" Kissinger asked.

"I'll be damned if I know," Brognola said. "Before this, I just figured him to be another Foggy Bottom, Bolshevik who thought he was promoting peace and world brotherhood through benevolent socialism. God knows there are more Communists in the State Department than there are in Moscow anymore. But now I don't know. He might actually be a trained agent."

"Working for who?" Greene asked.

"That's what Aaron's going to have to find out for us and fast."

AARON KURTZMAN HAD already started to run Carlsworth's particulars as soon as Brognola and his ad hoc team left for the abortive snatch. So far, though, he wasn't coming up with anything out of line. He couldn't find any of the usual markers of a government official gone bad. There were no unexplained expenditures, no expensive real estate or cars, no vacation homes in expensive resorts and no unexplained trips abroad. His bank balance wasn't even that high, and Kurtzman hadn't been able to find any offshore holdings.

That wasn't to say that this negative information cleared up the suspicions about Trent Carlsworth. A positive couldn't be disproved with negative information. It only indicated that he was either a hell of a lot smarter than the average spy, or that he was the most dangerous kind of agent—a man who was motivated by personal political beliefs, rather than money, to betray his country. Those agents left little or no trail to follow.

Nonetheless, Kurtzman started looking for traces of Carlsworth's political philosophy, which was also no easy task. With the State Department filled to the rafters with pinkos and flaming leftists, how did you tell the real Bolsheviks from their many admirers? Being a subscriber to the *Daily Worker* didn't automatically disqualify one from being an American Foreign Service officer anymore.

Again, he didn't find any overt signs of Carlsworth having been more than an all-American yuppie in training during his university years. There was no protesting for leftist causes, or any political activity at all, as far as that went.

His State Department missions, though, bore immediate fruit. Prior to his requesting assignment to the Latin American desk, his most important assignment had been an observer at the IRA–Northern Ireland peace accord brokered by Sean Collins. Immediately following that, he had started talking up

White Shield's activities with his superiors. Considering the juvenile peace-at-any-cost mentality of so many State Department officers, that wasn't unusual. Or was it?

Though he didn't have evidence that he could take to court, he trusted his gut on this one.

"I think I've found the bastard," Kurtzman called up to Brognola.

"What's the story?"

"He's working for Sean Collins—I'll bet my pension on it. He's been sucking up to him since they met at the Ireland peace talks."

CHAPTER THIRTEEN

Peru

Rockhill's country safehouse turned out to be all the Lima station chief had said it would be. Its location halfway between Lima and the coalition territory made it safely remote, but still within easy reach of the capital and the target zone by chopper.

At one time, the small stucco-walled and tile-roofed house had been the center of a large farm, and it had a stone compound wall enclosing the main house and the outbuildings. Inside the walls, Rockhill's people had set it up well to accommodate operations. The Japanese portable generator was almost new and had several drums of fuel. The compound wall was wired with security devices, and the kitchen was well stocked with bottled water and freeze-dried food.

As Able Team got settled in, Hermann Schwarz set up the satcom gear and radioed their location back to the Farm so it could be passed on to Phoenix Force. As soon as they arrived, they could really get the show on the road.

THE TWO BLACK SPECKS that appeared over the high mountain valley soon became recognizable as a pair of UH-60 Black Hawk helicopters on loan from Special Operations Command. One of the birds was painted in the standard olive drab, but the other was in the matte-black-and-charcoal-gray camo paint scheme of the special-ops birds. As it got closer, the dark ship was also seen to have the special-ops modifications of an air-to-air refueling probe, a 25 mm chain-gun pack and an SAR—Synthetic Aperture Radar—Jungle Penetrator winch. Jack Grimaldi had found himself a hell of a ride this time.

Lyons was a bit surprised to see Yakov Katzenelenbogen step off of the special-ops aircraft. Hal Brognola usually liked to keep the Israeli tactical officer close to the Farm, but it looked as if he'd managed to slip his leash this time.

"Welcome to the armpit of Latin America," Schwarz greeted him.

Katz looked around the bare mountain plain. Beyond the small villa, its stone enclosure wall and a couple of outbuildings, the area was bare except for a few outcroppings and the odd patch of scrub brush. "It doesn't look any worse than some of the rest of it I've seen."

"The local beer really sucks."

"The local beer always sucks unless you're in

Holland, Germany, Denmark and maybe northern France.''

"Don't forget jolly old," David McCarter added as he carried his mission bag off the Black Hawk. "We still make some decent brew."

"Welcome to Peru, David," Lyons greeted him. "Have they located any hard targets for you guys yet?"

"Your activities in Lima stirred up a lot of calls back and forth," Katz explained, "but the Farm's still having problems trying to pinpoint the exact points of origin. The best we've been able to do so far is to locate them as having come from somewhere in the middle of a several-hundred-square-mile area in the jungle along the border with Colombia."

"In other words," McCarter stated, "they have bugger all, but we're going to thrash about in the bush anyway and see what we can come up with the hard way."

The olive-drab chopper turned out to be their supply bird, and its crew quickly off-loaded Phoenix's mission equipment. As soon as it was empty, it lifted off for a long flight back to Panama.

EVEN THOUGH PHOENIX FORCE had been in the air from Panama for several hours, the first thing the men did was break out their weapons and equipment and go through their mission preparation. They'd sleep after they were ready to go into action at a moment's notice.

While the commandos went through their prep, Grimaldi serviced and checked over his aircraft. The plan was to use it for a series of mini-air assaults, what had been called eagle flights back in Vietnam, where those tactics had been invented. The Israelis had fine-tuned the procedure, as well, to the point that it was now one of the most efficient ways to utilize a raiding party.

They wouldn't have the air support that usually went with these kinds of operations, so they would go for stealthy insertions instead of sanitizing the landing zones with firepower before setting down. If they really had to have aerial firepower, though, the Black Hawk had the 25 mm chain-gun pod mounted under its nose.

The side-mounted SAR winch with a Jungle Penetrator basket could be used as the commandos' quick-extraction route. With the auxiliary winch controls in the cockpit, Grimaldi could make the pickups by himself. The basket could carry three men in an emergency, so the Phoenix Force team could be lifted out in only two loads.

The last thing he did was top off his fuel tanks from the fuel bladder that had been delivered on the supply bird. It would allow him to do his own on-site refueling, although, in an emergency, he had been cleared to take on fuel at one of the DEA airstrips.

When the chopper was ready, the pilot went inside to find something to eat. The in-flight meal service in the Black Hawk consisted of McCarter handing him a fruit-and-nut bar.

THAT EVENING, the Phoenix Force warriors had a quick meal of MREs, got suited up and checked over their weapons again while Katz and Lyons briefed them.

"Okay," Lyons said, "since Katz has graced us with his presence, he'll be running the show here. Gadgets will be taking care of the gadgets while Pol and I keep an eye on our butts. This place is supposed to be a CIA and DEA safehouse, but that doesn't mean that the opposition isn't aware of it."

"And speaking of the opposition," Katz said, grinning, "the Bear has finally found something to do. They located what they think is a semipermanent guerrilla camp occupied by between one and two dozen men."

"How did they find that one and not what we're really looking for?" McCarter asked. The fact that the clock was ticking down on Bolan wasn't being mentioned, but neither had it been forgotten.

"This site is on the edge of the jungle, and the trees are thin enough that satellite sensors were able to get good readings from it," Katz explained. "It's as simple as that."

"Let's take a look at it."

Katz turned the portable monitor so the men could see its display. The satcom radio not only gave them instant communication with the Farm, but it also provided a data link that allowed their computer to "see" what Kurtzman was getting from the spy satellites.

The Phoenix Force warriors were used to looking at the satellite readouts and could read them as easily as a map. The ground-imaging radar was showing two ridgelines sixty yards apart following the path of a stream. The camp was in between the ridges.

"Aaron will be watching this site in real time when you go in," Katz said, "so check with him when you reach the assembly area."

No one knew exactly how many fighters the rebels had in the coalition area, but it was just a few. Phoenix Force usually worked against the odds, but the amount of firepower the PLFP could bring to bear was more than they usually had to deal with. If there had been any change in the opposition at the target, they would need all of the early warning they could get.

After going over the chopper LZ, the route in, the assembly area and the pickup zone, T. J. Hawkins tapped the bottom of the magazine in his Heckler and Koch subgun. "Okay," he said. "As we used to say in the Rangers, it's time to get out there, kill people and break things."

McCarter had done his military time in the British SAS and, while they were a little more delicate in talking about what they did for a living, the bottom line had been the same. The only way that any military force ever accomplished its mission was to bring death and destruction to people who simply refused to see things their way.

The trick was to always make sure that only the right people got killed and only the right things were blown up. That was the difference between a paramilitary force like Phoenix Force and their enemies. On this operation, their primary mission was to find a friend, but they would bring death and destruction to the people who were holding him captive and anyone else who got in their way.

PILOTING HIS blacked-out Black Hawk through his night-vision goggles, Grimaldi flared out and brought the ship to a smooth landing in the clearing. The modifications made the big bird as easy to pilot in the dark as it was in broad daylight. The modified rotor blades barely whispered as they cut through the air.

The instant the landing gear touched down, the five Phoenix Force commandos exited the aircraft and went to ground facing away from the ship. The FLIR hadn't detected anyone in the vicinity of the LZ, but a prudent man didn't put his life in the hands of a sensor readout.

"We're clear," McCarter said to Grimaldi over the com link.

"Roger," the pilot sent back as he twisted his throttle and gently pulled up on the collective control to change pitch on his rotor blades. The whisper of the silenced blades turned into a soft roar as they bit the cool night air and pulled the chopper into the air. "Good hunting."

As soon as Grimaldi had cleared the area, Phoenix Force left the LZ and hurried for the tree line. Once inside the trees, the men again halted to check their surroundings before moving out again.

This was a commando raid in the grand tradition. They were on the ground to kill people and destroy things. Should they come across intelligence information in the process, so much the better, but that wasn't the primary objective. They were there to bring war to their enemies. Because of that, each man was carrying a double basic load of lethal equipment. The plan called for them to be on the ground for no more than twelve hours, so the extra weight could be borne for such a short gig.

After satisfying himself that their insertion had gone unnoticed, McCarter clicked the com link to signal the move out. As silent as ghosts, the Phoenix Force commandos faded into the Peruvian jungle.

Taking up a line formation, they moved quickly but cautiously to the assembly area a quarter-mile short of their objective. So far from any source of man-made light, their night-vision goggles gave them a very clear, glowing green view of their surroundings.

WHEN THEY REACHED the assembly area, the five men went into a defensive circle while Manning checked in with the Farm for the intel update.

Aaron Kurtzman was quick to give his report. "I have thermal readouts for three campfires more or less in a triangle right alongside of the stream. From the minimal amount of metal returns, I'd say that there's only a dozen or so of them armed with small arms. There are no indications of anyone else in the vicinity, so it looks like you have them all to yourselves."

"Roger," McCarter acknowledged. "We'll be moving out shortly."

"I'll be here."

With Kurtzman's confirmation of the target environment, McCarter opted for a U-shaped ambush with the base of the U on the ridgeline to the south. He, Encizo and Manning would be the killer team at the base. Hawkins would take the east end of the stream, and James the west to seal off the kill zone.

The setup was right out of the jungle fighter's handbook, but some things were difficult to improve upon. The only escape route for the PLFP gunmen would be up the steep slope of the northern ridge, and it was in direct line of fire from the killer team.

PHOENIX FORCE WAS in no hurry, so the commandos took an hour to silently move into position. Their enemies were experienced jungle fighters and would be alert for the slightest sign of anything out of the ordinary. Hawkins and James had the most dangerous routes in. Since they were without backup, they had to make doubly sure that they weren't detected.

Thirty yards from the edge of the enemy camp, Calvin James spotted a figure backlighted by a low cook fire. The PLFP guerrilla was keeping an eye out, but without night-vision goggles, he really couldn't do a good job. Even with the cook fires kept purposefully low, the light threw enough shadows that there was no way he could adequately cover his front.

James knew the limitations the sentry was working with and was glad for them. But those limitations also affected him. His night-vision goggles had an automatic light-blanking feature that kept him from being blinded when he looked toward the campfires.

Moving up to within twenty yards of the sentry, James found a depression that concealed him but still left a clear line of fire at the guerrilla. From the pocket on the side of his assault pack, he brought out his silenced .22-caliber Ruger semiauto pistol with a red dot laser sight, then double-clicked his com link.

"Do it," McCarter whispered over the com link in reply.

Resting his right wrist on his left forearm, James gently squeezed the trigger to activate the pistol's laser sight. Through the green glow of the NVG, the red sighting dot appeared dark orange. When that orange dot was centered one inch above and one inch forward of the man's ear, he pulled the trigger the rest of the way.

The puff of air from the end of the sound suppressor as the subsonic .22-caliber Long Rifle round left the muzzle was no louder than a sleeping baby's cough. The plastic piston-tipped round entered the sentry's head a fraction of an inch from James's aiming point. The penetration drove the piston down to the base of the bullet, causing it to mushroom to the size of a dime as it drilled deep into the man's brain.

The sentry was brain-dead before his body even knew it.

A guerrilla lounging away from the fire turned his head when he heard the sentry's body hit the ground and started to raise his weapon. It was the last thing he ever did.

The southern ridgeline erupted with gunfire as the killer team cut down a handful of the rebels in the first burst. One of the bodies fell into a fire, showering sparks that glittered in the commandos' night-vision goggles.

On the arms of the U, James and Hawkins held their fire until the guerrillas lunged for their weapons, then they opened up from the sides, as well. Staring into their own campfires had destroyed the rebels' night vision, and they were returning fire blindly.

Facing an assault from three sides, the survivors

of the first few bursts turned and scrambled for safety up the northern ridge. None of them made it more than halfway.

THE FIVE COMMANDOS quickly searched the bodies for identification and documents. As they expected, they found little of interest beyond Peruvian and Colombian currency. Rebels rarely carried anything incriminating on their persons.

"David," Manning called out, "did you check out these assault rifles? They're almost brand-new, and they're AKMs."

The AKM was the second generation of the famous AK-47 assault rifle. The *M* meant "modified." While the original milled-steel receiver AKs were the most common military long arm in the world today, the lighter AKMs with their stamped-steel receivers weren't often found in guerrilla forces. For these people to be armed with new AKMs meant that someone was running arms to the PLFP.

"Where were they made?"

"East Germany."

"That figures."

"If we're about done here," Hawkins said, "Calvin and I want to leave some surprises."

"Do it," McCarter said.

James and Hawkins went to six of the scattered bodies and placed hand grenades under them. As soon as the fragmentation grenade was lodged firmly in place with the spoon held down by the body's weight, they pulled the pins to arm them. Now when the PLFP sent someone to find out what had happened to their outpost, the first man to roll a body over would become a casualty, too.

It was true that after the first blast, the surviving would-be rescuers would instantly become very cautious and would use ropes to move the bodies so the booby traps would explode harmlessly. But Phoenix Force was running a psy-ops play on the opposition as much as they were trying to eliminate them, and anything that made the rebels nervous would pay off in the long run.

There was no way that the five men could cause the PLFP enough damage to put them out of business. They could, however, put them in fear. And as every would-be terrorist knew, fear could be a great ally. Word that the bodies had been booby-trapped would get around quickly, and the rebels would start asking themselves who was hunting them. Anyone who hated them enough to do that had to be taken seriously.

"We're done," Hawkins said. "Six easter-egg surprises just waiting to be found."

"Okay," McCarter said. "Let's go."

On the way out, Manning and James left one more surprise for whoever came to investigate their handiwork. The Phoenix Force warriors made sure that they left an easily seen trail leading away from their kill zone. After two hundred yards, they stopped and set up a Claymore mine with a laser detonator, a textbook mechanical ambush. If anyone followed their obvious trail, they would break the laser's beam and the Claymore would detonate.

They slipped into the jungle, heading for the pickup zone to call Grimaldi for a quick flight on to their next target.

Phoenix Force was on a rampage and had to keep moving.

CHAPTER FOURTEEN

Stony Man Farm, Virginia

The report on Phoenix Force's first raid was a very welcome break to the monotony that had the Computer Room firmly in its grip. Unlike with a usual Stony Man mission, time was dragging for the Farm crew. They were ready to do what they did so well as soon as they could locate a target location. But having to wait to find that place was wearing on everyone. Knowing how high the stakes were this time, all they wanted to hear was that Striker had been located.

But if they couldn't hear that, hearing about Phoenix Force's success was second best.

Even so, Hal Brognola was particularly antsy, but he was trying to keep calm, and his supply of antacid tablets was helping with the facade. He would have much rather been in Peru himself directing the operation up close with Katzenelenbogen. But the President had expressly forbidden him from going to the war zone so as not to increase the Farm's exposure. SOG's most valuable asset was at risk as it was, and the President wasn't willing to risk its leader, as well.

Barbara Price was also on edge. With Trent Carlsworth in the wind somewhere, they were back to working the communication intercepts as the only way of developing their lead. "How long do you think it's going to take to locate a target area out of those intercepts?" she asked.

"I'll be damned if I know," Brognola said. "Hunt and Akira keep saying that the jungle is so thick that it's blocking too much of the signals to home in on them. They said it was something called frequency shadowing or some such, and I don't know what in the hell they're talking about."

"The intercepts work well enough in Iran and Afghanistan," she said.

"But they don't have triple-canopy jungles over there," he reminded her gently. "But maybe the Phoenix raids will create enough additional traffic that they'll be able to get a better fix."

Considering that Stony Man routinely performed technological feats of stunning brilliance in the conduct of their operations, being hung up on what should be simple wasn't easy to take.

"How much longer do you think he can last out there?" she asked, changing the subject and posing the question that every man and woman in Stony Man wanted to know the answer to.

Brognola was well aware that she knew the answer herself and only wanted encouragement, but he had to be brutally honest with her. Anything less would be cruel.

"Until we have more information on exactly what he's facing down there," he said calmly, "there's really no way to know. But don't forget that he's been through worse than this before and came through."

Price knew all they could do was trust in Bolan and wait.

Peru

SEAN COLLINS WAS a man beset with troubles. If it wasn't bad enough that someone was attacking the White Shield and coalition facilities in Lima, and Belasko was haunting the jungles around his camp, now he had an enemy unit operating within the coalition territory. The attack on the border-patrol outpost had been totally unexpected.

When the outpost didn't check in with the camp as scheduled, he'd had a bad feeling and had dispatched Ramon Sabatas to investigate. Now he was back, and Collins had never seen him this agitated. The PLFP guerrilla leader was a veteran of more battles than he could count, and the Irishman had come to depend on his rock-solid steadiness. This time, though, he was blazing.

"They were professionals who did that, I tell you," Sabatas said, fighting to keep his voice even.

"Not those stumbling idiots from the national army. Not even the government Rangers the Yankees have tried to train are good enough to have done that."

America's efforts to upgrade and train Latin American antiguerrilla forces hadn't been uniformly successful. Some government units had been turned into first-rate jungle troops. But in all too many other instances, they had just become better-equipped bumblers. There was a real good reason that Peru had suffered through more than thirty years of internal strife—the government simply couldn't put a decent army together.

"Those were nineteen of my best men and they were slaughtered like schoolboys."

"Could you tell how large the enemy force was?"

"That is why I am concerned," Sabatas replied. "There were only five of them. We found the positions they fired from and recovered their expended ammunition. The head stamps on the cartridge cases show them to have been manufactured in Taiwan. That indicates to me that they were some kind of special-operations unit."

Collins didn't have a direct link to Peru's president, but one of his most trusted cabinet members was on the White Shield payroll. The minister would have warned him of any Peruvian army operations, so it couldn't have been the Peruvian Rangers or paratroopers.

"We know it wasn't the government," Collins

said. "So who do you think they were, the infamous CIA you are always telling me about?"

"Over the years, the Yankee CIA has done some very stupid things, yes," Sabatas said. "But a wise man tries to stay out of their way. They also have shadow units that they send in on very important missions, and they are as good as any man who has ever carried a gun."

"But the American President had thrown his weight behind the coalition," Collins pointed out. "He has almost as much to lose as I do if the treaty doesn't hold."

"Think of what you have told me of your own war against the English," Sabatas said. "The government in London would say one thing, but their intelligence services and their SAS would do another. Peru is far from Washington, and maybe the American President does not know what is happening down here. It would not be the first time. Remember the Contras."

"What's happening is that the treaty is not holding, and you know what that means."

"And do not forget Belasko," Sabatas reminded him. "He is still a threat."

Sabatas was obsessed with Belasko, but when compared to the treaty being broken, his nuisance attacks weren't of much importance to Collins. For him to get the funding he needed, the fighting had to stop. Much of the plan hinged on his receiving the Nobel Peace Prize and, while that was supposed to be in the bag, he hadn't yet been named the laureate. There was still the off chance that if the peace didn't hold, he would be passed over for the honor.

"With everything else that is going down," Sabatas said, "I do not understand why you are keeping the DEA man alive. If we no longer need him, kill him and be done with it."

Collins wasn't a jungle-warfare expert, but he was a good tactician. It was obvious that Belasko was staying in the neighborhood for a good reason. And the only reason for that could be Denning. Belasko was sticking close so he could keep an eye on the DEA man and try to find a way to rescue him.

"It's true that I'm not sure how much use Denning is going to be to us," Collins said, "but, as long as he is here, I think Belasko will stay in the area, too. And dead or alive, Belasko is valuable to us."

"So you believe the Arab's story, then?"

"Yes, I do." Collins nodded. "As outlandish as it sounds, it makes a certain amount of sense. And if Belasko is who Mamal says he is, he was assigned to guard Denning for a good reason. Since it is obvious that he is not willing to abandon his assignment, it means that Denning is also more important than he appears to be. So until I know who he actually is, as well, I'll keep him alive as bait.

"Plus," Collins added, "I am confident that Belasko will not be able to evade us for much longer.

No matter how good he is, he is only one man and we have the numbers on our side. The cartel tracking teams you asked for should be here this afternoon.''

"Is Rivera coming?"

"That's what I was told."

Sabatas nodded. "Good, his people are some of the best in the area. I'll send them out as soon as they get here."

WHAT TROUBLED COLLINS more than Belasko being loose was that he hadn't heard back from Trent Carlsworth about the mysterious American's background. He really didn't need Carlsworth's information to know that Belasko was a dangerous man, but he always liked to know as much as possible about his enemies.

He had been trying to get through to the State Department man for more than a day now, but every time he called, he got the man's voice mail with a message saying that he would be out of the office for a few days. Carlsworth's voice sounded a bit strained, and that troubled him. The thought crossed his mind that Carlsworth might have been found out. If that was the case, it would be troublesome to his plans, but it wouldn't be a real blow.

Having a high-level State Department official on the payroll was never a bad thing. He could never tell when he might need an inside line to the plans of the American administration. But, on second thought, since the Yankees would tell Peru's president of anything they planned to do, maybe Carlsworth was expendable.

THE SUN WASN'T YET high in the sky, and a mist still hung low to the ground when Bolan left his tree and set out for his morning manhunt. Now that he had replenished his ammunition supply in the camp raid, he could step up his hit-and-run raids. But rather than simply assassinating every rebel who came into his sight picture, he was going to work a psy-war operation on them instead. When he could tell that his target was one of the Indians, he wouldn't shoot to kill, but only to wound. But when he saw that the target was plainly a city man with a large mixture of Spanish blood, he would kill him.

He wasn't going to spare the Indians because of any humanitarian concern, but because it was an effective combat tactic. The purpose was to take out Collins's cadre and leave his troops leaderless. Also, every man he wounded was a man who would have to be cared for. It was true that the PLFP had more manpower than he had ammunition even now, but psy-war tactics usually yielded results far greater than the actual ammunition expended.

Also, the Indians who made up most of the PLFP's fighters were truly tribal people. And while the Spanish priests had forcefully converted them to Christianity centuries ago, they still held closely to their ancient beliefs. To them, the jungle was inhabited by dozens of gods, spirits and demons. Some of them took the shapes of birds and animals, some hid in the trees and rocks and some were even in the winds. For the duration, he would become one of those demons.

The modern industrial world might make light of those ancient beliefs, but they were very real to those people. And if they thought that they were going up against one of their jungle demons, so much the better. It would work on their minds and make them tend to see things that weren't there.

It was a role he had played before, and it wouldn't take much to do it again. In the lingo of mayhem, it was a force multiplier and it was the only help he had available.

AFTER JACK GRIMALDI had dropped off Phoenix Force the night before, the commandos had marched overland to the hills on the southern border of the new coalition territory. The target Katz had identified there was a coalition compound in the little town of Chapatas, which had once been a Peruvian national police station. Under the terms of the treaty, the compound with its barracks, armory and headquarters buildings had been handed over to the PLFP intact.

Part of being a sovereign nation was to control one's borders, and the coalition had regarrisoned it with PLFP rebels as a border checkpoint on one of the roads leading into the new territory.

There were enough people in Chapatas that Phoenix Force was forced to make its prestrike recon from a hill overlooking the little town. They had no information about the mood of the civilians about their new masters, so they couldn't risk going in closer and being spotted.

"We're going to have to be careful going in there tonight," Encizo said. "There are too many houses close to that place."

"I've got the ticket on handling this job," Hawkins said, grinning. "And we won't even have to go down there to do it. We can do it from here."

"What's that?" McCarter asked.

"Well, if I'm not mistaken, I think I spotted a hundred-gallon propane tank at the end of one of the buildings. My bet is that the building's their mess hall and the propane is running their cook stoves. If there's any gas pressure at all in that thing, we have a nice little FAE bomb on-site already. All we have to do is find a way to remote detonate it."

FAEs, or Fuel Air Explosives, were a development of the Vietnam War where huge propane tanks had been parachuted from low-flying C-130 cargo aircraft and detonated before they reached the ground. These Daisy Cutters bombs, as they had been known back then, had been used to create bare-ground helicopter LZs in even the densest triple-canopy jungles of Southeast Asia.

If it was detonated properly, that hundred gallons of liquid gas should be more than enough to destroy the thirty-foot-long mess hall.

"That's no trick setting the tank off," Manning stated patting the stock of the 7.62 mm M-21 Springfield sniper rifle slung over his shoulder. "I can put an AP round in it to crack the tank, then fire a second tracer round to set it off. Just let me get within eight hundred yards of it so I don't have to worry about tracer burnout."

"That's a thought," Hawkins said. "It'll save me having to sneak down there to place a remote-controlled bursting charge on the damned thing."

"We won't get the effect that we would if the tank was inside of the building to contain the gas," Manning commented. "But if it's even half-full, we should be able to take out most of that mess hall."

"And whoever's in it," Encizo cautioned. "They have their women and children in there with them, and we don't want to cause any collateral damage if we can help it."

That was always a problem when fighting irregular forces, particularly in Latin America. The guerrillas often brought their women into their camps to cook and wash for them, as well as to share their beds. And since day care wasn't big south of the American border, the women brought their children with them. Accidentally killing women and children would be very counterproductive to what they were trying to do.

"We'll watch who goes in there tonight," McCarter said, "and see if we can get a clear shot without endangering the noncombatants."

"In the meantime," Encizo said, "I'm going to get caught up on my sleep, and I recommend that the rest of you do the same. We're going to have to haul ass out of here as soon as we detonate that thing tonight."

"A nap sounds about right to me, as well." Hawkins started making himself comfortable.

"Not you," McCarter said. "I want you to take first watch."

"You really know how to spoil a lovely afternoon, boss."

RAMON SABATAS WASN'T HAPPY to receive the reports from the two patrols he'd had in the field that day. He had sent his more "civilized" patrol leaders with them, hoping that they wouldn't be so caught up in the tales of El Tigre, as the Indians were calling Belasko. But all that had happened was that they had been killed.

Two of the Indians had been wounded, as well, one from each patrol, shot in the legs. If he didn't know better, he would think that Belasko had purposefully killed the leaders and wounded the men so they would have to withdraw back to camp. But no American could be that clever.

It didn't matter now, though. Rivera and his men had arrived, and he would send their first patrol out in the morning. Tonight they would stiffen the perimeter so the Indians didn't see El Tigre.

CHAPTER FIFTEEN

Outside of Chapatas

As soon as darkness fell, Phoenix Force left its hilltop day site and moved closer to Chapatas. Since the little village was far from a power line, the villagers stayed close to home once the sun went down. Except for the coalition compound, the soft glow of kerosene lamps was the only illumination that could be seen, and there wasn't even much of that.

The single naked light bulb on the pole in front of the main building in the PLFP compound didn't provide a lot of light. It was enough, though, to reflect off the white propane tank Hawkins had spotted.

When the commandos moved into the firing location they had spotted during the day, they took up security positions. They didn't expect to be bothered, but they took no chances. While they guarded his flanks, Manning got settled to scope out his target. That single light illuminating the tank was bright enough that he had to adjust the light-intensifying night optics on his sniper scope to compensate for it being in his field of vision. But with the scope dialed down, he still had as good a sight picture as if it had been broad daylight.

Once the range—a little less than eight hundred meters—was dialed in, he turned to David McCarter. "We ready?"

"Do it."

Manning lined up the crosshairs, took up the trigger slack, filled his lungs with a deep breath and let it out slowly. When his lungs were deflated, he fired.

The 7.62 mm armor-piercing round hit almost in the center of the rounded end of the propane tank. The bullet's steel core easily punched through the relatively thin steel skin and continued through the tank and out the other side. The sudden release of pressure into the warm air flashed the liquid gas into a vapor, bursting the tank open with a loud bang like a huge pinpricked balloon.

Being heavier than air, the propane acted more like a thin, fast-moving liquid than it did a gas as it flowed onto the ground. And as the gas expanded, it mixed with the oxygen in the air.

Manning counted down sixty seconds to allow the propane to mix adequately before he fired into what was left of the tank. When he reached the end of his long count, he triggered his M-21 again, and this round was a tracer.

The red phosphorous burning in the chamber in the end of the projectile's boattail was more than hot enough to set off the fuel-and-air mixture. With a white flash, the propane detonated like a thousand-pound bomb.

More than half the length of the concrete-block mess hall simply disappeared. Most of it was instantly turned into fist-sized fragments that shot through the rest of the building like cannonballs. The smaller pieces flew into the air in ballistic curves to fall back onto the tin roofs of the surrounding buildings like concrete hail.

The dust cloud was still billowing when the survivors stumbled out of the remaining half of the building. Phoenix Force had spotted about two dozen rebel fighters inside before the blast, but only six staggered out into the dark. The blast had obliterated the unprotected light, but the darkness was no protection for them.

"Do you want me to tag the survivors?" Manning looked up from his sniper scope. Now that the light was out, he had switched over to full night-vision mode.

"No, let them go this time," McCarter said. "We'll let them think that this was an act of God."

"I thought we wanted them to think that they are under attack?"

"We do." The Briton smiled. "But it doesn't hurt for the rank and file to think that God's pissed off at them, as well."

"Paranoia, the gift that keeps on giving," Hawkins stated.

"Particularly when someone really is attacking you—that's when it works best."

Their business at Chapatas concluded, the Phoenix Force commandos faded back into the mountains for an hour's march to their planned pickup zone and a rendezvous with Grimaldi.

IF SEAN COLLINS DIDN'T have enough trouble already, the report that the border outpost at Chapatas had been attacked by an unknown but significant force stunned him. As with the attack on the border outpost, this wasn't supposed to be happening. And although he had all his intelligence sources working on it, he hadn't been able to find out who was behind these attacks.

This time, Ramon Sabatas hadn't been able to determine how big the attacking force had been. But from the damage they had done to the compound's mess hall, it had to have been more than the five-man unit who had hit the jungle outpost the day before. And more significantly, they had to have been supported with heavy weaponry, maybe a mortar or some kind of rocket launcher, to have destroyed the building that way.

Again his first inclination was to blame the Peruvian government, but he knew better. He also knew, though, that the Yankees hadn't been officially involved. His first call had been to the Peruvian cabinet minister he had in his pocket, and the man had claimed not to know anything.

YAKOV KATZENELENBOGEN MARKED the PLFP compound at Chapatas in red on his map. Keeping computer lists of the Phoenix Force and Able Team strikes was all well and good, but he liked to see what he was doing on paper. There was something about looking at a map that imprinted the information more firmly in his mind.

The Phoenix Force warriors were causing as much damage as they could, but there were only five men and Katz could have used a dozen teams like them. The coalition was starting to react to their pinpricks—their communications traffic had increased tenfold. But it was still a slow process trying to make anything usable out of that raw traffic. His fear was that it would be too slow to get the results they needed in time to save Bolan and Denning. With the restraints they were working under, though, he knew that they had no choice.

What made this mission different from what Stony Man usually did was that they weren't reacting to a threat either to the nation or to the world at large. Nothing was really on the line this time except a man's life. Two, actually, if Dan Denning was still alive, as well.

Even though they had the backing of the President, this was a very sensitive mission because of White Shield's international status and Collins's peace-activist notoriety. The fact that they had uncovered what looked to be a major worm in what was being presented to the world as a shining apple made no difference right now. Until they had solid proof, White Shield was bulletproof.

That didn't mean that there wasn't a great sense of urgency about what they were doing this time. Every hour that Bolan was wherever he was, his life was in danger in a unique way. No one was more aware of that than he was, but there was no timeline imposed by circumstances or some madman's plan of destruction.

Katz always did his best work when his back was to the wall and the clock was loudly ticking in his ear. This time he could only try to keep up the pressure on the coalition and attempt to force an opening. Phoenix Force's raids were doing exactly that, and he had another one in the hopper for them as soon as they returned.

"YOU LADS DID okay in Chapatas, David," Katz told McCarter when the commandos disembarked from the Black Hawk. "There's been a storm of messages flying back and forth on that one. Much more than after the first hit."

"What was our body count?" McCarter asked the only question he cared about, because it was the only thing that he and his men had any control over.

"It looks like you got at least a dozen."

Now that he knew the damage, the Phoenix Force

commander had only one question for his operations officer. "What do you have in line for us next?" he asked.

"Come inside."

Inside the small command post, Katz looked at his map for a few moments. The coalition territory was the size of a small European nation, and trying to cover it with a single five-man strike force was stretching things to the breaking point. But that was where Grimaldi came in.

"How about a change of scenery?" Katz asked McCarter. "Aaron has spotted what looks like a cartel convoy moving south from Colombia into the coalition territory. They picked it up on satellite radar first, then confirmed it with an optical scan. It looks like a troop movement."

"What do you want us to do?"

"I figure I'll have Jack fly you down there. You shoot up the convoy and pull back to the PZ, he lifts you out and flies you south to the other end of the coalition territory to continue your raiding."

"If I didn't know you any better, Katz," McCarter said, grinning, "I'd say that you were trying to confuse the bastard. He'll think there's yet another group moving against him. It's enough to make a paranoid bastard like him really crazy."

"I thought it might, and it will also anger his cartel supporters. They aren't going to like having their people chopped inside coalition territory."

"Let's grab a meal and a few hours of sleep. We'll reload and be ready."

COALITION LAWYER Roberto Richart couldn't believe his eyes when he drove up to the front gate of his villa. Trent Carlsworth was the last person he expected to see there. "What on Earth are you doing here?"

"The Feds came after me," a weary, travel-worn Carlsworth answered, "and I had to run."

"But why here?"

"Where else was I to go?" Carlsworth snapped. "They came after me because of my connection to you people. You've got to hide me."

Richart knew that Carlsworth was Collins's inside man in the American State Department, but if he had been found out, his value to the coalition had come to an end. Being an ex-cartel front man, Richart was a good judge of a man's value. With this Yankee on the verge of panic, he didn't see him as a man to be depended on in any case. Nonetheless, he knew better than to follow his first impulse and simply have this stupid man eliminated out of hand. A decision like that could only come from Collins himself.

But first he had to get him off the street. If he ended up in the hands of the police, there was no end to the damage he could do.

"Come in," he said as he clicked his automatic gate opener. "You can stay in my house until I can contact Collins. There are a great many things going on right now, so it may be a while before I can get to talk to him. But you will be safe here until then."

"Thank you. I really appreciate your hospitality."

Richart just bet he did.

AFTER ACCEPTING a drink, Carlsworth explained what had forced him to take flight. When he was finished, Richart regretted having offered his house to this bungler. Calling Ambassador Biggins was one of the most stupid things he had ever heard of. It didn't matter that the woman was an old family friend; she was a complete fool. Bringing her into this was beyond belief and had probably sealed her fate, as well. Collins couldn't afford to let her live, either.

"I have to leave again," Richart said. "But let me show you around."

Richart took his unexpected houseguest on a quick tour of his modest villa. It wasn't as grand as his boyhood home back in Santiago had been, but it was very comfortable and befitted his lifestyle as a well-connected lawyer.

Ending up in his den, Richart walked over to his desk, opened a drawer and pulled out a .38 Smith & Wesson stubby. "You do know how to use this, don't you?" he said as he offered the weapon to Carlsworth.

"I've never fired a gun."

Richart didn't let his face show the disgust he felt. This pampered Yankee wouldn't last a week on his own outside of his sheltered existence in the States without the protection of the State Department.

"This one's easy to use," he said. "You just point it and pull the trigger."

"But I thought you said that I'd be safe here?" Carlsworth was on the edge of panic and trying hard to hold it in.

"You are safer here than out on the street, yes," Richart explained. "But not taking precautions to protect yourself is foolish. You will be no good to Collins if you are dead."

"I'll take it."

Carlsworth gingerly put the pistol in his coat pocket, uncomfortable with the unfamiliar weight. He knew he was in trouble here if he needed to carry a gun. The problem was that he had nowhere else he could go that the U.S. authorities couldn't come after him.

"Just make yourself at home," Richart said, "and I will be back later this evening. I will try to get a message to Collins and let him know what has happened and that you want to see him."

"When do you think I'll be able to talk to him?" Carlsworth asked.

"That's difficult to say," Richart replied carefully. "He's rather busy right now. But I am sure that he will make time for you as soon as he can."

"Tell him..." Carlsworth paused. "I mean, please ask him to make it soon."

"I will do what I can."

EVEN THOUGH he was seriously suffering from jet lag, Trent Carlsworth was too wired to even try to sleep. He roamed the villa for twenty minutes, making himself familiar with his new surroundings. Richart had told him about the guards outside and had warned him not to go out on the grounds, so he was restricted to the house.

Clicking on the TV, he watched a game show that was more inane than the ones he remembered as a kid. He tried to find CNN International, but there were only two local channels, and apparently Richart didn't have whatever served as cable. He tried to find something to read, but other than a couple of month-old *Time* and *Newsweek* magazines, there was nothing in the house to read in English. His conversational Spanish was quite good, but he wasn't used to reading more than street signs and menus in the language.

He opened his suitcase, purchased in the Mexico City airport, and took out his cellular phone. The battery was still charged, so he flipped it on and placed a call to his home communication center. He could access not only his voice mail, but could also transfer his call to his office phone or any other D.C. number from his satellite cellular phone.

Going to a window so he would have a clear shot to the satellite, he quickly punched in his home phone number. There was the familiar dead-air sound as the signal from his phone went up to the satellite and was retransmitted to Washington, D.C. When it connected, he punched in his voice-mail code and listened. Strangely enough, no one had left any messages for him. Usually he had at least three or four calls a day from his friends and associates.

Apparently the word that the Justice Department was after him had spread quickly, and no one wanted to risk contamination by contacting him. He had known some of his co-workers since high school, but he knew the realities of life. If he was on the way down, no one would claim to even know him. That's just how the game was played. He considered calling his office voice mail, but knew better. The number would have been blocked out.

He briefly thought of calling the only other person he knew in Peru, Ambassador Samantha Biggins, but quickly put that out of his mind. There wasn't much the woman could do for him now. And with the word out about him, letting her know he was in town would be tantamount to turning himself over to the nearest cop. He was completely on his own now.

Taking his phone recharger out of the suitcase, he switched it over to the Latin American 50-cycle setting, plugged it in the wall and put the phone in the cradle. Now he could leave his phone switched to receive for the off chance that anyone did want to try to contact him.

CHAPTER SIXTEEN

In the Jungle

Bolan had been in the woods long enough now that he had completely reverted to his jungle persona. His night vision was back to being as good as a human's ever got, and his hearing and sense of smell had been completely cleansed of the pollution of "civilization." Even his body had tuned itself to the jungle, and now when he moved through the brush, he hardly disturbed the leaves in passing.

Though Bolan was comfortable with where he was, the jungle creatures still weren't too sure about him. They gave him a wide berth and didn't contest his right to be in their territory. Even the undisputed king of the South American jungle, the universally feared jaguar, didn't challenge his passage. He also didn't give his customary coughs of warning. There was something about this man that made even him cautious.

Since Bolan had bushwhacked the two patrols the previous day, he really didn't expect to find too many rebels in the woods today. If their commander was smart, he'd keep them close to the camp where they could watch out for one another. But making one's plans around what someone else might do wasn't conducive to longevity in the jungle. Even more than in any other combat zone, a man in the jungle constantly had to be on the offensive in order to defend himself.

After roaming for more than an hour, Bolan suddenly caught a whiff of something warm on the breeze and immediately recognized it. The distinctive smell of burning tobacco carried far on the cool morning air, and not even the heavy, overlaying smell of the jungle could mask it. The Indian guerrilla fighters rarely smoked when they were on an operation because they knew how far the odor traveled. This meant that there were new players in the bush, men who either didn't know the rules of the game or who didn't fear being detected.

Before he made his move on them, he needed to find out which category these newcomers fell into. But in the event that they were unafraid of being found rather than just being careless, he would take extra care.

In triple-canopy jungles, it was often possible to travel through the trees several yards above the ground for miles without having to get down. Considering the density of the brush at ground level, moving through the trees could be considerably faster than trying to break trail.

Taking the high route, Bolan moved from tree to tree in the direction of the odor. Following the wind direction, he vectored in on the ever stronger smell to try to get ahead of them.

Twenty minutes later, Bolan was twenty feet up a tree at the edge of what passed for a clearing in this kind of jungle, watching a ten-man patrol pass below him. From their uniforms, weaponry and features, they weren't the same Indian PLFP troops Collins had at his camp. They had the well-fed look of cartel troops, which was no surprise to the Executioner. The Irishman would be much more comfortable working with a drug lord's troops than with Indians.

They moved like experienced troops, but like most men operating in dense jungles, they were watching their surroundings at ground level. They weren't unaware of the trees around them, but they expected their prey to be on foot as they were. While it was a natural assumption, it was also dead wrong this time.

The man on drag at the end of the file was alert and stopped every few yards to check their back trail. But, like his comrades, he wasn't looking up into the trees. Even had he been, though, he wouldn't have spotted Bolan. The soldier was well hidden in the foliage.

With the drag man making such an inviting target, Bolan decided to take him down first. Parting the leaves with the muzzle of his AK-47, he took aim and squeezed off a single round.

The 7.62 mm bullet took the gunman in the base of the skull for an instant kill.

The rest of the patrol instantly took cover, but with the density of the vegetation muffling the sound, it was difficult for them to determine where the single shot had come from. One of the gunmen crawling back to check on his fallen comrade briefly appeared in the open, so Bolan put a bullet in his head, as well.

That done, he left his sniper's nest and, still keeping to the trees, quickly worked his way around to the front of the patrol. Now that he had the drag pinned down, he could shut the front door on them.

So far, these troops were showing that they were veteran jungle fighters. Novices would be nervously burning up ammunition right now, blasting the jungle around them in hopes of hitting someone. These gunmen were looking for a hard target before they fired and gave their positions away.

When one of the rebels at the front of the column broke cover to move forward in an attempt to find a way out of the kill zone, Bolan tagged him with a round through the chest. He cried out as he collapsed.

This time, the rest of the patrol had had enough. They finally opened fire, some of them raking the nearby trees with long bursts. It wasn't aimed fire because they hadn't seen anything to shoot at. It was purely defensive fire and a complete waste of ammunition.

Some of that ammunition, though, was being wasted in raking the trees, so it was time for Bolan to withdraw. He traveled through the trees for a hundred yards before dropping back down to the ground. He had no fear that he would be followed. At least not for an hour or so. It would take the gunmen that long to realize that he no longer had them in his sights.

RAMON SABATAS HAD almost expected the report he got from the cartel patrol leader when the survivors returned to the camp bearing the bodies of their dead. Three highly skilled jungle fighters had been killed by an assailant they hadn't spotted even once.

Rivera, the cartel commander, was deeply angry and wanted to replace his casualties and go back out after the Yankee, but Sabatas talked him out of it.

It had been proved to him the hard way again that whoever this Belasko was, he was no amateur jungle fighter. That these hardened Cubans and Colombians could be sucked into an ambush like that showed that the Yankee was better than the best jungle fighters in the region. Sending even more of these troops out there would be a waste of warm bodies.

Were there something to be gained from it, he

had no problem with sending these men out there to be killed. But he sincerely doubted they could do any better against Belasko a second or a third time than they had done today. They would die, and they were of more use to him guarding the perimeter against the Yankee's night attacks. At least here they had clear fields of fire.

Sabatas had come to the conclusion that the only way Belasko was going to be stopped was for him to go after the man himself. There were two old Indian trackers in his unit who had worked with him before on similar assignments. They were the best jungle trackers he had ever known, and the three of them should be able to clear the jungle of this bothersome Yankee.

Collins wasn't going to like his being away from the camp, but there was no point in sending even more men out there to be slaughtered like sheep. If Collins wanted Belasko eliminated, it was going to have to be done his way. There were times when only extreme measures would work, and this was one of them.

ROBERTO RICHART'S MESSAGE about Trent Carlsworth showing up in Lima was the last thing Sean Collins wanted to have to concern himself with right now. But he would have to make the trip himself to deal with it, as he wasn't about to have the American brought to the camp. Carlsworth had proved his incompetence and could no longer be trusted.

Calling Ramón Sabatas to his office, Collins told him, "Something has come up in Lima that I have to take care of personally."

Sabatas was surprised to hear Collins say that. With the attacks that had taken place in Lima, he was safe only as long as he stayed in the coalition territory. "If I may ask," he said, "what is it?"

"Carlsworth was found out and he fled to Lima. I have to find out what happened to him and take measures to protect us. So, while I'm gone, I want you to keep up the pressure on Belasko. Like I said, I still want him alive if possible. But if you kill him, make sure to bring the body back."

Knowing that he would have to put his personal hunt off for a few days, Sabatas came up with a new plan. "I can get him to come to us," he said. "Let me tie Denning to a pole and skin him alive. He'll show up quickly enough."

Collins wasn't averse to using the DEA man for bait, but he didn't think that it would have to come to that. "Not yet," he said. "But you may get your chance later. When I learn why Carlsworth was forced to leave Washington, I will have a better idea of what's going on here. Until then, just keep the camp secure."

"You haven't much time left," the PLFP commander reminded him. "Remember that the Nobel committee is coming to Lima to monitor your progress.''

''At our last meeting, I told them that this was going to be a long process. They have to understand that we are building a new nation in the jungle, and these things take time.''

Sabatas knew what was taking the time was getting in the military supplies he needed to build up his forces to be able to withstand any attack. As soon as the drug lords and the Brotherhood were satisfied that Collins was going to be able to survive politically, the shipments would be made.

Stony Man Farm, Virginia

AARON KURTZMAN'S RIGHT HAND snaked out to punch the intercom button to Hal Brognola's office. ''Hal, I think I've finally got a hit on Carlsworth,'' he said.

''About damned time,'' Brognola growled. As with all of the Stony Man crew, his frustration level on this mission was through the roof. ''What is it?''

''I've been monitoring his home phone and Internet service provider. He's got a full service system there, voice mail, call forwarding, a message service, the whole nine yards. Anyway, I picked up two international cell phone calls to his message service about four hours apart.''

''Did you get their point of origin?''

''Damned straight,'' Kurtzman said proudly.

"Lima, Peru. And I even captured the frequency for the originating cell phone, which, by the way, is registered in his name. Either he's down there or someone nicked his cell phone and headed south."

"It's him, all right. But how the hell did he get down there?"

"Probably through another Latin American country under a false passport. He did work for the State Department, so that would be no trick for him to prepare false documents. Since we didn't get his photo and particulars out to all the INS and customs stations for almost a day, he probably slipped through before then."

"Send that to Carl and tell them to go after him immediately," Brognola said. "But tell him that I want that little bastard alive. He's got a lot to answer for."

"I'm sending it now."

Tracking down Carlsworth's cellular phone wasn't going to be as easy as asking the phone company where they were running a land line to the side of a house. But it wasn't going to be all that difficult, either. His cellular phone was nothing more than a small radio capable of reaching a communication satellite deep in space. And like all radios, its transmissions could be detected and pinpointed. The next time he used his phone, its signal would be intercepted and traced.

WHEN KURTZMAN CALLED, Able Team left its Blazer at the safehouse for Katz and McCarter, and hitched a ride on Grimaldi's chopper back to the Lima airport. A quick call to Station Chief Cary Rockhill got them the loan of a van and a quick ride back to their safehouse in the city. After grabbing Gadgets Schwarz's bag of electronic tricks, they headed for one of Lima's better residential districts.

"This is about the middle of the area Katz told us to look at," Schwarz said as he looked up from the map he had been checking.

"I'll pull over," Lyons said from behind the wheel.

The embassy motor pool van they had borrowed from Rockhill had Peruvian plates on it, so no one was going to take much notice of it parked in one of Lima's upper-scale residential neighborhoods.

Blancanales punched in a number on his cellular phone. "It's ringing," he said as Schwarz switched on a radio speaker tuned to the cellular-phone frequency.

"Hello," a voice said in English.

"Please," Blancanales said in Spanish, "may I speak to Mr. Menendes?"

"I am sorry," Carlsworth answered in the same language. "You must have the wrong number. There is no Señor Menendes here."

"Thank you."

"What did you get?" Lyons asked Schwarz, who

was looking at the readout on his radio-signal direction finder.

"I've got it down to a four-block area. We need to go to the middle of that and try it again," he said as Lyons hit the ignition and shifted into first. "Turn right at the second street down."

"This should do it," Schwarz said when they were a dozen blocks away from their first call.

Blancanales punched in the number again, and again the voice answered in English. "Hello?"

"I'm sorry, sir," Blancanales said in Spanish. "I must have the wrong number again."

"I got him that time," Schwarz said triumphantly. "He's in the villa at the end of the block on the right."

Lyons dropped the clutch, shifted into first and pulled away from the curb for a drive-by recon.

The target building wasn't the largest villa on the block, but it sat on a two-hundred-by-two-hundred-foot lot. Like the rest of the homes in the area, it was surrounded by an eight-foot masonry wall topped with broken bottles set in concrete. A wrought-iron gate closed off a driveway that branched off to a garage on the left and the house on the right. There were a couple of trees in the front yard and a garden in the back.

"There's no sweat getting in there," Schwarz said. "That's not a real good place for him to hide."

"We don't know who he's hiding with," Blancanales pointed out. "We have to find out who lives here before we start going over the wall and busting heads.''

Lyons was frustrated at their lack of progress in Lima so far and wanted to go in after Carlsworth immediately. But he knew that Blancanales had a good point. Busting in on an unknown situation was a good way to get into a major dustup, and they needed Carlsworth alive.

''What's the address, Pol?'' Lyons asked.

Blancanales looked for the street sign. ''Calle del Sol number 41.''

''We'll run it past Rockhill and find out who lives there.''

CARY ROCKHILL WAS HAPPY to go to Able Team's safehouse for a conference. Even if he didn't know what was really going on, being on the periphery of this operation was better than waiting for Madam Ambassador to ask him another dumb question about Peruvian culture. As long as he had worked for the Company, he had never understood why the CIA station chiefs were always given the cover of ''cultural attachés.'' To most station chiefs, culture was knowing that Jack Daniel's whiskey had a black label.

''You know,'' Rockhill said, ''you guys are starting to really give the coalition a serious case of the red ass. But I don't know how much of their concerns are really a result of what you've done and how much is because someone has picked up on your activities and is following your lead.''

''Well,'' Schwarz said, ''if it's low-down, nasty and very destructive, we did it.''

''I kind of figured that. I didn't think that you guys were much into painting political graffiti on walls like the locals.''

''All of our graffiti is explosive.''

''This time,'' Blancanales explained, ''we're after a fugitive State Department flunky who we have reason to believe was involved somehow with the 'deaths' of Denning and Belasko. He was tracked down here to Lima, and we located him in a villa in a residential district.''

Like all government spooks, Rockhill knew the old ''don't ask, don't tell'' drill by heart. He didn't need to know how this fugitive had been tracked down, so didn't ask.

''The purpose of all of this,'' Blancanales tried to explain in an unclassified manner, ''is that we need to grab someone who knows where Collins is hiding in the jungle. We haven't been able to locate his camp on our own yet, and we haven't been able to draw Collins back into Peru so we can ask him. This guy might know.''

''Let me make a phone call on that address,'' Rockhill said. ''I have a contact who won't ask me why I'm asking.''

''That's the only kind of contact to have,'' Lyons said as he handed Rockhill the phone.

"This is Lima," the station chief said after talking to his contact, "so it'll take a while. But it shouldn't be too long."

"We don't mind waiting, do we, guys?" Schwarz grinned.

"Right."

CHAPTER SEVENTEEN

Lima, Peru

Cary Rockhill looked thoughtful after receiving his callback on the address Able Team had given him.

"Your man is keeping interesting company," the station chief said. "The villa is owned by a Señor Roberto Richart, who just happens to be the chief counsel for the coalition. He's believed to be Chilean by way of the wrong part of Colombia. We haven't been able to prove that he has a link to the cartels, but all the signs are there. We've been trying to hook him up for months now, but haven't been able to get anything hard on him yet."

"If he's hiding the man we're looking for," Lyons growled, "he's hooked up big time. And if he's not real careful, the coalition is going to lose their chief lawyer."

Rockhill knew that with the intense international scrutiny of White Shield and the coalition, tagging a well-known lawyer for the peace group was bound to cause waves. But he wasn't about to try to tell this three-man wrecking crew how to handle its business. Their introduction documents allowed them to nuke the damned city if they felt like it.

"Have you any idea what kind of personal security this guy might have?" Schwarz asked.

"According to our information, the coalition gave him a four-man bodyguard, and we can assume that they stay at his villa. But I doubt that they're much more than gatekeepers, so I don't think you'll have any trouble with them."

"How are they likely to be armed?"

"Probably the usual hardware for around here—AKs and pistols."

"Is there any way that you can provide a ground plan of that villa in the next couple of hours?" Lyons asked.

"There's probably one somewhere in the city archives," Rockhill replied. "But my contact in the city government doesn't work in that department, and there's no telling how many months it would take to find it going through the usual channels. These people are well behind the cutting edge when it comes to information retrieval. Down here, things like that are done by a poorly paid clerk, not a search engine.

"But," he added, "I can promote a low-level aerial recon courtesy of the embassy chopper. The pilot works for me, so you'll be covered."

"Let's do it," Lyons said.

THE AERIAL RECON of Richart's villa revealed more or less what Lyons had expected from the street recon. The lot was walled on all four sides, and the wrought-iron double gate in front was the only entrance. A three-car garage stood to the left of the main house, and a gardener's hut was in back. The CIA man had thoughtfully provided a Polaroid camera, and Lyons took several snaps to study later.

After the quick flight, the two went back to the safehouse to finish up.

"When are you going in?" Rockhill asked.

"Early this evening," Lyons replied as he reviewed the notes and photos he had taken. "I don't want him getting away on us."

The one thing Rockhill really appreciated about working with these guys was that they didn't mess around. When they found a target, they moved in on it. It was nice watching professionals at work. "Since you're going after an American citizen this time, do you need any backup?"

Lyons shook his head. "I appreciate the offer, Cary, but we have to keep this one even tighter than our primary mission. This guy's State Department Latin American desk, and he was instrumental in getting Washington to line up behind White Shield in the name of ending the world's regional conflicts. He's dirty and on the run, but he's well connected. We have to keep this tight until we can find out how many others in the foreign service are involved."

"Other than Madam Ambassador, you mean."

Lyons didn't smile.

FOR THE EVENING'S EXERCISE, the men of Able Team outfitted themselves in their full night-combat kits—blacksuits worn with Kevlar vests and assault harnesses, night combat cosmetics, rubber-soled boots and night-vision goggles.

Since they were working in a foreign city with only the thinnest cover, they opted for carrying their silenced 9 mm MP-5 SD subguns. Nightly gunfire had been a feature of life in urban Peru for years, but a firefight breaking out in an upscale residential district might attract the unwelcome attention of the police.

Rather than cut the power to 41 Calle del Sol and alert the guards, as well as the residents, they decided to leave the lights on when they went over the wall. There weren't that many on the grounds anyway, just a pole light outside the garage, two small lights on either side of the front entrance and one above the back door.

Nonetheless, while Lyons and Rockhill had been making their aerial tour of the neighborhood, Schwarz had taken the time to rig one of his specialized toys to the power pole feeding the villa. The remote detonator for the microcharge on the line's fuse link was in his pocket ready to cut the power with the push of a button.

Since their attire made them a bit suspicious, they

parked the van at the curb, covering their planned entry point. "We're clear," Blancanales said after checking the street.

Sliding back the side door, Schwarz and Blancanales took out what looked like a four-foot-long rolled rug and laid it at the bottom of the wall.

Usually, going over a glass-embedded wall like the one they were facing meant a choice between risking gashing arms and legs trying to go over it quickly or taking the risk of being seen by doing it slowly. This time, though, they had a new entry aid Schwarz had come up with—a weighted Kevlar blanket to lay over the glass.

After peering over the top of the wall and making sure that the way was clear, Blancanales and Lyons lifted the blanket up to cover the broken bottles, which gave Schwarz a safe, quick passage over the wall. Dropping to the ground, he snapped his night-vision goggles over his eyes and scanned the grounds.

The guards, wherever they were, weren't taking care of business. The life of a villa guard in most of Latin America wasn't that rigorous. Their presence alone was usually enough to insure that the villa was left alone. But the recent attacks on White Shield and the coalition should have been a clue that life in Lima wasn't running in status-quo mode. However, if the guards wanted to make their job easier, that was perfectly okay with him.

Double clicking his com link, Schwarz signaled his partners to join the party.

INSIDE THE VILLA, Roberto Richart was playing the perfect host to his unwelcome visitor. Trent Carlsworth had rested from his trip, so he was a little less frantic than he'd been the day before. But he was still barely tolerable. Carlsworth was one of those insufferably arrogant Americans who gave all the rest of them such a bad name in Latin America.

Richart could hardly believe that Sean Collins had placed any faith in the man at all. But turning an American official was so tricky that he guessed the Irishman had simply taken what he could get. It was true that Carlsworth had been quite helpful in bringing the White Shield agenda to the table in Washington. But that usefulness had come to an end now that he had been discovered. And that's what Collins would tell Carlsworth in person tonight.

"But why is he coming at night?" the American asked. "He doesn't have to hide. He's an important man now."

"As I have tried to explain." Richart had to start each sentence with that phrase, and he was getting tired of saying it. For a foreign-service officer, Carlsworth was as dumb as dirt about the realities of politics.

"Lima is not your Washington, D.C. The so-called peace treaty is only an uneasy cease-fire between factions that have been at war for thirty years, and it is not holding very well. There have been two major attacks against White Shield and several minor ones. Sean is in great personal danger, and his only hope of surviving long enough to see his plan come to fruition is to not take unnecessary chances. And as you know, without him there is no White Shield, and the coalition falls apart.''

''I would have thought that the peace-prize nomination would have given him the same kind of blanket protection it did for men like Mandela and Arafat. No one would dare attack them.''

''Oslo is a long way from Lima,'' Richart said dryly. ''Most of the people who want to kill him haven't even heard of Oslo. All they know is that he has made it very difficult for them to continue their struggle. Fascists or Communists, it doesn't matter, they both want him dead.''

WHEN LYONS and Blancanales joined Schwarz inside the wall, they covered his flanks while he took the point again. They didn't have a layout of the villa, but the kitchen was usually found at the rear of the house, and the guards would likely be close to the coffeepot.

When Schwarz got close enough to look through the windows, he flipped up his night goggles and saw two men sitting around a small table drinking beer. They had been told to expect four, but those two would do for a start.

Dropping back down, he clicked in his com link.

"I have two at a table in what looked like a kitchen."

"We'll do them," Lyons came back.

Around the back of the house, Lyons and Blancanales crouched low and kept an eye on the grounds for the missing two guards while Schwarz tried the door lock. When the handle turned, he eased the door open and found that there were no interior locks.

He clicked his com link, and Blancanales and Lyons joined him. "Ready?" Schwarz whispered.

"Do it."

Schwarz clicked the switch, and the fuse link on the power pole failed.

The instant it did, the three commandos were through the door, their silenced MP-5 SDs spitting subsonic 9 mm rounds.

The two guards Schwarz had spotted through the window died before they could get out of their chairs. When a third stumbled out of a washroom still pulling up his pants, Blancanales put three rounds into his chest.

As one, the trio turned and ran for the stairs.

SEAN COLLINS HADN'T BEEN in Lima for several weeks. Once the final stages of the treaty negotiations had been worked out, he had moved into the jungle to keep out of the firing line. Only something as important as finishing his business with Trent Carlsworth could have gotten him to risk coming back. As soon as he learned exactly what had happened in Washington to make Carlsworth have to flee, the American would cease to have any value to him. And like all useless things, he would be eliminated.

Approaching the villa on foot, the Irishman used his duplicate key to disable the alarm and unlock the front gate. He was halfway around the side of the house when the lights suddenly went out. Drawing his 9 mm pistol from the back of his belt, he hurried to the rear door.

WHEN THE LIGHTS in the villa abruptly winked out, the streetlights were still shining, which told Richart that he was in trouble.

"What's happening?" Carlsworth barely kept from shouting as he went into a full-bore panic.

"Keep quiet!" the lawyer snapped.

The thud of boots running up the stairs told Richart that more than one man was coming for him. He wasn't a coward, but he knew there was no way out of this one.

"On the floor!" Blancanales shouted from the landing in Spanish.

"Don't shoot," Richart answered as he raised his hands. "We are not armed."

"Which one of you is Carlsworth?"

In his panic, Carlsworth lost his Spanish. He had no idea what was being said or who these people were. He recognized his name, though, and knew that he was in danger. Cursing himself for ever coming to Lima, he edged deeper into the shadows.

When he bumped against a table, he felt the pistol in his coat pocket. Richart had told him that all he had to do was point it and pull the trigger. His hands shaking, he drew the revolver and aimed it.

Lyons caught the motion out of the corner of his eye and spun to face the threat, his Python clearing his shoulder leather.

"Ironman!" Blancanales shouted. "Don't shoot!"

It was too late.

The Python roared, and the .357 slug slammed Carlsworth back against the wall as if he had been hit in the chest by a baseball bat. The snub-nosed .38 fired into the ceiling before falling from his nerveless fingers.

"Damn!" Schwarz dropped to his knees beside Carlsworth to see how badly he was hit. Considering that this guy had made the mistake of drawing down on Lyons, he knew it was a waste of time. But he had to check for a pulse anyway.

"He's dead."

Richart stood where he was and held his hands stock-still over his head. Whoever these Yankees were, they weren't to be taken lightly. He knew that he should be able to talk himself out of whatever mess he was in. But to do that, he had to stay alive.

WHEN SEAN COLLINS REACHED the rear of the villa, he found the back door open. A prudent man would have done anything other than enter the darkened house, but the Irishman hadn't always been a peace activist. He had taken part in almost a hundred hits and a man never forgot the smell of gunpowder. Leading with the muzzle of his pistol, he slid through the door.

He paused inside to let his eyes adjust to the dark and spotted the body of one of Richart's security guards on the floor by the door to the side room.

When the shouting started, he flattened himself against the left side of the stairwell and, training his pistol on the empty landing, quickly went up the thickly carpeted stairs. He was only halfway up when the shots rang out and he heard the voices speaking English.

The landing at the top of the stairs was in deep shadow. He looked in through the open door of Richart's study and saw three black-clad, armed intruders. One of them had Roberto Richart up against the wall while the other two knelt beside a body on the floor, the American Trent Carlsworth. The faint light from the streetlight shining through the window allowed him to make a positive ID.

He wouldn't learn what had gone wrong in Washington now, but the intruders had taken care of silencing him, and that had been the ultimate goal. The man had been weak, but informants usually were. That's why they could be so easily turned. That had eliminated one problem for him, but had created another one that was even more serious.

The mystery commandos had Richart and, since they had known enough to connect Carlsworth to him, they were unlikely to turn him loose before interrogating him. The lawyer knew more about Collins's operation than anyone other than himself, and the man couldn't leave the room alive.

Collins had been in enough shootouts in darkened houses to know how this was going to go down. Since he was armed with a pistol, he would get only one good shot before the commandos reacted, and they were armed with subguns. Killing one of them would make him feel better, but it would be a waste of that one shot. Richart would remain in custody, and he couldn't allow that to happen.

Shielding his body behind the thick doorframe, he had a clear line of sight to the Chilean lawyer. At such close range, he sighted in on his forehead and squeezed the trigger.

LYONS HEARD the 9 mm round sing past his head. Even though it was too late, he reflexively dropped into a crouch and his Colt roared twice. The powerful .357 rounds, though, couldn't penetrate the interior masonry wall.

Schwarz ripped off a burst through the open door before sprinting across the room.

"Watch your ass!" Lyons shouted after him.

By the time Schwarz reached the door, the hall

was empty. "He's gone!" he shouted as he headed down the stairs.

Blancanales rose from checking Richart's pulse. "So's this one."

Lyons dashed down the darkened stairs after Schwarz.

"DAMN!" SCHWARZ SAID as he raised his night-vision goggles. The grounds were clear, and there was no sign of whoever had sneaked past them in the villa. "The bastard pulled a rabbit on us."

"It had to have been a guard we missed," Blancanales said as he joined his partners. "But I don't know where he could have been hiding."

"It doesn't matter," Lyons growled. "Let's get the hell out of here. I've got to let Hal know about this rat screw."

"We can't win them all, Ironman," Schwarz said, trying to be philosophical about the disaster.

"I don't want to hear that crap," Lyons snapped.

CHAPTER EIGHTEEN

Stony Man Farm, Virginia

When Carl Lyons reported the results of the raid on 41 Calle del Sol to the Farm, Hal Brognola let all his frustrations hang out. Since nothing else on this mission was working as it was supposed to, he had unrealistically pinned his hopes on taking Carlsworth into custody and interrogating him.

"Dammit, Ironman, you know we needed that bastard alive."

Lyons knew that, unfair or not, he had to take the hack on this one. He, too, had been hoping that Carlsworth would be the break they so desperately needed.

Nonetheless, he did want to explain. "The idiot snuck up behind me in the dark," he said. "I saw the gun in his hand and had no choice. Plus, I'm not too sure that he had what we needed anyway. He hadn't been in Peru long enough to have learned much."

"And Richart?" Brognola asked. "Did you at least take him alive?"

"No," Lyons said. "One of the bodyguards tagged him by mistake while we were trying to save Carlsworth."

"So, it was a successful mission. We just don't have anything to show for it."

"I'm afraid that's about it, Hal. I'm sorry."

"So am I."

Brognola put the phone down and stared at nothing for a few moments. The Trent Carlsworth situation had been resolved, and the traitor had paid for his crimes. The resolution, however satisfying it might be, hadn't contributed to resolving the greater problem of finding Collins's camp and freeing Striker and Dan Denning.

Brognola had made a habit of a mental discipline he had picked up from Bolan, that of visualizing the outcome of any action even as it was ongoing. This process didn't cut down on his situational awareness, another critical mental discipline, but it did help him focus. He was totally focused on getting Bolan back, but with each passing hour it was getting harder and harder for him to visualize the outcome he wanted. In a situation like this, time was never on your side.

Automatically thumbing two antacid tablets from the roll in his pocket, he got up and headed for the Computer Room and a cup of Kurtzman's coffee. As long as he was torturing his stomach, he might as well do it up right. With all the advances that had been made recently in mass organ transplants, he really should look into getting his entire GI tract replaced with something made of stainless steel.

When he entered the Computer Room, Brognola found Barbara Price going over Hunt Wethers's latest attempts to make sense out of the muddle of communication intercepts they were downloading. The NSA and DIA satellites had been monitoring radio and phone traffic in and out of Lima and the coalition territory for days now, but the desired results hadn't been forthcoming. Even the damned electrons seem to be conspiring against them this time.

"I've never run into this kind of problem before," Wethers said. The normally calm and collected computer master looked absolutely frazzled, which wasn't like him at all. His detailed, disciplined, academic mind was the left-brain half of Stony Man's collective intelligence.

Where Aaron Kurtzman was a world-class intuitive genius, Wethers had an equally skilled but completely methodical mind. Kurtzman could instantly see around corners no one else even knew were there. Wethers routinely made the impossible work for him by the tenacious application of sound basics and a refusal to take no for an answer. The difference between the two men was more of a matter of style than it was a difference in the results they obtained.

Both men produced results few others could match, but they were usually results that the other one wouldn't have arrived at easily.

"Why isn't it working this time, Hunt?" Price prompted him, knowing full well that she was in for a lecture. Before being recruited for the Farm crew, Wethers had been an academic superstar in one of the nation's foremost computer-science departments. Though he had transitioned well to the free-swinging world of clandestine operations, he still liked to lecture.

"As I mentioned before," he began, "we're still trying to find a way to compensate for the density of the jungle vegetation so we can fine-tune the data we're getting. Then, we're also getting some kind of echo from many of the transmissions, as if the rebels are using ground-plane antennaes to keep from having their signals intercepted."

Brognola knew better than to interrupt Wethers when he got on a technical roll, but this time he just couldn't resist. "What in the hell is a ground-plane antenna?"

"It's just a piece of antenna wire laid out in the precise azimuth of the intended receiving station. Often they're buried to keep them from being damaged by enemy attack. Anyway, the signal travels along the wire in the direction that it's aimed, and you don't get the 360-degree signal radiation that you do from a normal antenna. Because of that, we can't find the nexus of the transmission and—"

"I want all of you in the War Room immediately," Brognola abruptly broke in. "And I want Katz on the line for this little conversation, as well. If what we're doing isn't working, I'm not going to waste any more time doing it. We have to come up with something else that will work, and we don't have much time left to do it."

WITH CARLSWORTH and Richart both dead, Able Team was back to the old square-one position again. They had stuck to the game plan so far, but for all the good they had done, they might as well have stayed home. It was time to do something different if they could figure out what would work.

Early the next morning, they invited Cary Rockhill to the safehouse for an after-action skull session and to get the outside take on their last operation.

"The hit on 41 Calle del Sol had quite an impact," the station chief said. "The local media are reporting it as yet another violent expression of the growing resistance to the coalition treaty. Two organizations no one has ever heard of before have already taken the credit for it. The president issued a press release saying that he will personally insure that those who killed such a selfless man who had devoted his entire life to peace are brought to justice."

"What's the take on Carlsworth being found with him?" Lyons asked.

"He's being identified as an American tourist

from Boston named Francis Nelson, which was what was on the passport he was using. Nothing has been said about what he was doing there or of his having any connection to the coalition. He's just identified as being Richart's houseguest."

"Good," Lyons said. "See that his body goes home to Boston. Someone will take care of it from there."

"You guys are three for three here in Lima as far as getting away clean," Rockhill said admiringly. "What's your next move?"

"To be honest with you," Lyons said, "since both Richart and Carlsworth ended up dead last night, I really don't know. We've kind of run out of bright ideas for the moment. We've been trying to rattle Collins and force him to make a mistake, but I've got to admit that it isn't working. The bastard's hanging tight.

"So, I guess we'll just have to keep on doing what we do best. We'll take another shot at White Shield and the coalition to keep them from getting too comfortable. Where did you say that they've set up their new headquarters?"

Rockhill grimaced. "Inside the Lima air force base."

"The what?"

"The Peruvian air force's headquarters is right outside town and with the coalition under attack, the president gave them permission to move their operation inside the base for security reasons. Your tank stunt really scared the living shit out of them.''

"Can you get us a layout of the place?" Schwarz asked.

"Of the base?" Rockhill was startled.

Schwarz nodded.

"You're not going to attack government units, are you?"

"Not if we can help it," Lyons said seriously. "We're really trying to help these people, not kill them. But if our target is there, we have to go after them."

"It's the collateral damage I'm worried about," Rockhill replied carefully.

Collateral damage was government shorthand for the wrong people getting killed in a military operation. And in this case, the wrong people would be Peruvian airmen, their dependents and other civilians. These guys had carte blanche to do damned near anything they wanted, but...

"If it's the buildings you're worried about, Uncle Sugar can always rebuild them," Lyons said. "And as far as the soft targets, we only want the bad guys. They should be easy enough to sort out. They'll be the guys not wearing Peruvian air force uniforms."

"Well," Rockhill said cautiously, "there might be a problem about that, as well. I guess you guys already know about it, but there's a delegation from the Nobel committee showing up the day after tomorrow to see how the peace treaty is working out, and they'll be staying in the new coalition headquarters at the air base."

Lyons and Blancanales exchanged glances. That was a piece of intelligence that hadn't been passed on to them yet. "We were out of town for a while," Lyons said, "and we missed that one."

"Is Sean Collins scheduled to make an appearance at this meeting?" Blancanales asked.

"We don't know," Rockhill said. "But our sources inside the coalition and White Shield aren't that good. In fact, they're damned near nil."

"In that case," Schwarz said, "there's no point in delaying in hopes of catching him there. So, we need to do whatever we're going to do real soon."

"On that note, gentlemen," Rockhill said, standing, "I'm going to excuse myself. As much as I'd love to be in on this, I can't afford to let myself know anything about your plans. Plausible deniability and all that. You know the drill. But I'll get a map of the airfield complex to you within a couple of hours, and it will be marked to indicate the buildings the coalition is occupying. More than that, I can't risk it at this point in time. I know you understand."

"Thanks, Cary," Lyons said. "We'll get back to you on this."

"That's okay. I'll just read about it in the papers."

"This one might make TV, too," Schwarz added.

Rockhill shuddered.

As soon as the CIA man left the safehouse, the trio went into planning mode.

"Before we go too much further with this idea, Ironman," Blancanales said, "let me have Katz check this out with the Farm. If we whack some visiting international dignitary by mistake, there'll be hell to pay and we don't want to get in too deep here. We're trying to rescue Striker, not bring the government down."

"We're in well over our belt buckles already," Lyons said, "and Striker's in a hell of a lot deeper than that. If a bystander happens to collect a stray round—" he shrugged "—it might be worth taking the flak if it helps break this thing loose."

The former LAPD cop looked up, the pain showing on his face. "We're going nowhere right now, Pol, and Striker's hanging. We've got to do something."

"Let me call Katz anyway, Carl," Blancanales said. "He might be able to come up with an angle we can use to our advantage instead of just busting in and tearing the place up for the hell of it."

"Make it quick."

Stony Man Farm, Virginia

KATZENELENBOGEN's call to the Farm about Able Team's plan to hit the coalition's new headquarters was a welcome interruption to another mission planning session that was going nowhere.

Hal Brognola liked the plan; it was vintage Able Team—get in there, kill people and break things—and he could see Lyons's hand on it. He was well aware that the accidental deaths of either Peruvian military personnel or international observers would be detrimental to their real objective. But he also knew that the more pressure Collins was under, the greater the chance that he would get careless and make a mistake.

As soon as Striker and the DEA man were safe—and the big Fed still stubbornly refused to see another outcome to this operation—he was going to take Collins down one way or the other. Continuing to hit the coalition would be a big part of that. When the various groups who had signed on with White Shield kept seeing that the man couldn't even protect his headquarters, they might have second thoughts about what they were doing.

"Do it," he told Katz. "But tell Ironman to try to keep the collateral soft-target damage to a bare minimum. He can trash the building, but I want him to go easy on the people, even the coalition types."

Katz laughed. "I'll try."

"Try hard. The Peruvians are still on our side, and I'd like to keep it that way."

"While I've got you on the line," Katz said, "I need to brief you on Phoenix's next target. I'm sending them to the Colombian border after that cartel convoy Aaron picked up. Regardless of what they're hauling, it won't hurt to take it out."

"Take them out," Brognola growled, "and any damned thing else you can find. Just keep hitting them."

"HE DIDN'T ASK how we were doing with the radio intercepts," Barbara Price noted when Katz signed off.

"You know Katz," Brognola replied. "He doesn't have as much faith in such things as the rest of us do. He likes his intelligence to come from his field sources instead of from cyberspace."

Brognola's eyes swept the table. "The real problem is that we're not getting what we need from either source this time. I know that everyone's working as hard as they can with what we do have, but this operation isn't working. We need new ideas, and we need them fast."

His eyes swept the conference table. "I know that I don't have to remind anyone what we're trying to accomplish this time, and I'm not going to insult your intelligence by giving you some bullshit pep talk. But if any of you have personal gods you haven't talked to lately, this might be a real good time to do it."

After a long moment of silence, Brognola stood. "Let's get back to it, people."

CARY ROCKHILL WAS as good as his word, and the information on the Lima air base was delivered to Able Team's safehouse in a matter of a few hours. Along with an overall map, there were detailed drawings of the building the coalition had taken over.

As Lyons expected, the airfield showed signs of having been grafted onto an earlier military base as was so often the case in Latin America. Since early airplanes had been primarily used for scouting, it was most often a cavalry unit that first got a dirt landing strip.

The good news was that the coalition's building was set well away from the others. That would limit unintended damage. The bad news was that being the headquarters of the Peruvian air force, the base was locked up tighter than a vestal's knickers. Getting inside wasn't going to be as easy as going over a villa wall.

"Now all we have to do is find a way to get past the guards at the main gate," Schwarz said.

"And back out again," Blancanales added. "Don't forget that part."

"We may just have to blast our way out," Lyons said.

"I think I've got our way in," Blancanales said. "With the foreign delegations coming in here, what's more natural than a media circus following them around? If Aaron can whip us up the necessary credentials, I can be the Hispanic American reporter again. Rockhill should be able to get us the Peruvian endorsements we'll need."

"Do it," Lyons said.

"I'll start getting some goodies together," Schwarz added.

CHAPTER NINETEEN

In the Jungle

When Ramon Sabatas showed up outside Sean Collins's bamboo building headquarters that morning, he didn't look much like the veteran guerrilla-force commander he was. He looked like just another one of his Indian fighters. Except for his height and a thinner, Spanish cast to his features, he could hardly be told from the two Indians who were accompanying him on this personal manhunt.

If he was going into the jungle after Belasko, he was going to do it on his own terms. That meant getting into a particular mind-set that he normally didn't have to use, and what he wore was part of it. He wasn't hunting poorly trained government troops or a part-time peasant militia this time. He was going after a man who had proved to be almost as good in the bush as he was.

Which of the two of them was actually the better jungle warrior would be played out within the next few days, but Sabatas had no doubts about the outcome. He had to admit that the Yankee was good, and he wouldn't make the mistake of underestimating him. He had seen the bodies of the men who hadn't given the Yankee his due.

But no matter how good Belasko was, he hadn't been born to the environment he was now in. As far as Sabatas was concerned, there was no place on Earth that was more unforgiving of strangers than the jungle.

Sean Collins had never seen his field commander in his Indian-hunter persona and was more than a little surprised by what he was seeing.

"You look more like one of the natives than they do," he said. "You could pose for *National Geographic* or whatever they call that magazine."

Instead of the jungle boots he usually wore, Sabatas had rope sandals on his feet. He wore well-washed cotton pants and a loose shirt instead of multipocketed military fatigues. In place of a webbed field belt and assault harness, a rope belt was tied around his waist and another rope slung a bag of provisions over his shoulder. A second bag held ammunition and his combat supplies. A canteen wrapped in brown cloth hung from his rope belt next to a sheathed fighting knife.

A soft cotton headband held his hair back, and his face was banded with semipermanent black-and-dark-green skin dye the Indians brewed from plant roots. He knew that it would take weeks for the last of the dye to wear off, but the face paint, too, was part of his preparation.

"To hunt like an Indian," he told Collins, "you have to become an Indian, and part of that is to completely leave the white man's world behind."

"How long do you think this will take you?" Collins asked. He didn't like having his troop commander taking off like this. He spoke Spanish, but not the local languages, which meant that he had to rely heavily on Sabatas and his subordinate troop commanders to get things done. "We're in a critical phase right now."

Sabatas's dark eyes locked on the Irishman's blue ones. "It will take as long as it takes. And while I am gone, Romero can handle the troops almost as well as I can. You should have no problems with them."

Without a word, Sabatas turned to go, and the two Indian trackers fell in behind him. Using only hand signals, he led them into the jungle. Until this manhunt was concluded, none of them would speak except in an emergency. In seconds, the three had completely disappeared, barely disturbing the vegetation in their passing.

THE THREE MANHUNTERS headed for a little cluster of huts in the immediate area. The Indians who lived there were even more primitive than those who made up the bulk of Sabatas's rebel force. They wanted no part of outside society and couldn't be hired for anything more than being jungle guides, and then even only occasionally. Though these people had no use for money, sometimes they would hire out in exchange for steel tools and weapons, or glass containers. A good hunting knife would get the services of a man for a handful of days, and Sabatas doubted that his mission would take more than that.

Sabatas spoke several of the regional Indian dialects, but he let his Indian trackers negotiate for him this time. As was the way with these people, the talks started off slowly with a conversation about the weather followed by news of each other's tribes. The Indians had their own sense of time, and they wouldn't be hurried, so he didn't even try.

The negotiations took up most of the morning and involved talking about everything except what Sabatas had come to talk to them about. After talking nonstop and snacking on jungle delicacies, including several varieties of roasted spiders and insects, they finally got around to talking business. From that point on, the discussion went quickly and was concluded in an hour.

The man who finally took the job was over forty years old, which made him an old man for a jungle Indian. It also meant that he was experienced, and, more importantly, because he had survived that long, he was good. In the jungle, men who were less than good didn't survive long enough to become forty.

When they were ready to go, the new tracker took little with him beyond a small pouch on a cord around his neck and a bow with a quiver slung over his back. The new knife he had been given was stuck in the waist of his loincloth.

Again, using hand signals, Sabatas and his three Indians disappeared back into the jungle.

BOLAN HAD BEEN SLEEPING in the trees for so long now that the birds and animals were no longer afraid of him. To the denizens of the jungle, he was just another animal who sought refuge in a tree at night.

After hitting the nearby river and foraging in the brush for breakfast, Bolan made a quick circuit of the areas he had been watching to look for signs of enemy movement, but came up empty. It had been two days since he had encountered one of Sean Collins's patrols and, since the rebels were keeping close to their camp, it was time for him to make another midnight visit.

There was no way for him to know if his plan was working as he had intended. For all he knew, Dan Denning might well be dead by now. But he was going to keep the pressure on Collins as long as he could on the off chance that the DEA man was still alive.

Before he returned to the camp, though, he was going to make a detour and visit a small Indian village he had located during one of his sweeps. It was only a collection of a few huts beside a small patch of cultivated land, but the dozen or so Indians who lived there might be able to help him. Living off the kills of hunting and the fruit of the jungle was keeping him alive, but he needed a better diet. A few beans or a little corn meal would go a long way to keeping his strength up.

There was a danger in approaching the Indians, but he needed to find more portable and nourishing food.

He didn't have anything to trade for what he wanted, so he would have to do what so many others had done to them before, steal what he needed at the point of a gun. He didn't want to do it, but he had no choice. When this was over, he'd make sure that they were well paid for everything he took.

On the way to the village, he would stop by the river again and fill his one canteen. To keep from becoming dehydrated in the jungle heat, a man had to drink at least four quarts of water a day, and his canteen only held one. That meant that he had to refill it at every opportunity.

SABATAS AND HIS THREE Indians were sweeping through the jungle in what Bolan would have called a clover leaf. Along their axis of advance, they moved out well to both sides in sweeping, overlapping, circular patterns looking for signs of their prey. It was a grueling process and would go on throughout the day, but it was the only way they were likely to pick up his sign. One man moving alone didn't leave much trace.

Two hours later, their path took them close to the main river that cut through the area before joining the other headwaters of the Amazon. Sabatas signaled for his guide to check it out. Like everything else in the jungle, Belasko would need to drink often, and this was the primary source of water in the area.

Over the smell of the water, the guide Indian caught the faint scent of a white man. It wasn't as strong as he expected, which told him that this particular white man had to have been eating native foods for the past several days. Though he didn't stink as badly as most of them, enough of the unmistakable stench was there. Stepping back out into the open, he signaled his find to the other Indians.

One of Sabatas's Indians caught the signal and passed it on to his boss. The rebel leader signaled in return for his men to spread out and search the area thoroughly for any sign that Belasko had been in the area. If he had, they could set up an ambush for his return.

OVER TIME, the fast-flowing river had cut a deep channel into the limestone that formed the bed rock of the region. Also over time, the inhabitants of the jungle had worn several paths into the resulting cliffs so they could get to the water. Like the rest of the creatures in the jungle, Bolan used their pathways to reach the riverbank.

He had drunk his fill and refilled his canteen at the river and was now halfway back up the rock face of the cliff. Suddenly he was aware that he was no longer alone in this part of the jungle. It wasn't as much anything he had seen, heard or smelled as it was a gut feeling. But such feelings needed to be heeded.

Making his way back to the top of the cliff, he unslung his AK, settled down motionless in the brush and became a part of his surroundings.

For a number of reasons, the small yellow spider Bolan had lain down beside didn't fear the big warm-blooded predator who had intruded into its realm. For one thing, like most insects, it simply wasn't smart enough to be afraid. Secondly it carried a neurotoxin venom in its fangs that few warm-blooded mammals could survive. A little nip usually was enough to insure that no animal bothered it more than once.

Bolan felt the spider crawl across his lower leg and ignored it. As part of his accommodation to living in the jungle, he had become immune to the insects that made up so much of the biomass of the tropics. To take notice of them by swatting or brushing them away was to stand out as an intruder. And if he was being hunted as his senses told him he was, he couldn't afford to be noticed.

REACTING TO the guide's hand signals, Sabatas ordered his two trackers to spread out and move toward the cliffs overlooking the river. If Belasko was hiding there, there was no place for him to run and they had him. While the Indians moved through the brush, he took to the trees, climbing a dozen feet into the air until he found a well-concealed perch that gave him an overview of the cliff.

BOLAN SPOTTED a movement to his right and, slowly parting the vegetation in front of him, saw an Indian in tribal dress, including face paint, and armed with an AK-47. Apparently, Collins had called in his Indian allies to take over for his guerrilla fighters.

Where there was one Indian, there might be more, so he patiently waited to see whether he could spot anyone else. With his back to the river, he couldn't retreat and would have to fight it out where he was. First, though, he had to know how many men he was facing.

Suddenly, his right leg felt as if it had been dipped in liquid fire. A cry of pain slipped past his lips as his nerves spasmed. The pain was so intense that his body reacted without his instructions, bringing him to his feet.

FROM HIS OBSERVATION POINT in the tree, Sabatas saw the disturbance in the brush and brought his

AK up to bear on it. When his target suddenly appeared, he fired.

His target's leg collapsed as Sabatas fired, sending him backward. But, in falling, he turned just enough that the 7.62 mm round that had been aimed at his heart cut a shallow grove along his left chest.

Off balance from the bullet's impact, his left foot slipped on the slick rock and he tumbled backward into space.

Sabatas rose from his hiding place and shouted his war cry. He had killed.

Climbing down from the tree, he ran forward to the edge of the drop to see if he could spot the body, but the spray of water from the falls obscured the pool below and he saw nothing. He could work his way down the stream to the bank below and search for the body, but he knew that it wasn't worth the effort. He had no doubt that his shot had been true. He had caught a glimpse of bright red on Belasko's chest as he turned and fell.

Whoever and whatever the American had been, he was dead now and that was the end of it. Collins had said that he wanted the body brought back so he could sell it to the Arab, but Sabatas didn't deal in carrion. He created it wholesale, but he didn't sell it retail. If the Arab wanted the body, he could look for it himself.

His job done now, the guide slipped back into the jungle for the walk back to his village. He had earned his pay and wanted to go home and use it.

His bamboo hut needed to be repaired, and the steel knife the white man who tried to look like an Indian had given him would make that an easy job now.

EVEN THOUGH his consciousness was fading, Bolan knew that he was in the river and he fought his way to the surface before he blacked out. The swift current had him in its clutches and swept him over the water falls. He fought to stabilize himself as he fell again, but he completely lost consciousness halfway down.

He plunged into the deep pool at the bottom of the waterfalls like a rock, but the air in his lungs brought him back up to the surface. With his conscious mind shut down, some survival system buried deep in the recesses of his brain kept his head above water as he was swept along.

A few yards from the base of the falls, the stream turned turbulent again as it coursed through rocks that had fallen from the cliffs over the years. A series of rapids churned the water to a white froth, and he was buffeted and slammed from one rock and whirlpool to the next. The rocks were well rounded, so he hit most of them only glancing blows.

After two hundred yards of white water, the torrent shot him out and sent him downstream into calmer water. Once past the rapids, the river flattened out and became shallower, slowing the current dramatically. The last rapids had rolled him over so that he was lying face up, and he floated because he was still breathing. As long as his lungs stayed full of air, he wouldn't sink.

As he floated downstream, the coldness of the mountain water had lowered his metabolism and circulation enough that the spread of the neurotoxin had been retarded. Since the spider's poison was a complex organic chemical composition, it deteriorated in contact with the oxygen in his blood. His liver also attacked it with enzymes to try to break it down into something less toxic and damaging to his system.

Twenty minutes and almost a mile later, the current had carried him to a shallow pool formed by a bend in the river. Where the river curved, a sandbar had built up over the years until it was only a few inches below the surface of the water. Once out of the main flow, he slowly drifted toward the sandbar and stopped when his head touched it. The current kept pushing him against it, and the eddies swirling around his head scoured the sand away until they carved out a place for it to rest firmly with his face clear of the water.

To a casual observer watching from several yards away, he would have appeared to have been drowned. One would have had to go closer to see that his chest was still slowly rising and falling.

Had this observer gone even closer and laid their fingers on his carotid artery, his pulse would have been very slow, but strong.

Mack Bolan was alive.

CHAPTER TWENTY

In the Mountains of Peru

In the part of Peru that had been surrendered to become the coalition territory, the northern border with Colombia was no longer guarded by the Peruvian military. Neither was it more than barely patrolled by the government of Colombia. With the signing of the treaty, it had become a virtual no-man's-land, which was exactly what Collins had wanted to happen. His main ground supply routes would run through that area, and he didn't want his people to have to dodge government patrols, either Peruvian or Colombian.

On both sides of the border, this was an area of remote jungle, the only habitations being small, scattered Indian villages. Most of it was unmarred with roads, and what few roads there were, were marked on the maps as being seasonal. This was also a region that traditionally had been an area of small coca tree plantations hidden in the jungle.

The main road from southern Colombia into the

coalition territory was of the few that wasn't marked on the maps as being seasonal. It wasn't paved, but it was a fairly good all-season route that bypassed most of the villages in the region.

The first village inside the old Peruvian border, however, was a well-known way station along this route. The locals, mostly Indians, did a good business catering to the men of the truck convoys that rumbled through on a fairly regular basis. The fact that most of their customers were working for one or the other of the drug cartels didn't bother them. What city people did was of no interest to them, and the only laws that concerned them were those made by their elders.

These outsiders paid well for hot food, something to drink, a place to sleep and someone to sleep with. These visitors were usually armed, as well, but the Indians had long been accustomed to seeing guns in the hands of their masters. It was a good symbiotic relationship. The news of the formation of the coalition territory promised that more convoys would be making the long drive, and the villagers were ready to service their crews.

JACK GRIMALDI DROPPED Phoenix Force at an LZ several miles away from the border village. Since this was an inhabited area, they couldn't risk having an Indian spot the Black Hawk coming or going.

An hour and a half's march brought them to a hillside overlooking the little town nestled in a valley between two hilly areas. The village consisted of two dozen huts and a dozen more small concrete-block houses off both sides of the road. Three larger structures in the middle of town edging the road were obviously roadhouses—combination taverns, restaurants, hotels and brothels. The village didn't have what could be called side streets, merely beaten footpaths between the clusters of huts. So the convoy vehicles were parked along the side of the road in front of the roadhouses.

"Do you want to take them out down there in the ville?" Hawkins asked as he checked the avenues of approach through his field glasses.

"I don't think so this time," Encizo answered. "If we do that, the next bunch of thugs who come through are likely to take it out on the people down there. I think we should wait until they move out again and ambush them along the road."

"Rafe has a good point," McCarter said. "Let's go light on the locals if we can. The map shows good ambush sites to the south."

There was no way that the cartel troops in the village could have known of Phoenix Force's presence, but they still moved back up the hill and picked an easily defensible site. If a wandering Indian stumbled onto them, he would be sure to report it to the cartel men.

"Maybe I should drop in down there and try to count noses," Hawkins suggested as night fell.

"That would give us a better idea of what we're up against and all that."

"You're going to try to find a spare case of beer you can liberate, you mean," James said, grinning. "I'll go down with you to watch your back."

"I'll go," Encizo told James. "If you try to use your Chicago Spanish down there, you won't last past the first *'¡buenas noches!'*"

"And," he added, turning to Hawkins, "I'll go alone. You're way too much of a gringo to even be a mercenary."

"Bummer."

WITH GARY MANNING WATCHING over him with the night scope on his sniper rifle, Encizo started down the hill. With all the brush on the hillside, Manning couldn't keep him in sight for the entire distance, but once in the valley he would be in open view until he reached the huts.

At the edge of the village, Encizo found cover and took a long look at the final approach. Since he was trying to pass for a cartel gunman, he wasn't wearing his night-vision goggles. "It looks okay to me," he whispered over the com link back to Manning. "What do you have?"

"It's clear on the way in," the big Canadian replied. "I don't have any sentries. Most of the action looks to be around the bars and cathouses."

"I'm moving in now."

"Watch your ass, Rafe," McCarter cut in.

"Always."

One of the roadhouses had a portable generator, and the sounds of a boom box playing salsa cassettes carried outside. The raucous music was a perfect mask for any noise he might make. Not that anyone else was being quiet. Men were shouting, singing and laughing. Occasionally he could hear a woman's voice joining in on the party. He probably could have brought a brass band with him and no one would notice.

It took little time for him to make the rounds of the taverns and roadhouses. In each one, he poked his head in as if he were looking for a buddy, took a quick estimate of the number of men and left. He knew, of course, that he was only counting the drinkers, but he wasn't about to try to count the gunmen in the back rooms with the girls.

He was on his way back out when he heard a rough male voice behind a hut followed by a girl's scream. He knew better than to let himself get drawn into whatever it was that was going down, but the girl sounded young. Cursing himself, he drew his fighting knife and stepped around the corner.

A man in camouflage fatigue pants and a T-shirt had an Indian girl pinned on the ground in front of him. He was holding her down with one hand around her throat and was fumbling at his belt with the other. The thug was too busy concentrating on rape to be aware of what was happening around him, and that's the way Encizo liked it.

By the time he crossed the ground, the would-be rapist finally had his pants open and was positioning himself over the girl. Reaching down, Encizo grabbed the man's hair with his left hand and jerked his head back while his right stabbed the knife into the side of his throat.

The blade ripped through the thug's throat from side to side, severing both the jugular and carotid and taking his windpipe with it. The man blacked out so fast from the massive loss of blood that he didn't even have time to scream and was dead in ninety seconds.

The girl had passed out, probably from shock. After pulling the body off her, Encizo checked to see that she was still breathing. When he found that she was, he grabbed the gunman's body under the arms and dragged him off, leaving the girl to wake up on her own.

"I'm on the way back up," he said into his radio a few minutes later.

"THERE'S ABOUT SIXTY of them down there," Encizo reported, "and they aren't nice people. We'll be doing everyone a favor by zeroing them."

McCarter caught the look on his face and asked, "What happened, Rafe?"

"One of them grabbed a young Indian girl on her way home and wouldn't take no for an answer."

"Are they going to miss him?"

"Maybe." Encizo shrugged. "But they won't find him. I dropped him in a pit latrine."

"What are they packing?" Hawkins asked.

"Nothing special, AKs and a few new M-16s. No grenade launchers that I could see, or RPGs either."

"They're making it too easy for us."

"They're cartel scum. It can't be too easy."

IT WAS WELL PAST DAWN the next morning when the cartel troops finally dragged themselves onto the road and climbed on board their vehicles. Since they believed that they were safe inside the territory of their new allies, they weren't on the lookout for trouble when they left the village.

A mile and a half south of the village, the road wound into the mountains again. A little farther on, the road was cut into the side of a ravine, and that was where McCarter set up a simple linear ambush along the uphill side of the road. The convoy would drive into the kill zone, and Phoenix Force would shoot it up, then escape over the ridgeline. Any survivors they left behind wouldn't be in any shape to chase them.

Traveling as lightly as they were, the Phoenix Force warriors didn't have the best weapons in the world for pulling off this kind of convoy ambush. An RPG would have made the job a lot easier, but this would have to be pulled off with small-arms fire and a few grenades.

When the convoy entered the kill zone, Gary Manning opened up with his rifle, putting a 7.62 mm NATO bullet in the head of the driver of the first vehicle in the convoy, an open-topped four-wheel drive. In his death throes, the driver jerked the steering wheel to the left and drove off the cliff.

The driver of the two-and-a-half-ton truck following behind it slammed to a halt, his cab passenger jumping out and running to the edge of the cliff to look for survivors from the crash.

With the lead truck halted, the other trucks were forced to stop, as well. Troops being troops, most of the men shuffled out of their transport to see what was happening. When the road was crowded, McCarter gave the word. "Take them out."

Manning's next shot punctured the right front tire of the lead truck before he switched to the last truck in the column. The trucks could drive on flat front tires, but it was difficult—doubly difficult when someone was shooting at the drivers.

With the second shot, the cartel troops realized that they were under fire and reacted. Since most of them had left their weapons in the trucks when they disembarked, the result was chaos.

For the first few seconds, Phoenix Force had everything its way. It was more of an execution than a firefight. The handful of gunmen who had been too hungover to want to gawk at the wreck were the first to reach their weapons. Even with adrenaline pumping them, it still took a few shots before any of the return fire was even close.

When one of the cartel gunmen proved to be a cooler head and a better shot than the rest, he pinned Hawkins down for several nasty moments.

"Get that bastard off me, Gary," he said over his radio to Manning as bullets sang over his head.

"Got him spotted," Manning sent back. When the scope's stadia lines intersected with the gunman's chest, the big Canadian fired and saw him fall back.

"Thanks, buddy," Hawkins called out.

Along with taking his own shots as he found them, McCarter was watching the progress of the firefight. Even having gotten the drop on the gunmen and drawn first, as well as second and third blood, there was simply no way that the five of them were going to be able to keep the upper hand. Sixty to five wasn't good odds no matter who had taken the first shots.

"That's it," he called over the com link. "Pull back."

"One more," Manning said as he centered his scope on the gunman who looked to be trying to rally his comrades. Drawing attention to yourself in the middle of an ambush was always a sign of having a death wish. The squeeze of his trigger made that a fact.

When that man dropped to the ground, the commandos started to fall back over the ridgeline behind them. A scattering of AK fire followed them up the hill, but most of the fight had been taken out of the cartel troops.

AN HOUR LATER, Phoenix Force had reached its planned PZ and went into a defensive perimeter to wait for Grimaldi's aerial taxi service.

"Fly One," Manning transmitted, "this is Rover One. We're Papa Zulu, over."

"This is Fly One," Grimaldi replied. "Roger, copy Papa Zulu. I'm eight mikes out, mark it, over."

"This is a no-smoke Papa Zulu," Manning reminded him.

"Roger. Copy no strawberry, lime or goofy grape."

The Phoenix Force warriors were several miles from the ambush site, but they still didn't want to be noticed if they could help it. Because of that, they didn't want to pop a smoke grenade to guide Grimaldi in for his pickup. Instead, as soon as the Black Hawk appeared in the sky, Hawkins stepped out into the clearing and stood with his back to the wind with his assault rifle held stiffly up over his head with both hands. This was the traditional signal for the chopper pilot to land in front of him.

Grimaldi flared the helicopter out for a landing only three yards in front of Hawkins. The tip wash from the rotors buffeted the ex-Ranger as he automatically ducked his head. The disk of the spinning rotor blades was well over his head, but old habits were hard to break.

The five commandos scrambled on board in no time flat, and Grimaldi pulled pitch to lift out of the clearing an instant later. He had been on the ground less than sixty seconds.

ONCE THEY WERE in the air, McCarter slid into the copilot's seat. Putting on the spare flight helmet, he got on the radio to Katzenelenbogen to report their kill.

"We got the lead vehicle with the officers," he reported, "at least a dozen and a half of the troops and damaged all four trucks. They won't be bothering anyone for a while, and Collins is going to have to go to the cartels again if he wants reinforcements."

"Good work," Katzenelenbogen told him. "If you feel up to it, I have another mission you might want to drop in on for a few hours."

"What is it?"

"Kurtzman came up with a report of armed rebels moving south out of the coalition territory back into Peru proper. We don't know what they're doing or where they're going, but it might be worth while looking into. We've pinpointed a couple of trails that are their likely avenues of movement."

"Send them."

Katz sent the coordinates and, when he checked

the map, McCarter saw that they could reach one of the suspected trails in twenty minutes.

"I'll have Jack insert us on the first one," he called back. "We'll watch for the rest of the day and see what turns up. If we dry hole there, we'll come back to your location, refit and try the next site."

"Sounds good."

THIS TIME GRIMALDI LANDED Phoenix Force less than a klick from its intended ambush site. This would be a straight hit, again designed to throw the coalition off balance. If Collins was moving troops, Stony Man wanted to make sure that he knew they were being watched.

After reconning the immediate area, the commandos settled in to see if they got any business. They had been in position for several hours when Hawkins broke in on the com link. The ex-Ranger was a hundred yards up the trail in an early-warning outpost.

"I have eight," he whispered. "No, nine, coming our way and they're moving fast."

"Break off and come back," McCarter said.

"On the way."

The enemy patrol was moving quickly, almost as if it was being pursued. They weren't keeping much of an eye on their back trail, so something else had to be pushing them along. Whatever it was, it was making them careless, and they would have to pay for that lapse.

"Fire," McCarter transmitted.

This time the fight was more one-sided than it had been at the convoy ambush. There were fewer troops to deal with, and the terrain was perfect for a classic L-shaped jungle ambush. Few of the Indians even got a shot off.

A blaze of 3-round bursts from the commandos' MP-5 subguns swept the kill zone, taking out three of the patrol in the first seconds. The other six tried to react, but only got off a few scattered shots before going down themselves.

After the last shot died away, Phoenix Force moved out to clear the kill zone. They didn't expect to collect much in the line of field intelligence from this patrol, but it didn't hurt to take a few minutes to look while they waited for Jack Grimaldi to return.

"We've got one still alive," Manning said as he knelt next to a slight figure who was keeping very still trying not to give himself away. "He took a round in the leg, but looks okay other than that."

McCarter saw that the wounded guerrilla was little more than a teenager. He wasn't in the mood to take prisoners, but sending boys into battle had always been a big no-no with the tough Briton, and that swayed him. Growing up was hard enough without someone shooting at you.

"See if you can patch him up," he told James.

The wounded boy instantly relaxed when he saw James open up his medic's bag and pull out his medical supplies. A doctor was a doctor no matter what his skin color or the uniform he was wearing. If they were going to kill him, they wouldn't waste time treating him first.

"See if you can get his story while Calvin's working on him," McCarter instructed Encizo.

The Cuban slung his rifle and squatted beside the boy.

After a long exchange, Encizo looked up. "He doesn't speak very good Spanish," he reported, "but he's saying something about having to leave where they had been because of El Tigre, the Jaguar. He says that a jaguar demon wearing the shape of a man has been hunting in the jungle around the *patrón*'s camp, and they had to flee or be killed."

"What the hell does that mean?" McCarter asked.

"He says that his boss brought a white man into the camp, but that he escaped and he was taken over by the spirit of the jaguar god when he went into the jungle."

"Bingo." McCarter grinned. "That can only be Striker. Ask him how long ago he saw this killer jaguar who walks like a man."

"He says he attacked their camp at night three days ago and the next day, he killed many of the men who went out in the jungle to hunt him down."

"Who is this boss he's talking about?"

"He says that he doesn't know his name," Encizo said, "but that he is a white man with red hair and blue eyes."

"That's got to be that bastard Collins." McCarter's eyes narrowed. "There can't be two red-haired Irish bastards in this jungle."

"Ask him where the camp is."

Another intense discussion had Encizo shaking his head before it was finished. "He says that he doesn't know how to tell us how to get to the camp in a way that we can understand. He says that it's two days' travel for him, three for men like us, but that we couldn't follow the signs he sees on the trail because we aren't Indians."

"Tell him to give us a try," McCarter replied. "We might be a little smarter than he thinks we are."

Encizo shook his head again in frustration. "I'm not getting much out of this. He's using a lot of Indian words that he doesn't know the Spanish equivalent for, and I sure as hell don't understand his dialect."

"Damn," McCarter said. "At least ask him which direction it is from here."

When Encizo translated, the Indian boy looked around for a long moment, and then pointed in a northwesterly direction.

"Make that 321 degrees from here," Manning said, glancing down at his wrist compass.

"Do we leave him here or fly him out?" James asked as he started repacking his bag. "He's ambulatory, but just barely. It's going to take him days to get to the next village from here on his own."

"Let me ask him," Encizo said, "and see what he wants to do. If we take him to a medical facility to heal, the authorities might slap his ass in jail, and we owe him a big one this time."

"Good point," McCarter said.

When his choice was explained to him, the young Indian had absolutely no interest in being taken to a hospital anywhere. Indian jungle fighters like him who went to hospitals usually ended up in a Peruvian prison.

"Now what?" Encizo asked when he passed on the boy's choice.

"Now we call for Grimaldi to pick us up."

"And take him with us?"

"Why not?" McCarter said. "As far as I'm concerned, he's earned a trip to damned near anywhere he wants, so ask him where he wants to go."

Encizo spoke to the boy soldier again, but he shook his head emphatically and pointed off to the side of the trail. "He says thanks," the commando translated, "but he wants to wait here for his uncle."

"How's his uncle going to know where to find him?"

"He says he's here right now. He bugged out of the ambush and hid."

McCarter laughed.

CHAPTER TWENTY-ONE

Stony Man Farm, Virginia

Aaron Kurtzman almost came out of his chair when Katzenelenbogen called from Peru on the satcom link. "I think we finally have a line on Striker," Katz said tersely.

"About damned time," Kurtzman growled. "What is it?"

"It isn't much," Katz admitted, "but Phoenix ambushed a rebel patrol that turned out to be a small group of Indians fleeing from Collins's camp. There was a survivor, a boy really, and he told them that their jaguar god had taken over the soul of a white man and that he was killing his *patrón*'s men in the jungle."

"That sounds like Striker." Kurtzman smiled. "And the *patrón* is Sean Collins, right?"

"The Indian didn't have a name, but the description he gave fits him."

"Did you get a location for this camp?"

"The kid didn't speak much Spanish, just enough

to get by in combat, and Rafe isn't too good on the local dialects, so they couldn't get exact directions. He did say though, that the camp was northwest a two-day march for him from the ambush site and, for the Indians around here, figure that at forty to forty-five miles a day. He also pointed in the direction he thought the camp was in.''

''Where was the ambush?''

Katz gave him the coordinates, and Kurtzman superimposed them on the map of the region on his screen. ''And what direction did he point to?'' he asked.

''Three hundred and twenty-one degrees.''

''Good,'' Kurtzman said. ''I'll run this through the machine and see what I can come up with. I'll do a two- to three-day fan out from the ambush site and superimpose it over what commo intercepts we have and see if we can find a nexus.''

''We'll be waiting.'' Katz signed off.

THE REPORT that Bolan was alive electrified the Stony Man Farm crew. The worried faces everyone had worn since the chopper crash so many days ago almost instantly evaporated to be replaced by broad grins. If Bolan was haunting the jungle like a jaguar, he had to be okay.

''But if he's free,'' Price said, frowning, after Brognola gave her the news, ''why hasn't he gotten out of the area and gone for help? There must be a village or a small town somewhere around there that has a radio or a phone so he could contact Lima. I don't understand.''

Brognola had the same question, but he wasn't going to let it dampen his spirits. "My thought is that he may be trying to protect Dan Denning," he said. "If he's causing enough trouble for the rebels, they might concentrate on trying to find him instead of working on Denning for information."

"But can't they still question Denning even if Mack isn't there?"

"They could, of course," he replied. "But we don't know what the situation is there. There must be a good reason for Striker to be doing something like that. He always has a good reason for what he does."

She had to agree with Brognola's assessment. Every time outsiders hadn't understood why Bolan had done a particular thing, it had become instantly clear when he was asked about it later. She would just have to trust him again on this one.

"Do you think he can hold out long enough for Phoenix to find him?"

Brognola knew what she wanted to hear, but he also knew that he had to stay true to what few facts he had at this time. "He has a much better than average chance of survival, of course. But this time he's in the jungle with people who were born there, and the jungle doesn't play favorites. He certainly has the skills and, if he still has his luck, he should be okay."

Price knew that blind luck was always a player in any combat situation. More men died in firefights from unaimed bullets than from anything else. But luck could always be coaxed to favor a man when he added skill and experience to the mix. And no man had more skill or experience at raw survival than Mack Bolan.

"But," Brognola added, "we're going to do what we can to add to that luck."

He turned to Kurtzman. "Get me a hard copy of everything you have," he said. "I'm going to take it up to the Man."

"But what are you going to tell him?" Kurtzman asked. "None of this is hard enough to prove anything yet."

"As you say, it's not much. But as far as I'm concerned, it's enough to convince him to break loose the one thing in the arsenal we haven't been able to use yet. I'm going to ask him to authorize a Blackbird and a Night Owl run over this place."

"All right!" Kurtzman grinned. If he was running the world, he wouldn't even go to lunch without first having an SR-71 check out the parking lot to spot the empty slots for him from sixty thousand feet. "Now maybe we'll be able to see what the hell's down there."

MACK BOLAN AWOKE with his head resting on sand and his face barely above water. He was so cold that he could hardly feel his body, but he didn't think that he had been hurt badly. Taking a deep breath, he managed to roll over and still keep his face out of the water.

His arms and legs were numb from the cold, and it was almost impossible for him to crawl. But he kept struggling, moving mere inches at a time until he was in a patch of sunlight on the narrow beach completely out of the water. He immediately lapsed into unconsciousness again from the effort.

The spider's neurotoxin wasn't gone from his system, but it was rapidly being biodegraded into a relatively harmless, but long acting psychoactive drug. This compound was similar to the "toad sweat" so popular among certain groups of thrill seeking American college students and Indian shamans who wanted to travel through the spirit world of the jungle.

The powerful poison wouldn't kill him now, but it sent his mind to a place that few men, and certainly no white men, had ever been.

In the spirit world Bolan found himself in, he saw his body lying on the sand as if he were looking down from a great height. Somehow he could look into his body and see that although it lay almost motionless, it was alive.

He was pondering being in two places at once when he saw a jaguar, a fully grown male, cautiously approaching him. This was the king predator of this jungle, but he felt no fear. He knew without knowing that the magnificent cat wouldn't harm him.

The animal's golden eyes glowed as if reflecting a fire. Its daggerlike fangs showed stark white against the red of its open mouth and tongue. Its nose was flared as it sniffed the odor emanating from this intruder. It wasn't the man smell the creature had learned to expect from these two legs. The two legs were usually meat to the jaguar, but not this one. This one wasn't to be killed and eaten.

Now that Bolan's body temperature had come back up to almost normal, blood again seeped from the gouge that Sabatas's bullet had cut across his left breast. The wound was so shallow that it had clotted almost as quickly as it had started to bleed again.

Even though the cat had no inclination to eat Bolan, it was curious and sniffed at the blood that tracked the soldier's chest. It then leaned over him and licked at it. A second lick firmly locked the taste in the animal's sensory memory, and now it would recognize Bolan forever.

When Bolan felt the big cat's raspy hot tongue against his chest, he knew that he was back in his body. He felt the scrapes and bruises from his trip through the white water and the pain across his chest from the bullet wound, but nothing seemed to be broken.

Now that he was conscious again, he could hear, but it took a while for him to recognize what he was hearing over the background noise of the jungle. It was a rhythmic, resonant, rasping sound, rising and falling as if air were rushing across the strings of a bass.

The jaguar was purring.

Unafraid, and lulled by the sound and the warmth of the sun, Bolan went back to sleep.

Stony Man Farm, Virginia

HAL BROGNOLA'S door-to-door turnaround time from the Farm to the Oval Office and back was almost a world record. He'd had his pilot set down on the South Lawn instead of the Justice Department landing pad he usually used to save the transit time in D.C. traffic.

Out of habit, though, after landing at the Farm, he didn't say a word until he was back inside the farmhouse.

"We're a go for both the SR-71 and the TR-3 recon runs," he announced. "We lucked out on the Blackbird because one of them just came out of a maintenance stand-down at Palmdale, and it was scheduled for a test flight anyway. Because of that, a flight crew is already in workup and the Q tanker is standing by. It will launch as soon as the cameras can be loaded and the tanker fueled up."

The Lockheed SR-71 Blackbird was almost forty years old, but it was still the pinnacle of aviation technology. And, as such, it wasn't a "kick the tires and light the fires'' kind of airplane. If the entire suite of Blackbird-specific support equipment, systems and crew wasn't available, it couldn't even have the engines started. In fact, its boron-based fuel wouldn't even burn at ambient air pressure and temperature without a chemical booster.

"How about the TR-3?" Kurtzman asked. "We need it for the under-the-trees shots."

"It's staging out of Elgin in Florida and will hit the IP right after the SR departs the search area. That way we'll have good overlap on the coverage and won't have to worry about time framing on the data."

"Somebody up north likes us." Kurtzman grinned. He wasn't used to the Farm getting everything they needed handed to them on a platter. All too often they had to "borrow" it when someone's back was turned.

Brognola smiled back. "That someone didn't need too much reminding that he owes Striker more than he, or any other President, can ever repay. This is crunch time, and he knows it."

Price knew how the Oval Office scenes went, and she could read between the lines. "How hard did you have to lean on him, Hal?"

"Not much," Brognola answered honestly. "He's not too happy at having gotten sucked in on this White Shield thing, and he'll be real glad when we have enough information to get it shut down. He's ready to admit that he got suckered, but he has to wait until it's all over before he can come clean on it. That's the only way he can keep from looking like a complete idiot to Congress.''

"I'll reserve judgment on that," she said, "but, it's nice to have him completely on board for a change.''

"Let me get Katz in on this," Brognola said. "I want Phoenix ready to exploit anything we find.''

Kurtzman's hand flashed out to key the satcom radio. "Coming up.''

CHAPTER TWENTY-TWO

In the Jungle

Ramón Sabatas entered Collins's camp like a conquering hero. The two Indian trackers flanking him loudly told everyone within earshot that the jaguar man had been hunted down and killed.

Most of the Indians, though, crossed themselves or made ancient signs of protection when they heard the news. Killing the man who had been possessed by the spirit of the jaguar could only bring them bad luck. The jaguar had been present at the beginning of the world, and the sun had sent him to rule over the jungle and all who lived in it. When the spirit of the jaguar visited a man, he was to be honored, not hunted down and slaughtered.

"You won't have to worry about Belasko anymore," Sabatas reported to his paymaster. "We caught up with him, and he's dead."

"Good," Collins said. "It's about time something went right. Now maybe the damned Indians will calm down and do what I pay them to do. I have more-important things to worry about than one man hiding in the jungle. I still wish I had been able to find out who he was, though.''

The Irishman glanced over to the well, where the two Indian trackers were washing off their face paint. "Where's his body?" he asked. "At least I need his head.''

"When he was shot,'' Sabatas explained, "he fell into the river and went over a waterfall. He's halfway downstream to the Amazon by now if he isn't fish food already. Believe me, he is dead.''

"Dammit, Sabatas,'' Collins roared, "the Brotherhood was ready to pay well for proof of his death. I've had a hard enough time reminding Mamal that his Islamic brothers aren't in charge of the coalition. I've only been able to keep him in check by promising him Belasko dead or alive. He's not going to like this.''

The more Collins had talked with the Arab, the more he realized that the Islamic Brotherhood had its own ideas about how his operations would be run. They saw the coalition as a springboard they could use to launch attacks deep into the underbelly of the Great Satan of the United States. Their fanaticism was so overwhelming that it closed their minds to anything less than total warfare. Subtlety wasn't to be found in the Arabic revolutionary lexicon.

"The Arab dog can die as easily as Belasko,'' Sabatas said bluntly. "Much easier, in fact.''

Collins was sorely tempted to take up his field commander on his offer, and he had little doubt that he would have to order Mamal's death before this was over. But he was hoping to get the promised financial support and equipment from the Brotherhood before he had to terminate their relationship with Mamal's blood.

"It will be a while yet," he replied. "But I promise that I will give him to you."

"Good." Sabatas had had his fill of the Arab's arrogance, as well. He intended to put the man naked in the jungle and hunt him down as he had done with Belasko. But instead of killing him with an AK, he'd use the Indians' poisoned arrows. They could take hours to kill a man.

DAN DENNING HAD SEEN Sabatas and the two Indians leave the camp earlier that day. Now they were back and they were most certainly celebrating something. He didn't want to have to think about what that was. But when Sabatas walked up to his cage with a smirk on his face, he knew what was coming.

"Your protector is dead," Sabatas stated. "My trackers and I ran him down and shot him like a dog. So don't hold out any hope that he's going to come back for you. You are completely mine now."

Denning didn't doubt that Belasko was dead. The rebel would never tell him that he was if there was any chance of his being proved wrong. He did, though, seriously doubt Sabatas's self-serving version of the events. If Belasko had died, it hadn't been because he had made a mistake. He hadn't seen Belasko as a man who made too many mistakes. Something about him shouted competence in everything he did.

But the jungle was a treacherous place, and even the best could fall victim to an accident. The fickle finger of Fate was all too active in Belasko's line of work.

"Are you going to kill me, too, now?"

"Not yet, amigo." Sabatas laughed. "You still have value to us, and when you die, it will probably be at the hands of one of the drug lords. The cartels feel that they owe you for all the trouble your agency has been to them, and they will pay us well for the pleasure of watching you die."

"I may die as you say," Denning said, trying to keep calm, "but I can assure you that I won't be the only one who's going to get killed. If I were you, I'd be looking to protect my ass. Collins is a fool to think that he's going to be able to get away with this. And you—" Denning slowly smiled "—are an even bigger asshole for working for him."

Sabatas flushed with anger. "I would watch my mouth if I were you, DEA man."

"What are you going to do, kill me? You've already told me that you're going to do that, and frankly it's starting to get a little old. I'm tired of hearing it."

"You will live to regret that you said that." Sabatas turned and walked off.

Denning savored his small victory. It had been pure bravado, a useless gesture, but it had felt good. He hoped that he would be able to remember it when he was dying in pain. And he hoped that wherever he was, Belasko had heard him say it.

Going to the side of the cage where he had made his makeshift bed, he lay down. Whatever happened next, he wanted to be rested for it.

WHEN BOLAN NEXT OPENED his eyes, he was in the middle of a glowing golden-green world. The sun lancing through the trees looked like molten gold and glittered off the ripples in the water like gemstones. The jungle around him looked like something from a fairy tale. He could make out each individual leaf and vine, and they shimmered as if they were made of thin glass. He blinked his eyes, but the vision didn't go away.

He was parched and had an acrid taste in his mouth. Smelling water, he rolled over and crawled toward it. At the edge of the pool, he lowered his face into the water and drank. After a few swallows, he raised his head to make sure that he was alone. He immediately sensed that he wasn't, but the creatures watching him weren't his enemies.

When he had drunk his fill, Bolan looked around again. The landscape still glowed in shimmering shades of iridescent gold, green, blue, red and purple. His eyes were able to strip the natural camouflage from the animals around him, revealing them clearly against the glowing backdrop. His enhanced sense of smell also told him that he wasn't alone at the watering hole, but he wasn't afraid. He neither saw nor smelled any enemies among those who watched him.

He remembered dreaming about a jaguar, a magnificent male who had come up to him while he had lain on the beach. For some reason, the cat hadn't taken advantage of his helplessness. In fact, he had a vivid memory of the animal lying beside him as if it were guarding him. In his current state of mind, though, that wasn't a strange thing at all. It seemed to go with the world he found himself in. For some reason, he felt a kinship with the big cat as if he had lived with it for years. It felt like a comrade.

Slowly getting to his feet, he moved away from the water to allow someone else a chance to take a drink. Now that he had quenched his thirst, he was suddenly ravenously hungry. He was still too weak, though, to want to move very far.

The only weapon that had made the trip down the river with Bolan was the knife sheathed on his belt. It stayed with him because it had a tie-down that had held it in its sheath. When a slight rustle in the bushes at the tree line revealed a small animal that looked like a cross between a rabbit and a large hamster, light glinted on the blade as Bolan whipped the knife at the creature.

The soldier walked forward slowly and removed the knife.

Then he used it to skin the animal and to cut the meat from the bones. He was so hungry that eating the meat warm and bloody wasn't a problem.

After eating, Bolan felt better than he remembered feeling in a long time. But then, his memory didn't go back very far beyond falling into the river. Fleeting glimpses did come to his mind of a man he was supposed to be guarding. He didn't remember who the man was, only that he was a friend and that he had to get back to him. He also vaguely remembered that he had enemies in the jungle.

When he felt his strength returning, Bolan went to the edge of the water again to drink. When he was full, he turned to leave the river.

As much an animal as a man now, Bolan faded into the jungle and unerringly set a course back toward the camp where his friend was being held prisoner. Inside the animal he had become was still the soul of a man who had a duty that he wouldn't forget. The name of the man he was returning for didn't surface in his mind because it wasn't important to him. The face and smell of the friend, though, was strong enough in his mind to guide him.

BOLAN WAS HIT by another wave of hunger that drove all other thoughts from his mind. He vaguely remembered that there was something important he was supposed to be doing. He kept getting flashes of a man's face and a sense that the man was important, but he couldn't bring it to focus. Every time he tried, it made his head hurt. All he could concentrate on was finding something to eat fast.

The jungle wasn't a fast-food outlet, but neither was it a wasteland for someone who knew what was good to eat. In Bolan's condition, he craved protein. With his senses sharpened even more by his hunger, his nose tested the air and his eyes searched the brush for his next meal.

Bolan was drawn to a large tree whose foot-thick branches drooped down over a faint game trail. Wrapped around the branch was the sinuous, dappled form of an eight-foot python patiently waiting for an unwary animal.

The snake smelled Bolan as he got closer, but his smell wasn't something the python recognized as being dangerous. It was only when its slitted eyes snicked open that it saw danger approaching. The reptile's walnut-sized brain was processing this information when Bolan vaulted into the limb behind the creature.

The snake's head was coming around to get a better look at this intruder when Bolan clamped his left arm around the snake, right behind his head, and hammered down with the knife in his right hand.

The knife went in at the base of the python's

arrow-point-shaped head, severing the spinal cord and driving into the reptile's brain.

Though technically dead, the snake went into tail-whipping convulsions. Bolan kept his grip as the powerful muscles tried to throw a coil around him to peel him off. When he felt the contractions weaken, he pulled the snake loose from its perch and dropped to the ground with it.

After eating his fill, Bolan left the rest to whoever wanted to fight over it. That, too, was the way of the jungle. His hunger sated, he smelled water and went toward the smell and found a small pool in an outcropping. Cupping his hands, he drank cool water until he could drink no more.

Suddenly feeling sleepy, he climbed a tree to find a comfortable place to sleep off his meal.

Stony Man Farm, Virginia

THE MOOD in the Stony Man Computer Room was tense but hopeful. Everyone was keenly aware that this was the last chance they had to try to find Bolan. If this mission by the world's two greatest aerial spies didn't develop something they could use, they had to start thinking of going into mission closure. Either that or send Phoenix Force deep into the coalition territory on a suicide recon. Neither option was thinkable.

"The SR has lifted off from Palmdale," Kurtzman announced, "and is headed for its first refueling hookup. It has gone into radio silence, so the only way we'll know what's happening is when we start getting the first of the recon feed."

The computer crew was ready to intake the recon sensor information and start working it into something they could use. The post-Gulf War refit of the Blackbirds had included real-time sensor downloading capability, so they would get whatever the SR saw almost as soon as the spy plane saw it.

Barbara Price and Hal Brognola stood off to the side waiting to see what could be seen by the spy planes. Both of them knew what the other was thinking, but neither spoke. Putting their thoughts into words was too dangerous. Certain things, once spoken, took on a life of their own. As long as there was this chance, nothing needed to be said.

AT THIRTY-FIVE THOUSAND FEET, the Lockheed SR-71 Blackbird was flying at 520 miles per hour over the Caribbean Sea. But at that speed, it was only loitering, barely hanging in the sky. The triple-sonic spy plane hadn't been designed to fly that slowly unless it was coming in for a landing. But at that altitude, it wasn't trying to land—it had merely throttled back for a badly needed refueling before continuing its mission. The 172,000 pound aircraft used so much fuel taking off that the first thing it did after reaching altitude was to gas up.

The huge McDonnell-Douglas KC-10Q Extender aerial tanker in front of the Blackbird, however, was flying as fast as its three GE F-103 turbofan engines could push it just to match speeds with the SR. When both planes were in position, the tanker extended a flying boom to make the hookup. The refueling probe had small, adjustable control surfaces mounted on the far end so the boom operator could lock the nozzle into the fueling receptacle on top of the Blackbird.

Once the nozzle was locked in, the boom operator flicked on a signal light to let the Blackbird know that the fuel was being transferred. As with all Blackbird refueling missions, it was conducted in complete radio silence. There was no point in broadcasting to the entire world that an SR-71 was on the prowl. It might make someone nervous and tempt him to do something stupid like try to launch a SAM missile to intercept it.

The missile would not, of course, reach its target. The SR flew faster and higher than most ground-to-air missiles. But shooting at U.S. aircraft always raised the international temperature a few degrees and was best avoided.

When the fuel had been delivered, the boom was disconnected and retracted back into the KC. The Blackbird blinked its refueling lights to say ''thanks for the drink.'' When the pilot lit the afterburners of his twin J-58s, the thirty-four-thousand-pound thrust engines, flame shot back the length of the dagger-blade-shaped fuselage. In mere few seconds, the matte-black spy plane was a speck in the sky headed back up to sixty thousand feet, where it liked to operate.

Throttling back down to cruising speed, the KC-10Q went into a wide orbit over the Caribbean to wait for its bottle baby to come back to mama for another nip of the good stuff.

Less than an hour later, the SR-71 was back for another refueling. At over two thousand miles per hour, covering the coalition territory had taken only a few minutes. Most of the elapsed time had been spent getting the plane turned in the sky so it could make an overlapping run in the opposite direction. The cameras and sensors covered a sixty-mile-wide swath on each pass, so several runs had been needed to get the necessary overlap to create the recon mosaic.

With her tanks topped off again, the Blackbird lit her afterburners and the ship rocketed away, headed back for its home base in the California desert.

As befitted a mother, the KC-10Q would follow at her own slower, matronly pace.

CHAPTER TWENTY-THREE

Above Peru

Once the SR-71 was clear of Peruvian airspace, the TR-3 moved in to do its thing. Compared to its triple-sonic big brother, the subsonic Night Owl loitered through the night sky Peru like it was dragging an anchor. What it lacked in speed, however, the TR-3 made up for with its beyond state-of-the-art stealth design that made it all but invisible to any kind of radar, ground based or airborne. Where the SR-71 depended on its blinding speed to escape from its enemies, the bat-shaped TR-3 used stealth technology.

But flying invisibly through the sky wasn't of much use unless it could do something useful at the same time, and that was where the Night Owl's specialized battlefield recon sensors came in. With its sensor suite being mission configurable, it was far more versatile than the older Blackbird. In just a few hours, the ship could have a package installed in its sensor bay that had been tailored to fit a specific reconnaissance objective.

For this mission, the TR-3 was equipped with a sensor package that had originally been designed at great cost and effort to help the DEA find cartel cocoa plantations hidden in the Latin American jungles. Since it had been designed and built, however, the winds of political change had severely curtailed the U.S. military's participation in the war on drugs, so the system had never been used.

With its purpose gone, though, this specialized recon gear hadn't been scrapped as was so often done with expensive equipment that some bureaucrat had decided to cancel on a whim. This time someone had had the foresight to save the equipment for another day. What one Congress had done, the next one could undo. And since the money had already been spent, why waste it?

This package used special frequency-mapping radars that weren't blocked by vegetation no matter how dense. They could peer through the jungle to look for trees growing in straight lines or other signs of cultivation. It could also pick up habitations, fences, wells, fire pits and other signs of human inhabitants. The pilot didn't know what he was looking for down there, but if it was down there, he'd find it.

When the pilot's nav screen showed that he was at the end of this leg of his recon pattern, he put his black batlike spy plane into a tight high-banked turn using his GPS satellite link to put him right on course for his next run in the opposite direction. As with the SR's sensors, he had to fly overlapping runs to make sure that he didn't miss anything. But at the altitude he was flying, the recon swath he could cover on one pass was only twelve miles wide, not the sixty of the Blackbird.

The TR-3 had taken on a load of fuel right before crossing over the Peruvian-Colombian border, so he could afford to take his time and do this job right. There would be no shortcuts taken nor corners shaved on his watch. He was a man who took pride in his work.

Once the pilot was back on course for the next leg, he automatically checked his threat-warning screen and saw that the sky around him was clear, and no ground radars were looking for him, either. Peru didn't have much of an air force and even less in the line of antiaircraft defenses. Nonetheless, he'd had it drilled into him that there were old pilots and there were bold pilots, but there were no old bold pilots. He fully intended to live long enough to become an old pilot and collect his pension, so he kept his boldness firmly in check.

After four more passes over his target area, the pilot turned his stealth spy plane east for a rendezvous with his own personal tanker orbiting in wait for him over the Caribbean. He didn't burn fuel as fast as an SR-71 did, but it was a long flight back to southern Florida.

En route to the refueling area, he did a backup data dump, transmitting all of his sensor take again to the satellite, which in turn retransmitted it to the ground station. That way, if something hadn't come through on the first feed, it would still be available.

That done, he settled back and prepared to meet his gas station in the sky.

Stony Man Farm, Virginia

THE COMPUTER ROOM WAS crowded as the real-time sensor readouts from the TR-3 Night Owl were transmitted to a satellite for retransmission to the NRO ground stations and on to the Farm. Since the TR-3 was operating in the same hemisphere, the data was coming through with only a few seconds' delay from the instant it was gathered.

The SR-71's earlier sensor readouts had also been sent in real time, and that data had already been fed into the computer matrix and was up on the big monitor screen. Hunt Wethers was interlacing the new information over the Blackbird's baseline data, and it was matching up perfectly.

Brognola and Price stood beside Kurtzman's wheelchair, which was crowded in front of Wethers's workstation.

As the sensor readouts from the recon flights were tabulated, filtered, sorted, analyzed and massaged electronically, a picture began to form over the faceless expanse of jungle that was the coalition territory. The mapping program was starting to print out straight lines that didn't occur in nature.

"It won't be long now," Kurtzman announced as his fingers flew, adding layer after layer of data until a thick composite image was created. This particular patch of the jungle had significantly fewer trees than did the jungle around it. The vegetation density was less than half of the surrounding area. There were natural clearings in any jungle, but most of them weren't almost completely circular as this one was. The hand of man had obviously been at work here, selectively thinning and cutting, but leaving enough growth to still conceal what was going on below.

When the communications-intercept map was superimposed over this area, even with the imprecision from shadowing and the frequency echoes, it lined up enough to be a match.

The final touch was the deep-penetrating radar-data map from the TR-3's specialized package. It fit exactly over the first two images.

"That's it," Kurtzman announced with a finality no one would even think of questioning. Questioning him on this would be like asking why rain was wet. It just was, and it couldn't be any different.

Price had seen worse jungles around the world, but this had to be in the top half dozen or so. Even knowing where the camp was, Phoenix Force was going to have its work cut out.

After looking over the composite image, Brognola asked, "How is Collins getting in and out of that place? With the troops and material he has in there, he has to have easy access with the outside world."

"I have faint traces of paths in the jungle now," Kurtzman said as he moved his cursor to highlight certain areas. "They aren't roads as such, but they show signs of having been artificially thinned, as well. I suspect that this camp was set up by the PLFP a long time ago and has only recently been taken over by the coalition. He hasn't had time enough to create this out of raw jungle.

"And," he added, moving his pointer past the top of the map and dragging the image with it, "this town, San Simone, has to be his outlet to the outside world. It's only a two-hour or so walk from the camp. That's a long hike for a city dweller, but nothing for a guerrilla fighter. You will note that the town has what looks to be a chopper pad next to a building large enough to be used as a hangar. There's also a hard-pack road leading a couple of miles into the woods before it peters out."

"Get this down to Katz," Brognola ordered. "It's time we put an end to Sean Collins's career."

Peru

THIS WAS ONE TIME that Katzenelenbogen wished that he were back at the Farm instead of in the field.

Even with the multiple data links Gadgets Schwarz had set up, the information was slow coming through. While it was downloading and printing out, he was on the other line with Hal Brognola.

"How soon do you think it'll be before you can launch?" Brognola asked.

"It's hard to tell at this point. I want to pick David's brain to work up the plan, so it'll probably be another twenty-four hours. Also, I want to bring Able Team in on this, but they're working that new coalition site in Lima."

"Now that we have Collins's camp," Brognola said, "we can let the rest of this slide. I'll call Ironman and tell him to pack up and close that one out."

"Will do."

LIMA STATION CHIEF Cary Rockhill had been able to produce a Peruvian government endorsement on the media ID Kurtzman had faxed Able Team. They were now a news team from the Spanish-language edition of CNBC, who had come to cover the pending arrival of the Nobel Peace Prize Commission in the morning.

The Peruvian air force officer at the main gate to the air base courteously examined their credentials, then waved them through with a snappy salute.

"Damn," Blancanales said. "I sure hate to have to abuse that young lieutenant's hospitality."

"Into each life a little rain must fall," Schwarz said. "We may have to abuse him a little, but he should survive our visit and I can't say the same for some of these other people."

The building that had been taken over by the coalition had once been the headquarters of the cavalry regiment quartered at the base before it had been taken over by the air force. It was one of the two-story, tile-roofed, colonial-style masonry structures that gave Lima so much of its charm.

"It's too bad we don't still have our tank," Schwarz said when he got his first look at their target. "That place would be fun to take apart, and we could drive it through the wire when we were done."

"This time we'll just have to do it the old-fashioned way," Lyons stated.

White Shield was supposed to be a completely civilian organization, but that didn't mean that they didn't have armed in-house muscle. In accordance with their peaceful intentions, though, they didn't put their security forces in uniform and they carried their subguns slung inside their sport coats. It wasn't very subtle, but it maintained the facade. On the way to the media reception room, Lyons kept a close eye on those thugs.

"I'm afraid that I don't have you on the press roster, sir," the flustered man at the media registration desk told Blancanales.

"We are a last-minute addition to the CNBC

team," Blancanales said smoothly in Spanish. "The senior editor thought that a meeting of this magnitude should be covered by a Hispanic reporter. I was told that a fax had been sent."

"What's that name again?" the man asked as he thumbed through a pile of faxes and e-mails.

"Rivera," Blancanales said. "Just like Geraldo. But my name is Jesús."

"Here it is, sir," the man said, finding the CNBC e-mail that had originated at Stony Man Farm. The nice thing about e-mail was that no one ever questioned the return address that appeared on the screen. If people knew how easy it was to fake an e-mail address, no one would ever trust a single thing that came in over their computer.

"If you will just sign here, sir," the man said, pushing a clipboard across the table. "I will get you the room key and your press packets."

"Gracias."

The international press had been given quarters on one end of the second story of the building. The rooms had once been senior officer's quarters, so they were spacious and comfortable, but Able Team wasn't checking in for a long stay. Their luggage contained the tools of their trade, not clothing.

"Okay," Lyons said. "Get out there and make your recons. Be back here in an hour, though. I want to get this thing done and get out."

SCHWARZ HEADED straight for the kitchen for his part of the recon. In a region that was as prone to earthquakes as Peru was, underground gas lines weren't popular in Lima. Those who used natural gas to cook had propane-tank hookups. If that was the case here, it would be almost too easy to destroy the building.

The lights were on in the kitchen, but no one was present, so Schwarz took a quick look around. As he expected, there was a room off the main area that contained two large propane tanks. Only one would have been enough, but two would be twice as good.

He was closing the door when he heard a voice behind him. *"¿Señor?"*

Schwarz turned and saw a Peruvian in cook whites. "Ah..." he said a little too loudly as he mimed bringing a cup up to his lips. *"Por favor.* Coffee?"

The cook laughed. "You want coffee, *señor?"* he said in accented English as he took a cup from the rack. "No problem."

"Thank you."

"You want something to eat?" The cook smiled as he filled the cup. "Maybe, how do you call it, a sandwich?"

"No, thanks." Schwarz shook his head as he took the cup. "The coffee is enough."

"Maybe later."

"THIS IS GETTING much too routine," Schwarz said when he reported on his recon. "Every time we want to blow something up down here, the only way I get to do it is to set off the damned propane tanks. I'd really like a chance to play with a few bags of ammonium nitrate for a change or even some old-fashioned dynamite. Something nice and slow so I can control it better. This is going to spatter half of this building all over the base."

"All we need is whatever will do the job, Gadgets," Lyons said. "Blowing things up isn't an artistic endeavor."

"It is, too, an art form," Schwarz replied hotly. "It takes a lot of creativity to do what I do."

"After looking at the structure," Blancanales told Schwarz, "I think that the propane tanks alone will do it. This isn't a concrete-and-rebar building, so the blast will take out most of two major load-bearing walls on the ground floor, and the top floor will come right on down on top of it."

"Okay, okay," Schwarz said. "I'll do the tanks, but I want to make sure that cook gets out first. He makes a mean cup of coffee."

Lyons was pointing out the security guard posts he had spotted on the blueprint Rockhill had provided when his cellular phone rang. "What's up, Hal?" he said.

WHEN THE PHONE RANG in the duty officer's room, Cary Rockhill answered it. Ever since the three-man wrecking crew had come to town, he'd been spending his nights close to the panic button. "Rockhill," he said.

"This is Weiss," the voice on the other end said.

"What's up?"

"We're getting ready to move up-country again," Lyons replied, "but you might want to call your Peruvian air force buddies and tell them to evacuate the coalition building as quickly as they can."

"Oh, Jesus, what did you do this time?"

"Not much, but the coalition headquarters buildings look like a SEAL demo school has been wiring the place for a graduation exercise."

Rockhill felt as if he were walking on razors. The last thing he wanted to do was to get on the wrong side of this presidential hit team. But this was still his town, and he had good friends in the Peruvian military.

"Look," he said, "I sure as hell don't want to get in the way of your mission, but I don't want to risk the local EOD people trying to undo your work."

"Don't worry," Lyons assured him. "The packages look good, but most of them are dummies or flash-bangs. The ones that contain real explosives don't have detonators. It'll just be a two-day training exercise for the bomb squad."

"You guys are real bastards, you know that?"

"We do," Lyons said, "and I have to admit that we rather enjoy being bastards when it brings us results. You might be interested in knowing that we've finally located where we think Dan Denning is being held and will be moving on it ASAP.''

That was good news to Rockhill. "Is there anything me or my people can do to help?"

"Not right now, but I'll keep you in mind if we need backup. We're still real thin on the ground here."

"Anything you want from me is yours," Rockhill vowed.

"Thanks."

After Lyons hung up, Rockhill placed a call to a senior air force officer he knew well. "Carlos, Cary here. Look, we just got a call here at the embassy, and I think you may have a problem at the air base."

CHAPTER TWENTY-FOUR

In the Safehouse

By the time Jack Grimaldi returned from Lima with Able Team on board, Katzenelenbogen had downloaded the mission package from Stony Man and was ready for the mission briefing.

"I'm glad that someone has finally sorted this shit out," Lyons growled as he looked at the images. "We've been humping the pooch on this for far too long."

"What about the new coalition headquarters you guys were looking at?" Rafael Encizo asked.

"Gadgets kind of fell in love with the architecture, so we decided to leave it for someone else to blow up."

Katz looked concerned. He knew that Brognola had ordered them to pull out, but until they had proved this new information to be correct, they had to keep up their dialogue with the coalition. In this instance, they were communicating with explosives and not blowing up the building was a failure to communicate.

"You did leave calling cards, though, didn't you?"

"Believe it." Lyons grinned. "No one's going to be occupying that particular building for several days at least. Gadgets can do amazing things with a flash-bang grenade, a roll of wire and some black tape."

Katz chuckled. Sometimes you could send a powerful message by not sending one at all.

"BEFORE WE GET DOWN to cases on this," Katz said, "I want to make sure that we all know what we're getting ourselves into. We're going into the heart of the coalition territory to take on a force that we have no idea the size of. I can assure you, though, that there are a hell of a lot more of them than there are of us."

That statement of fact got a couple of chuckles.

"We really don't have enough information to be doing this," Katz continued. "And under normal circumstances, we wouldn't be. But I don't have to tell you that Striker's in a bind. According to what that Indian kid told us, he's been conducting some kind of harassment campaign against this camp. Now, if we had any way to get in communication with him, we could go in there, snatch him out and that would be it. Someone else could go in there and deal with Collins. But since that's not the case, we have no other choice but to go in there, find that camp and take it out.

"If he's still alive—" Katz wasn't one to mince words "—he'll hear the commotion and know that we've finally arrived. If he doesn't hear us, once we've secured our backs, we'll go out in the woods and keep looking for him until we find him."

No one had any problem with that objective. They would fight their way through two coalition camps if that was what it took.

Selecting an image from his menu, Katz flashed a map onto his monitor. "Somewhere within this kilometer-and-a-half circle is the camp we've been looking for. Now, the recon runs picked up traces of buildings, what looks like fire pits, a well, a few storage dumps and that sort of thing."

He paused before delivering the bad news. "What we don't have is any indication of their bunkers or fortifications. This tells me that they have taken their defenses underground, which means that we're going to have to be very careful on our final approach. If we get mousetrapped by hidden bunkers out there, we're finished.

"The IR traces indicate that there is somewhere between eighty and a hundred warm bodies down there. Now, we have no way of telling how many of them are trigger pullers and how many are water carriers. A rough estimate for this kind of operation in this part of the world would be eighty percent combatants, maybe a little less. So that means that we will have, more or less, eight dance partners apiece.''

That got a chuckle.

McCarter looked grim as he studied the map. ''This most assuredly is not going to be a piece of cake,'' he said. ''Going up against that many people on their own turf is going to be dicey at best. If we were making a raid we could just kip in, shoot the place up and kip back out again.''

''I think I can open a gap for you,'' Jack Grimaldi said. ''With the GPS fire-control system on that bird, I should be able to put my rounds dead onto the bunkers as soon as you can spot them for me.''

''It's the spotting them in time that bothers me,'' McCarter replied.

''No one's asking you to commit suicide, David,'' Katz said. ''If Jack can't open up a hole in that perimeter, we call off the assault.''

''And wait for what?'' the Briton asked bluntly. ''The political situation isn't going to change until Collins is either killed or taken into custody. The 101st Airborne isn't going to drop from the sky to give us a hand with this, no matter what. As long as this remains a black op, we're the only chance Striker has, so we have to deal with it.''

Stony Man Farm, Virginia

''THEY'VE LAUNCHED,'' Aaron Kurtzman announced. ''ETA to the first LZ is one hour.''

The tension in the Computer Room was thick, and Barbara Price suddenly felt the urge for fresh air. Once the teams were on the ground, she'd be riveted to the floor, but she wanted a break before she had to stand the death watch.

"I'm going outside, Hal," she told Brognola.

"You okay?" he asked.

"I'm fine, I just want to get a little air."

When Price walked onto the front porch, she smelled a burning cigarette. "Evening, Barbara," Buck Greene said.

"How's your 'stop smoking' program going, Buck?"

"Usually, it's pretty good," he said, grinning around the glow of his smoke. "Days like this, though, it doesn't work worth a damn."

She laughed.

"Look, Barbara," he said, turning serious, "I know that the teams are going to have their hands full down there. They're up against serious odds, and that's a damned big place. So, I talked to the men and we want you to know that I can put a blacksuit team together and have them standing by to go in a few minutes if we can help."

The blacksuit force rarely went "off campus." The blacksuits' duty was to protect the Farm from anyone who got close enough to be considered a threat. To say that Buck Greene took his work seriously was like saying rain was wet. For him to make this offer showed where his heart was.

"Tell the men I appreciate it," she said. "Striker would do the same for us."

Peru

JACK GRIMALDI MADE a high-level recon of the first landing zone with the Black Hawk's FLIR, forward looking IR radar. David McCarter flew the copilot's seat, manning the weapons and the fire-control radar. When the LZ showed clear, he dropped lower and checked it again with the night-vision equipment. When that showed no nasty surprises, either, he brought the Black Hawk to a hover right above the treetops.

Part of the concealment Collins had counted on when he moved his operation into this particular part of Peru was the density of the jungle. There were few, if any, clearings large enough to accommodate a helicopter. But that was exactly why the SAR Jungle Penetrator had been invented. The jungles in Southeast Asia had been just as bad. By crowding three men in the basket, Able Team could make it to the ground in one hoist.

The three Able Team commandos rode the Jungle Penetrator through the trees to the ground. When the bottom of the basket touched the earth, they jumped out and formed a small defensive circle. "We're clear," Schwarz radioed up to the Black Hawk.

"Roger," Grimaldi replied as he pulled pitch and

sent the chopper climbing, well out of sight and sound of the camp.

As soon as the beat of the rotors faded, Able Team moved out.

ON THE OTHER SIDE of a five-klick circle centered on Collins's camp, Grimaldi again made a preliminary high recon before dropping down for a closer look with the FLIR gear.

"We're go," the pilot called back to McCarter, "but it's going to be a basket job again."

"We're on it," McCarter called up from the SAR winch controls on the bulkhead by the door.

As Grimaldi held the ship steady in a low hover, Hawkins, Encizo and Manning stepped into the rescue basket for the first trip down. After strapping themselves in, Encizo gave a thumbs-up and McCarter swung out the basket's arm. On the way down, the three commandos turned their faces to one side to keep from getting slapped by the leaves and small branches the heavy basket dropped through.

As soon as the three men cleared the basket, McCarter winched it back up and stepped in with Katz and James. "We're go," he called up to the cockpit.

"Going down," Grimaldi said, controlling the second drop from the alternate set of winch controls in the cockpit.

This time the basket had an easier trip down as

it went through the same hole it had torn through on the first lift.

"We're clear," McCarter called up from the ground.

"And I'm out of here," Grimaldi radioed back as he hit the winch-retraction controls at the same time that he pulled pitch to break out of the hover. "Good luck."

Stony Man Farm, Virginia

"THEY'RE ALL on the ground," Aaron Kurtzman announced. Since Yakov Katzenelenbogen had decided to go with the raiding party, the tactical control of the mission had reverted to the Farm.

"I've got the Keyhole satellite feed coming in," Hunt Wethers added. "I've got the Black Hawk on-screen, but nothing else is showing so far."

Since that was what had been expected, there was no problem. It was planned that the ground teams would be tracked by the GPS. Once the firefight broke out, though, the satellites' IR sensors would help fill in the picture. It was a hell of a way to try to direct a battle, but it was the best they could do under the circumstances.

Barbara Price wandered over to the coffeepot and poured herself a cup. She was well over her limit for the day, but since they were going to be up all night, her stomach lining could look out for itself.

If it got too bad, she could always ask Brognola for a couple of his magic tablets.

Peru

AFTER CLEARING the LZ, Able Team moved out with Schwarz on point and Lyons and Blancanales working the flanks. With only the three of them, they were keeping a pretty tight formation. Even though they spent most of their time working the urban jungles, they hadn't forgotten their basic ground-combat skills. There were some things a man never forgot. But, even with night-vision goggles and the GPS, moving at night in this kind of terrain was difficult. The jungle fought them every step of the way.

COMING IN on the target from the other side, Calvin James was on point with T. J. Hawkins pulling slack. With the density of the vegetation, Manning was on close-in drag. In the center of the formation, Katz, McCarter and Encizo were maintaining their GPS location and transmitting the information to Grimaldi on a regular basis. The plan was to not get engaged going in. But if they stumbled into Collins's patrols or outposts, they would need the gunship on station ASAP and a minute or two could be critical.

JACK GRIMALDI HAD LANDED his chopper on the ground on a hilltop twelve miles away and was using it as a forward command post. Normally a helicopter on the open ground was a sitting target. But the Black Hawk was also equipped with a passive security system that kept a radar watch on anything that came within five hundred yards of its parked location.

With the radar keeping watch for him, Grimaldi was uploading the ground unit's positions directly into his fire-control computer each time they took a GPS bearing. If they needed fire support tonight, having the updated GPS data would allow him to get on the target a few seconds faster. With his satcom link hot, he was also in instant communication with the Farm.

Pulling his thermos from the pouch behind his armored seat, he poured a cup of coffee and settled in to listen to the radio and wait. The ship's batteries were switched over to standby, which kept the navigation, fire-control and com gear hot. Every hour, he would run the APU for fifteen minutes to keep the batteries charged up.

It was going to be a long night.

WITH THE GPS TO GUIDE the Phoenix Force commandos, navigation through the jungle wasn't a problem. Though it was slow going, they unerringly zeroed in on the enemy camp. The closer they came to it, the more cautious they were.

"We just entered a cleared fire zone," James reported over the com link.

"Hold there," McCarter sent back.

When Katz and the Briton reached James's position, they saw that the thinning of the jungle had been done artfully. Mostly it was the smaller trees and larger clumps of underbrush that had been cleared away, which left the large trees and the canopy intact.

"We're in a fire lane here," Katz said. "We need to pull back."

As silently as they had moved in, the commandos moved back into the jungle a hundred yards to wait out the dawn.

CHAPTER TWENTY-FIVE

In the Jungle

Jack Grimaldi had long since drunk the last of the coffee in his thermos. Like most professional warriors, he was a dedicated caffeine junkie and a late-night cup or three hadn't kept him from peacefully catnapping in his pilot's seat. A nice strong cup of java and the gentle hiss of the squelch coming over the earphones of his flight helmet were like a lullaby to him. Even with the chopper's security system activated and keeping watch over him, his sleep had been that of a warrior—wary. Even the slightest change in background noise would snap him instantly awake.

The night had passed uneventfully, but the change in light as dawn approached also triggered his internal warning system. He was fully awake and ready to go when McCarter's voice came in over his earphones.

"Flyboy," the Phoenix leader said, "this is Rover. Time to get it in gear. Over."

"Flyboy, roger," Grimaldi sent back. "On the way. I'll check in when I'm on station. Over."

"We'll be waiting. Out."

The pilot worked the fingers of his gloves tight before reaching out to flip the switches and punch the buttons to bring his two T-700 GE turbines to life. With a roar and a whiff of burning kerosene, the four-bladed rotor started to turn. His eyes swept the digital readouts as the turbines spooled up. Though he still preferred analog instruments, he had to admit that the digital ones were idiot proof and easier to read.

When a last glance showed that all the instruments were in the green, Grimaldi's left hand twisted the throttle and pulled up on the collective at the same time. When the Black Hawk rose into the air, he nudged forward on the cyclic and fed in a little right pedal to bring the nose around.

"Rover," he said, keying his throat mike, "this is Flyboy. I'm airborne and en route, ETA eighteen mikes. Over."

"Roger, copy, Flyboy," McCarter send back. "We'll be waiting. Over."

Grimaldi hadn't been given the best circumstances in the world to try to fly fire-support missions from a helicopter gunship, even from one as sophisticated as his special-ops Black Hawk. The jungle below was much too dense for him to see targets on the ground. Conversely, though, none of the enemy on the ground could get a clear look at him, either, which meant that no one would be firing Strella missiles at him or even antiaircraft rounds. There was no indication so far of the rebels having any heavy weaponry, but when a man was more than a few feet off the ground, it never hurt to be careful.

The only thing that made his mission even possible was the GPS blind-firing system this special-ops bird was equipped with. The system allowed the gunship to deliver accurate fire to ground targets under zero-zero visibility conditions of storm and darkness. This wasn't going to be exactly like firing into a fog bank or a blinding rainstorm as the system had been designed to do, but his visibility of the ground under the jungle's canopy was precisely zero.

THIS WAS ONE TIME that Carl Lyons didn't mind being assigned to cover the back door. If this thing went down as Katz had planned, he and his two partners should have more than enough work to keep them busy.

After moving into position the previous night, Schwarz had taken GPS readings and had radioed them to Grimaldi to load into his firing computer. The special-ops-issue GPS unit he used was calibrated to be accurate within one and a half yards, five feet give or take. If they did have to call on Grimaldi's fire from the sky, five and a half feet would be the new definition of what had previously been called "Danger Close" fire support.

The old definition had been one hundred yards.

THE SIX Phoenix Force warriors had broken down into three two-man fire teams for the initial assault. David McCarter was teamed with Katzenelenbogen, Rafael Encizo with Gary Manning and Calvin James with T. J. Hawkins. Going in individually would have made their force look larger, but against the kind of odds they had, it would have been almost suicidal to try to fight without someone watching their backs and flanks. Even in paired fire teams, it wasn't going to be easy.

"Rover," Grimaldi called down from his position high above the camp. "This is Flyboy. Any time you're ready."

"Roger, Flyboy," McCarter replied. "We're going in now. Out."

"And we're ready on the back door," Carl Lyons cut in. "Out."

The six Phoenix commandos rose from the damp jungle floor and started to move forward. They could smell wood smoke in the cool morning air as the Indian women in the camp started to prepare breakfast for the men. This was a slow time of day in a camp like this, when most of the inhabitants were more concerned with downing a couple of cups of coffee to start their day than anything else.

Phoenix Force appeared out of the mist like jungle spirits. Their camouflaged uniforms and face paint made them look the part, as well. The first guerrilla who spotted them blinked and looked again, trying to make sure it wasn't an apparition. He should have fired his AK instead. A single 3-round burst from an MP-5 cut him down.

Once the Stony Man warriors were inside the perimeter, more rebels appeared and the commandos opened up with a withering barrage. After the first long burst, they deployed into their fire teams, picked their next targets and started to move in. Breakfast was going to be a little delayed.

It took a few seconds for the guerrillas to recover from the surprise attack, but they returned fire and the Phoenix Force warriors were forced to go into fire-and-maneuver mode. Not all of the Indian fighters stood their ground to fight. Some of them assumed the camouflage-painted commandos were allies of El Tigre, and wanted no part of this fight. One by one, they laid their weapons down and turned away.

The remaining cartel fighters in the camp were made of stronger stuff, but even they didn't want to die in a fight that wasn't really theirs. When they saw their Indian allies start to desert, some of them also started to look for a back door. The problem was that the back door was closed and locked. And Able Team had the key.

"Get ready, Flyboy," Lyons growled over the com link. "Here they come."

Schwarz was handling the forward-air-controller duty and had his GPS transmitter at his side. The field glasses in his hand had a laser range-finding feature that gave him the near exact range to anything he could see through them. All he had to do was take a reading of the range and bearing from his position and call it up to Grimaldi to input into his fire computer. The autocannon would then put the rounds exactly on the target.

GRIMALDI GUIDED his helicopter into a left-hand, banked turn and swung the gun turret to the port side of the ship. This was basic Spooky Gunship 101 stuff and dated back to the Vietnam War. But this was the first time he had ever tried to do it without being able to see his target. When the fire-control computer told him it was in the right place in the sky, he squeezed the trigger.

The 25 mm chain gun didn't have the same ripping roar of the old 20 mm Vulcan cannon, but it was pumping out enough ammunition for anyone's need. He had the gun controls set on 12-round bursts to conserve ammunition and had dialed up a mix of half HE and half AP rounds.

Unlike heavier-caliber artillery shells that had delay fuses, most of the HE rounds would detonate high in the trees and the AP would drill deep holes in the ground. But a combination of the two ammo types was the best he could come up with. No one had ever seen a need to design a 25 mm HE round with a delay fuse for use in these types of situations. No one had ever fired an autocannon blind like this before, nor had ever needed to.

The chain gun chewed up the jungle like a giant chain saw stuck in overdrive. With the tracking system of the fire-control radar set on dispersed fire, the 12-round bursts made a slashing cut through the trees. As Grimaldi had expected, the HE rounds detonated in the trees, but most of the shrapnel from the exploding shells rained to the ground anyway. The 25 mm AP rounds were solid-core shot, and they simply drilled their way through whatever got in their road—trees or gunmen, it didn't matter.

The first burst hit off to one side of the assault, but it got the cartel gunmen's attention. Before they could figure out what it was, though, the second burst hit right in the middle of them.

"Check fire," Schwarz called up after the third burst. For this single-ship fire-support mission to do the job, they had to conserve ammunition. But, as brief as it had been, Grimaldi's rain of death from the sky had done its job. The guerrillas had been stopped in their tracks and, those who had been left on their feet, dropped their guns and turned to flee.

ON THE OTHER SIDE of the camp, Hawkins was doing the GPS readings for Phoenix Force. Since they were on the move instead of holding in static positions, he had to stay on top of it so someone didn't run into a hail of Grimaldi's 25 mm fire by mistake.

Outnumbered as they were, the commandos were keeping on the move, never staying in one firing position for more than a minute or so. Move and shoot, move and shoot—it was the only way they could hope to stay alive. And with the constant changing of position, Hawkins was using his own location as a base point for fire control.

"T.J.!" James's voice came over Hawkins's com link. "I need fire in front of me now! Azimuth two-three-five, range five-zero."

"Roger, Calvin," Hawkins sent back. "Copy two-three-five, range five-zero. Keep your head down. I'll get it coming."

"Jack," Hawkins radioed.

"I copied," Grimaldi called back. "What's his position?"

"From my last," Hawkins said. "Two-seven-one, add two-three."

"Good copy."

While Hawkins was using his GPS location as a base point for the computer, he had told Grimaldi that James was twenty-three yards from his position at an azimuth of 271 degrees. From James's position, the pilot was to fire his weapons on an azimuth of 235 degrees at a range of fifty yards.

This wasn't how Hawkins had been taught to call in air support, but no one had ever been in this situation before. Normally, for this kind of assault, he would have on-call artillery fire support and planned assault fires. But with no artillery standing by, Grimaldi's blind-firing gunship would have to do.

The beat of the rotors grew louder over the crackle of small-arms fire and the shouts of the combatants. Suddenly the coughing roar of the 25 mm chain gun drowned out all the other sounds of battle. With every other cannon shell being an HE round, their detonations in the trees echoed like rolling thunder.

"How's that?" Grimaldi asked after putting three bursts of twelve on target.

"I'm in business again," James radioed back. "Thanks."

"I aim to please."

IN BOLAN'S toxin-impaired state, his enhanced hearing picked up the sounds of battle from miles away. The sounds of gunfire wakened a part of his mind that had lain dormant since he had been poisoned. Like a stone thrown into a still pond, the impact of the sounds of battle sent ripples that shattered the calmness of his mind.

He suddenly remembered being a warrior himself. He clearly remembered times when the sounds of battle had been all around him. He remembered the smell of cordite and the feel of a weapon bucking in his hands. He caught glimpses of the faces of men fighting beside him and he knew that they were his comrades, his brothers.

He also remembered that he had left a comrade

in that camp, a man he had sworn to guard and protect. It didn't bother him that he couldn't recall the man's name or that he only had the vaguest memory of his face. He did remember clearly, though, that he'd been given the duty of protecting him. And he knew, without knowing how, that the attack he could hear in the distance had something to do with the man he had left behind. Since that was the case, his duty drew him to it.

He moved toward the sounds of battle at a loping run.

RAMON SABATAS WATCHED the battle with an experienced eye and didn't like what he was seeing. Whoever those Yankees were, and as few as they were, they were too good at mass slaughter for his Indians to stand and fight. The gunship the Yankees had brought with him was also cutting the heart out of his fighters. Most of them were veterans of the bloody civil wars that had raged through Peru for so many years. They had survived hundreds of small-arms firefights and even mortar attacks from government troops, but they had never had to suffer death raining from the sky.

Also, as any experienced combat leader knew well, in battle the psychological far outweighed the physical. The Belasko incident had shaken his Indians badly, and not enough time had passed to allow that to fade from their minds so they could recover their courage. With this unexpected assault on top of it, they were falling apart like government draftees in their first ambush.

He hadn't survived his long years as a mercenary soldier by fighting losing battles. Knowing when to fight and when to run away to fight another day was the most valuable skill a mercenary could have. This was one of those times that if he stayed, he was going to die.

He didn't feel at all guilty about abandoning Collins to the Yankees. The Irishman had paid him good mercenary wages, but he had also been an idealistic fool. He didn't know how these things were done in Europe, but in Latin America, idealism had to be tempered with common sense. He had come to Peru with grand plans and had been lucky at first in that the president was corrupt and his dreams of avarice were easily fed.

The establishment of White Shield in Lima had been a good start, and it had looked as if the foreign interest would make it a success. But the way that White Shield had suddenly come under repeated attack was a clear sign that Collins's program was doomed. Ramón Sabatas wasn't going to go down with anyone's ship.

Exactly what had gone wrong in Lima he really didn't know, but it was apparent that the Americans hadn't been willing to allow the rebel coalition to exist very long. This came as no surprise to him, but the Irishman had been convinced that his nomination for the peace prize would protect him from the Yankees. He was being proved wrong.

His decision made, Ramón Sabatas looked around to find his two Indian trackers. When the rebel commander spotted them, he used field signals to call them to his location.

"The Irishman is finished," he told them when they joined him, "and I am leaving."

The two Indians instantly nodded their assent. Sabatas was their boss and their loyalty had always been to him, not to whomever he had signed on with. If he thought it was time to leave, they would go with him.

After reloading their ammo pouches with fresh magazines, the three men started to work their way to the east side of the perimeter. Keeping low, they had little trouble evading the last few hot spots of the battle. It was as if the Yankees had intentionally left a door open for anyone who didn't want to stay and die.

On their way out, a couple of other men attempted to join them, but one look at the expression on Sabatas's face made them back off. He wasn't a man to displease even when things were going well, which they definitely weren't at the moment.

Once past the perimeter, Sabatas and his two trackers made for the safety of the jungle as quickly as they could. They were in jungle-camouflage battle dress instead of their tracking gear, but that wouldn't make then any less elusive in their home environment. They had a march of several days ahead of them before they would be completely safe.

CHAPTER TWENTY-SIX

In the Jungle

When shouts of *"¡No más!"* started to ring out in the camp, the fight was over. The last shot echoed into silence as everyone waited to see what would happen next.

Phoenix Force and Able Team kept their weapons ready until it was clear that everyone was in accordance. With their backs well covered, Blancanales and Encizo stepped out to order all the rebels to lay down their weapons and put their hands in the air. On command, Grimaldi dropped down low enough for his rotors to be heard on the ground and hovered nearby. The nervous glances sent skyward showed that everyone understood the threat he represented.

The Stony Man team quickly moved through the camp, their weapons ready and their eyes constantly searching for anyone who wanted to argue. The only rebels left in the camp were the dead, the wounded and those who stood by their women and children with their weapons at their feet, and their hands in the air. Other women silently tended to their wounded husbands and sons, carefully keeping their eyes averted from the men with guns in their hands. The custom in that part of the world was that women usually didn't have to fear for their lives when their men lost a battle. The worst that would happen to them was that they would be raped. But even that was a rare occurrence and didn't carry the heavy social sanction that it did in other parts of the world.

When the camp was cleared, the order was given for the men, one at a time, to unload their weapons and drop them in a big pile.

Once that was done, James broke out his medkit and started to tend the wounded. The first patient he saw to was Gadgets Schwarz. Playing close-in forward air controller had earned him a slash across the forearm from a razor-sharp chunk of 25 mm frag.

"That stings," he said as James washed the wound before wrapping it with field bandage.

"I can cauterize it with a hot iron if you'd rather."

"Smart ass."

THE OTHER MAN LEFT in the camp was Sean Collins. A long burst of fire from the chain gun had raked his headquarters, shattering the bamboo and bringing the flimsy building down on top of him. By the time he dug himself out, the fight was over. Not being suicidal, when he heard the commandos order the end of the resistance, he knew that it was too late for him to try to run. Instead, he got to his feet and held his hands up, as well.

As the only white man in the camp, he soon got the attention he feared. "Just keep them up," Hawkins ordered.

He kept the muzzle of his weapon centered on Collins as he keyed his com link. "I've got him."

Even though these commandos didn't use badges of rank, it was easy enough for Collins to see who was the man in charge. The hard-eyed mercenary wearing the maroon beret who strode forward was obviously their leader. The unwavering muzzle of the H&K subgun in his hand backed up the first impression.

"Where's Belasko?" McCarter asked, his clipped British accent showing.

Even though this commando was working for the Yankees, Collins knew an SAS man when he saw one and realized the extreme danger he was in. Whoever this soldier was, he had to know of his IRA background. The Provos and the SAS were the most bitter of enemies, and the SAS didn't like to take prisoners. With no photographers or TV journalists in the jungle, there was nothing to prevent his being shot in the back of the head and left where he fell. His only chance to stay alive was to tell everything he knew.

"My field commander told me that he was killed in a jungle ambush a couple of days ago."

"Who's your field commander, and where is he?"

"His name's Ramón Sabatas, and I haven't seen him since the attack started."

"What's his nationality?"

"Colombian originally," Collins replied, "but he's operated in many countries."

"Describe him."

Collins shrugged. "Early forties, typical Spanish blood, thin face, dark hair cut short, dark eyes, five-ten and maybe twelve stone."

"That's about a hundred and sixty-eight," McCarter said, automatically translating the weight into something his comrades could more easily understand.

"I'll check the bodies," Hawkins said.

"Where was this ambush your man reported?" Katz asked the Irishman.

"He didn't show me on the map," Collins replied, "and our maps of this region are notoriously inaccurate anyway. So, I'm sorry, but I can't help you there. All I know is that supposedly he was shot, fell into a swift-running river and went over a waterfall. Sabatas was certain that he was dead before he hit the water."

"Did your man actually examine the body?"

"No."

McCarter and Katz exchanged glances. Until

someone saw a cold body on a slab, the Executioner couldn't be counted out. And even then, they had better check his pulse twice. Bolan's death had been announced more than once and later proved to be false.

Collins caught the look the two men exchanged. Mamal might not have been right about Belasko having been the legendary mercenary of a hundred names, but he had certainly been someone of great interest to the Yankees. In retrospect, Collins really wished that he had taken greater precautions with the man, like locking him in irons and a chain. He would be a good bargaining chip right now.

"Who was the Arab we found?" Katz asked. Mamal had been dressed more or less the same as all the others in the camp, but he had insisted on wearing the curved dagger and a checkered neck scarf. The knife, the scarf and his hawk-nosed face had made the ethnic ID of his corpse easy.

"His name was Sayed Mamal," Collins said, "and he was a representative of the Islamic Brotherhood."

"Nice company you're keeping," McCarter said. "Another bunch of bloody murdering bastards."

Collins shrugged. "What happens now?"

McCarter smiled, but it wasn't reassuring. "Well, boyo, you're looking at spending the rest of your life in a small cell, very small if I have anything to do with it. You're going to have a long time to think about what a rotten IRA bastard you are."

"Oh, I almost forgot," McCarter added. "We got a call from the Nobel Peace Prize people right before we left to visit you here. They decided that they weren't going to give their prize to a murdering IRA bastard after all. They're going to give it to a syphilitic whore instead."

With a cry of rage, Collins lunged for a machete someone had dropped a few feet away.

When Hawkins swung his weapon around, McCarter shouted, "No! He's mine."

The Briton backed off long enough to lay down his weapon and draw his own machete from his assault harness. "Okay, boyo, let's play."

James had joined Hawkins and with Katz formed a rough circle around the two men. If McCarter wanted to do this, it was okay with them. If, however, it looked like Collins was starting to get the upper hand, they'd put a bullet in his head. It might not be fair, but who said life was fair?

"You SAS bastard!" Collins snarled as he swung the machete.

McCarter sidestepped the slash and riposted with his own blade, slicing a thin cut along Collins's arm.

Having once been a proper British soldier, McCarter had been trained in the long blade, as well as the short. Collins knew knives, but only to gut some unsuspecting prisoner or to cut a throat. Sword fighting and knife fighting were very different art forms, and what worked with one, didn't necessarily work with the other.

When McCarter saw how awkward the Irishman was with the machete, he knew he was facing a knife fighter, not a swordsman. He let a smile cross his face. "Is that the best you can do, boyo? That's right, I forgot. You're more into killing women and children in front of supermarkets with car bombs, aren't you?"

Collins yelled in rage and lunged at McCarter as if he were holding a huge knife.

The Briton stood his ground and, with a flick of the wrist, parried the Irishman's blade out of the way. His blade slid past Collins's arm and sunk deep into his belly. Jerking the machete free, McCarter paused a moment before slashing the brush-cutting blade across the man's neck.

Collins dropped his blade and staggered backward, his hands to his throat, before falling facedown in the dirt.

"I'm not sure the President wanted him killed," Katz said, keeping his voice even.

McCarter met his gaze without blinking. "If he doesn't like it, the next time he has a dirty little job he wants done, he can bloody well do it himself, can't he?"

There wasn't much Katz could answer to that.

CALVIN JAMES HAD just finished checking over Dan Denning when Katz and McCarter joined him.

"He's a bit bruised, he needs a bath, some good food and week or two worth of R and R, but he's okay."

"I'm okay," the DEA man confirmed. "I just need to get the hell out of this place."

"What can you tell us about Belasko?" Katz asked. "Do you know why he took off?"

"I think he escaped to try to take the pressure off me," Denning said. "He urged me to tell that Irish bastard everything I knew about our Latin American operations, but I just couldn't do it. And when they kept beating me, he took off in the middle of the night without saying anything to me about it. Apparently he grabbed a gun on his way out, because he started ambushing the patrols Collins sent after him."

Denning's face showed the anguish he felt. "I have to admit that it worked. Once he took off, Collins treated me much differently. I don't know if he wanted to use me as bait to trap Belasko or what, but the beatings stopped."

Katz had no trouble believing what the DEA man said about Bolan's motives. That sounded like something he would do without a second thought. He took his duties seriously, and he had been assigned to keep Denning safe.

Denning thought for a moment. "Actually the strange thing was that Collins also quit asking me about the DEA operations and started asking me about Belasko."

"What do you mean?"

"He wanted to know what I knew of his background, what agency he worked for, what we had talked about in Lima, that sort of thing. It was like he was trying to build a dossier on him."

Katz wasn't surprised to hear that. It fit right in with what Trent Carlsworth had tried to do from Washington. The unknown question was why he had wanted that information. Though it was a long shot, the presence of an Islamic Brotherhood officer in the camp could have had something to do with that. Bolan had been a thorn in the side of Arab terrorists for years. The Executioner had to have been recognized.

"For one man," Denning said, shaking his head in wonderment, "he sure did a hell of a lot of damage. Every patrol that went out after him came back carrying casualties."

"He is good at that." Katz smiled faintly.

"About him being hunted in the woods," McCarter said. "Collins told us that his field commander reported that he had tracked down Belasko and killed him. Do you know anything about that?"

"Sabatas told me the same thing, too," Denning confirmed. "In fact, he bragged to me about it. But he didn't come back with a body, so I don't know what to think."

"We're going out there to look for him," McCarter said. "And if you feel you're up to it, I'd like you to stay here with our pilot and help keep an eye on this mob. His chain gun can cover only so much.''

''Be glad to.''

''Go see him and get an AK.''

McCarter waited until the DEA man had walked off before asking Katz, ''What do you think?''

The Israeli shook his head. ''You and I have been at this game far too long to think that anyone is bulletproof, but both of us have seen him get out of worse situations than this. As soon as we get this mess sorted out, we're going out there to find him.''

''THE SATCOM LINK'S up and hot,'' Manning said. ''What do you want me to tell Hal?''

''Give him a report of the assault,'' Katz replied, making a quick tactical decision. ''And tell him that Collins is dead. On Striker, simply tell him that he's still in the jungle and that we're going out after him as soon as we have this secured.''

Katz felt there was no sense in putting the Farm crew through another grieving session until either Bolan or his body was found. If he was found dead, there would be time enough to mourn him then.

''Better yet,'' Katz said, quickly changing his mind, ''let me talk to him.''

Stony Man Farm, Virginia

HAL BROGNOLA WAS ECSTATIC when Katzenelenbogen broke the good news. His guarded comments about Bolan were, on the surface, believable. However, he had known Katz long enough to know that the wily tactical officer was holding something back. Exactly what, he didn't know, but his bet was that they didn't have a firm lead on him yet and were trying not to unnecessarily worry anyone.

It was a noble thought, but it was somewhat transparent, and he knew that Aaron Kurtzman would instantly pick up on it. But maybe Price would be so relieved to hear that he was safe that she wouldn't see beyond the surface.

"They don't have a firm lead on him yet, do they?" she asked bluntly after hearing him out.

Brognola sighed. It had been years since he had been able to put anything over on her, and it would make his life a great deal easier if he would stop trying.

"No, they don't," he admitted. "But they say that they have recent spottings of him. Now that they've taken care of Collins's operation, they'll be able to concentrate on finding where he's hiding out."

Even though she was more personally involved in finding Bolan than she usually was in a Stony Man mission, Price wasn't about to allow her personal feelings get in the way of doing what had to be done. Nonetheless, she couldn't keep from asking, "Is there anything we can do to help from here?"

"I'm afraid not," Brognola said gently, "but I told him to get in touch with us the minute we can do something."

CHAPTER TWENTY-SEVEN

Stony Man Farm, Virginia

Hal Brognola's report to the President on the red secure phone was well guarded, and he didn't voice his concerns about Mack Bolan's survival. Now that Sean Collins had been taken out, the President was focused completely on the second phase of the operation, which was putting the nation of Peru back together again under a stable government. He was eager to rectify the mistake he had made by lending his support to White Shield before his congressional critics crucified him.

The President's plan for the takedown of the coalition handed the issue back to the Peruvians themselves. But it was Peru's vice president Castillio instead of President Oswaldo Simone who would be in charge of that operation. President Simone was going to fall with the coalition he had so strongly promoted.

It wouldn't be another Latin American coup with tanks in the streets and politicians of the outgoing party hanging from the lampposts in front of the presidential palace. President Simone would be allowed to resign and even to keep his government pension. Vice president Castillio would succeed him, and he promised to hold new elections in three months. Peru needed to be guided by a firm hand, but it also needed to be a hand that the people had elected.

The odds were that Castillio would win the election in a landslide. He had done a good job as the nation's number two and was well liked throughout the country. Canceling the coalition treaty would only make him even more popular among those who had resented giving part of their country to rebel gunmen. Since most of his opposition was identified with the now discredited coalition, he should be a shoo-in to lead his nation.

So, while the U.S. President was so deeply involved with the fate of a brother politician, his mind wasn't on the fate of one of his operatives.

Brognola knew that the President would remember Bolan and ask about him in a few days. And by that time, hopefully, the Executioner's fate would also be known.

In the Jungle

AS SOON AS the jungle camp had been secured and everyone disarmed, Gary Manning, Calvin James and T. J. Hawkins quickly rigged enough trees in the middle of the camp with demolition charges to blow out a landing zone for the Black Hawk. A few wraps of det cord and a handful of C-4 in the right place could topple even the tallest tree, and Manning knew just how to do it. As each tree came down, the unarmed Indians dragged it out of the way.

As soon as the trees were cleared, Jack Grimaldi brought his helicopter to a hover directly over the hole that had been created in the jungle and slowly lowered the ship through it. The blasters had done a good job, and the opening gave him plenty of rotor-blade clearance.

"What's the drill?" the pilot asked as he stepped onto the ground.

"We're going to look for Striker," McCarter said simply. "If he's out there, we're going to find him."

"What about me?"

"Gadgets and the DEA man are going to stay here with you to keep an eye on things until these people disperse. I'm going to have their weapons loaded on board, and I want you to jettison them from ten thousand feet the next time you go over a mountain."

With the Black Hawk serving as a mobile command post, McCarter and Katz quickly worked up a plan. With so much ground to cover, the only thing they could plan was to stay in the jungle until they had covered every inch of it.

"Okay," McCarter said. "Carl, I'd like you and Pol to link up T.J. and Rafe to form one search team. Katz and I will go out with Gary and Calvin. Unless anyone has a better idea, we'll start doing cloverleafs, using this camp as our starting point. Gadgets can run the com center from the chopper, and Jack can air-drop us supplies as we need them and stay close for the extraction."

McCarter's face hardened. "We may bump into the remnants of Collins's Indian fighters. If we do, we'll offer them a break. If they want to walk away, we'll let them go. If they want to fight, we'll do that, too. But we're not going to let anyone get in our way."

"We need to get an ammo resupply before we go, then," James reminded him. "We kind of burned through our basic load this morning."

"It's in the chopper," Grimaldi said.

RAMON SABATAS and the two Indians were moving out at a good pace, but they weren't running. They had a long way to go, and only a fool would run when he couldn't see what he was running into.

Two miles away from the camp, Sabatas got a feeling deep in the most primitive section of his mind that someone was watching him. He had seen nothing and he had heard nothing, but his instincts were telling him that he was about to become someone's prey. The battle-tested mercenary hadn't survived as long as he had by not trusting his instincts, and he trusted them again this time. He instantly signaled a halt and dropped into cover.

Now that the sounds of combat behind him had ended, he knew that Collins's camp had been neutralized. Unless the Yankees had come in far larger numbers than he had seen, he knew that not all of the fighters had been killed. Many of them would have been able to escape to make their way out as he had done. Though they had been under his command for months, with the paymaster gone, Sabatas's authority over those men was gone, as well.

Sabatas knew how to become one with his surroundings as well as any of the other denizens of the jungle. Slitting his eyes, he let his gaze travel over the jungle in front of him, searching alternately high and low. His ears couldn't swivel like a cat's ears to zero in on a sound, so he slowly turned his head. His breathing slowed so that he could take in a full lung's breath, drawing the air through his nasal passages slowly to detect any scent that might be in the air. A scent of fear, sweat or gun oil.

He could neither hear, smell nor see anything alarming. The sounds were those he knew were normal for that time of day, and they weren't muted as they would be if men were hiding in ambush somewhere nearby. His mind, though, continued to warn him of danger. It was telling him that something was out there, and he would die if he ignored it.

Sabatas didn't particularly mind dying. The life of a soldier of fortune forced a man to confront his mortality. He usually confronted his mortality by taking the life of someone else. It was the oldest trade-off in the world—one man lived while another man died. As long as he could keep doing that, he would live.

He wasn't, however, going to go down without a fight. Whoever was out there wasn't going to take him while he was on his knees praying for Jesus to come out of the sky and snatch him up to heaven. He was a fighter.

First, though, he had find his enemy.

When he signaled to move out, he saw that only one of his Indian trackers was still with him. Miguel, the younger one, had deserted him, and only old Juan had stayed at his side. That angered him, but he would take care of that later. The jungle wasn't big enough to hide a man who had crossed him.

BOLAN WAS MOTIONLESS. Even his breathing was so low as to hardly move his chest walls. The poison in his system still affected his mind, and his eyes still showed him the extravivid, glowing vision of the jungle instead of what he would usually see.

Shimmering veils of colored lights surrounded every living thing that his gaze fell on. In his altered state of mind, he expected to see these auras, these glowing signs of the life force. Even though the toxins in his blood were breaking down more rapidly now, it was a slow process and they still held him tightly in what the shamans called the spirit world.

He sensed that this enemy, whoever he was, was moving toward him. He hadn't sighted, smelled nor heard him yet, but he knew that he was close and coming closer. The dark purple aura was growing stronger with each passing second, and the aura was that of a killer.

This man, and he knew he was a man because the aura wasn't that of a four-legged predator, was evil and a danger to all that lived here. Many of his kind were in the jungle today, but this one differed from the rest because he didn't have an edge of fear about him. Where the others were fleeing for their lives, this man wasn't. He was simply changing his territory.

Territory, and the need to guard it, was something Bolan had learned a great deal about since he had brushed up against the small spider. In the spirit world, territory was more than merely a space where an entity lived, ate and slept. It was a place where that particular life force belonged, the place where its existence meshed seamlessly with the other inhabitants of that particular area.

Bolan's mind kept sending him flashes of other territories he had fitted into when he had hunted before. Some of those were jungles of man's making with steel and concrete instead of the tangled green structures that surrounded him now. Sometimes they were seemingly endless expanses of little more than rock and sand. But wherever they were, he had once belonged to them the same way that he belonged where he was now.

He didn't question why he was in this territory. He simply was. This was *his* territory, and he had to protect it from all intruders.

Silently Bolan rose from his perch and descended to the jungle floor. The evil one was coming closer, and he had to be killed or he would make a wasteland of wherever he went next.

BOLAN WATCHED as a man came into his field of view, and he instantly knew that the evil he felt was emanating from him. What made this man so evil, he didn't know. He knew only that he was evil and that he had to die.

The Executioner drew his knife and went into the mental state that made him invisible against the jungle backdrop. His unshaved and unwashed face and the dried mud on his tattered clothing were effective camouflage, but it was the stillness that came over him that made him one with his surroundings. He, too, slitted his eyes and kept his mouth closed so as not to give his position away.

When the enemy passed within a yard of his position, Bolan sprang.

SABATAS COULDN'T BELIEVE his eyes, and he hesitated for a fatal moment. He had killed Belasko and had seen him fall into the river. Before he could bring his AK to bear, Bolan's left hand clamped around the barrel of the rifle.

The Colombian screamed defiance as he tried to free his weapon, but it was held in an iron grip. Focused on that tug of war, he didn't see what was in Bolan's right hand.

The knife he had taken from the dead rebel at the camp so long ago wasn't the Cold Steel Tanto blade he was accustomed to using, but it was good, thick steel and its previous owner had kept its heavy blade sharp. He slammed the broad point up under Sabatas's left rib cage and drove it into his heart.

The guerrilla gasped and his eyes fixed on Bolan's. "Who...?"

His feet kicked, and then he was dead.

CHAPTER TWENTY-EIGHT

In the Jungle

The Phoenix Force warriors stayed together after leaving the camp, until they were a thousand yards into the jungle. Then they split into their two search parties and went their separate ways. They would search out for five miles, then come back in toward the camp and continue that search pattern until they found him. None of them even attempted to put a time frame to this process. It would take as long as it took.

An hour later, the trail McCarter's group followed was empty one minute, and the next, Mack Bolan stood in their path as if he had materialized out of thin air.

On point, James drew down on the figure. As his finger tightened on the trigger, his eyes registered who it was he was about to kill. "Striker!" he called out.

Bolan stood with his hands held open at his sides as James walked up to him.

"Jesus, where you been?"

The rest of the search team hurried to Bolan's side, firing questions all at the same time. When the soldier didn't answer, Katzenelenbogen stepped up to him. "Look at his eyes," he said. "I think he's been drugged."

"I've got Jack on the way," McCarter said.

"I know you." Bolan turned to him, his voice still lifeless. "You have a strong heart."

McCarter reached out to wrap his arms around his comrade. "Oh, God, Mack."

Without waiting to be told, Manning fired up the satcom radio and put a call through to Stony Man Farm.

Hal Brognola answered instantly. "Brognola."

"We have him," Manning said simply, "and he's alive."

"Hand me that thing." Katz held his hand out for the radio microphone. "Like Gary said, he's alive," he reported, "but we need a specialized medical team down here immediately."

"How bad is he?"

"Except for being filthy from being in the woods," Katz said, "he looks okay physically. Calvin is checking him over now, but I think he's either been poisoned or drugged. I think he knows us, but it's like he's caught up in some kind of bad trip and is hallucinating."

"I'll get a team of CDC toxicologists and a

mercy flight on the way from Elgin ASAP," Brognola said.

"Tell them to be prepared for any kind of toxin. Whatever's wrong with him, it's major."

"I'll get them on the way as quickly as I can."

"Until they get here," Katz said, "I'm going to have Jack fly him to our country safehouse. Calvin and the embassy doctor can care for him there until you can get that team down here. I don't want to take him into Lima, because we wouldn't be able to adequately secure him. The only place we could take him would be the embassy, and we know it's been compromised."

"Do what you have to," Brognola said, "but get him out of the jungle."

"Extraction is on the way."

BOLAN WANTED to stay in the jungle. Life was simple there—hunt, eat, drink, sleep and repel all intruders.

It was a good life, but one that deep in his mind he knew wasn't his. His life was with these men, and the longer he was with them, the more he knew that was true. Even glimpses of their names were surfacing in his mind, as were snatches of the times they had spent together. He belonged with these men and would go willingly with them.

Bolan watched the helicopter draw closer through the breaks in the tops of the trees. In the depths of his mind, he knew that he was familiar with these things, and that they weren't to be feared. The Black Hawk went into a low hover to lower the SAR Jungle Penetrator, and he knew what it was doing. When the basket reached the ground, he automatically stepped into it and buckled the safety straps.

Calvin James stepped into the basket with him, and they were lifted into the air. Inside the chopper, he again automatically went to one of the canvas troop seats next to a window, sat down and strapped himself in.

Turning his head to look back, he felt a pang of regret as the chopper lifted off.

DON PENDLETON'S

STONY
AMERICA'S ULTRA-COVERT INTELLIGENCE AGENCY

MAN

DON'T MISS OUT ON THE ACTION
IN THESE TITLES!

#61898	DEADLY AGENT	$4.99 U.S.	☐
		$5.50 CAN.	☐
#61909	SKYLANCE	$5.50 U.S.	☐
		$6.50 CAN.	☐
#61911	ASIAN STORM	$5.50 U.S.	☐
		$6.50 CAN.	☐
#61912	BLOOD STAR	$5.50 U.S.	☐
		$6.50 CAN.	☐
#61918	REPRISAL	$5.99 U.S.	☐
		$6.99 CAN.	☐
#61923	BREACH OF TRUST	$5.99 U.S.	☐
		$6.99 CAN.	☐

(limited quantities available on certain titles)

TOTAL AMOUNT	$
POSTAGE & HANDLING	$
($1.00 for one book, 50¢ for each additional)	
APPLICABLE TAXES*	$ _____
TOTAL PAYABLE	$ _____
(check or money order—please do not send cash)	

To order, complete this form and send it, along with a check or money order for the total above, payable to Gold Eagle Books, to: **In the U.S.:** 3010 Walden Avenue, P.O. Box 9077, Buffalo, NY 14269-9077; **In Canada:** P.O. Box 636, Fort Erie, Ontario, L2A 5X3.

Name: _____

Address: _____ City: _____

State/Prov.: _____ Zip/Postal Code: _____

*New York residents remit applicable sales taxes.
 Canadian residents remit applicable GST and provincial taxes.

GOLD EAGLE

SMBACK2

James Axler

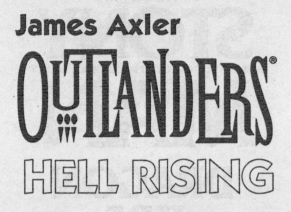

OUTLANDERS®

HELL RISING

A fierce bid for power is raging throughout new empires of what was once the British Isles. The force of the apocalypse has released an ancient city, and within its vaults lies the power of total destruction. Kane must challenge the forces who would harness the weapon of the gods to wreak final destruction.

On sale August 2000 at your favorite retail outlet. Or order your copy now by sending your name, address, zip or postal code, along with a check or money order (please do not send cash) for $5.99 for each book ordered ($6.99 in Canada), plus 75¢ postage and handling ($1.00 in Canada), payable to Gold Eagle Books, to:

In the U.S.

Gold Eagle Books
3010 Walden Ave.
P.O. Box 9077
Buffalo, NY 14269-9077

In Canada

Gold Eagle Books
P.O. Box 636
Fort Erie, Ontario
L2A 5X3

Please specify book title with order.
Canadian residents add applicable federal and provincial taxes.

GOLD
EAGLE

GOUT14

DON PENDLETON'S

STONY

AMERICA'S ULTRA-COVERT INTELLIGENCE AGENCY

MAN

DRAGON FIRE

The President orders Stony Man to place its combat teams on full alert when top-secret data for U.S. missile technology is stolen. Tracing the leads to Chinese agents, Phoenix Force goes undercover deep in Chinese territory, racing against time to stop China from taking over all of Asia!

Available in November 2000 at your favorite retail outlet.

Or order your copy now by sending your name, address, zip or postal code, along with a check or money order (please do not send cash) for $5.99 for each book ordered ($6.99 in Canada), plus 75¢ postage and handling ($1.00 in Canada), payable to Gold Eagle Books, to:

In the U.S.	In Canada
Gold Eagle Books	Gold Eagle Books
3010 Walden Avenue	P.O. Box 636
P.O. Box 9077	Fort Erie, Ontario
Buffalo, NY 14269-9077	L2A 5X3

Please specify book title with your order.
Canadian residents add applicable federal and provincial taxes.

GOLD EAGLE®

GSM49